Fluffy

JULIA KENT

Cover designer: Hang Le

Editor: Elisa Reed

Author website: http://www.jkentauthor.com

What Authors Say About Fluffy

"This book is life. **Funny, smart, and banter like no other. Fluffy is my top read this year!**" - *New York Times bestselling author Corinne Michaels*

"**Wickedly entertaining and clever**, with **spot on sexual tension and banter**, you won't be able to put this one down - nor will you want to!" - *#1 New York Times Bestselling Author Rachel Van Dyken*

"When I need an insightful, amusing, beautifully written book, I pick up a Julia Kent novel. So, it was this mindset that I read *Fluffy,* a book about an accidental fluffer. Yes, that kind of fluffer. I usually laugh often while reading Julia's work, but this time, I LOL'd and ROTFLMAO'd with every dang page. *Fluffy* **is the light and sweet side of Julia Kent, a perfect fluffernutter of romantic comedy: Very sweet, a little salty, and definitely delicious.**" - *USA Today bestselling author Blair Babylon*

"Fluffy is a laugh riot!I made the mistake of reading the book in public, and now there are places I'm not allowed to frequent anymore." -- *Amazon bestselling author Jami Albright*

To my amygdala.

Fluffy

BY JULIA KENT

It all started with the wrong help-wanted ad. Of course it did.

I'm a professional fluffer. It's NOT what you think. I stage homes for a living. Real estate agents love me, and my work stands on its own merits.

Sigh. Get your mind out of the gutter. Go ahead. Laugh. I'll wait.

See? That's the problem. My profession has used the term *fluffer* for decades. I didn't even know there was a more... lascivious definition of the term.

Until it was too late.

The ad for a professional fluffer on Craigslist seemed like divine intervention. My last unemployment check was in the bank. I was desperate. Rent was due. The ad said cash paid at the end of the day.

The perfect job!

Staging homes means showing your best angle. The same principle applies in making a certain kind of movie. Turns out a fluffer doesn't arrange decorative pillows on a couch.

They arrange other soft, round-ish objects.

The job isn't hard. Well, I mean, it is—it's about being

hard. Or, um, helping other people to be hard. In decisions about stripping down, I mean!

Oh, man...

And that's the other problem. A man. No, not one of the stars on the movie set. Will Lotham—my high school crush. The owner of the house where we're filming. Illegally. It's a rental house.

By the time the cops show up, what I thought was just a great house-staging gig has turned into a nightmare involving pictures of me with a naked star, Will rescuing me from an arrest, and a humiliating lesson in my own naïveté.

The job turned out to be so much harder than I expected. But you know what's easier than I ever imagined?

Having all my dreams come true.

Chapter One

Wanted: Professional fluffer for set. Experience required (no amateurs)! North Shore area. Immediate work, potential for more. 4 hours this week, cash paid at end of workday. Email or call.

Well, that's vague, but promising. I live north of Boston. I haven't heard the term *fluffer* used for house staging in a long time... maybe this is an older real estate agent?

A "set," huh? I know the industry is moving toward video to help drive sales. I'm a stager who used to work for Tolleson Properties, one of the biggest real estate brokerages in my area. I staged houses, model homes, and sometimes office space, until the owners decided to sell and retire.

Things with the new owner didn't exactly work out, but I don't want to think about that DEA raid.

My last day was exactly twenty-nine weeks ago.

How do I know it was exactly twenty-nine weeks ago?

Because this is week thirty, and my last unemployment

check should hit my account today. After that, it's all downhill.

And by "downhill," I mean I have to move back in with my mom and dad.

Immediate work sounds good, based on my bank balance and pending eviction. I send a quick reply.

To the Hiring Professional,

My name is Mallory Monahan, and I am writing to inquire about the professional fluffer position. I have six years of experience with staging and props, and am in search of freelance work that will use my expertise to draw out your best assets and help them rise to their fullest potential. My unique style never fails to set the right mood to bring your star properties to a happy ending. Clients tell me I have a special touch.

Please reply if you would like more information from me.

Sincerely,
    Mallory

I learned a while ago not to bother with a resume when you make the first inquiry. Too many spam filters, too many HR people not bothering. A brief, upbeat email is best, confident and businesslike.

I scan the rest of the ads. Ten-dollar-an-hour administrative assistant jobs. Lots of "Make $5,000 a month in your spare time" ads, which basically means the people placing the ads make $5,000 a month from suckers who sign up.

2

Call center jobs. Accounting and finance positions that are way out of my league. Fashion model come-ons. Medical testing for research studies. Can you really get paid $6,000 to live in a hospital and do nothing but sleep for seventeen days? If so, sign me up.

A lot of house-cleaning jobs, and licensed real estate agent positions, but nothing else for decorating, designing, or staging.

But hey–one job listing is better than none.

A quick look at my email tells me everything I need to know about my life. My bank balance is under the limit for free checking so an $18 fee is being assessed, according to my bank, putting me into negative-dollar territory. I have three spam emails from Nigerian princes offering to marry me or to save my life if I will transfer cash immediately. Two internet marketers want to sell me How to Find the Perfect Husband systems for the low price of $79 (Receive a free self-care pampering gift basket when you enroll in our annual plan! Includes skin cream guaranteed to make you look less desperate!). One egg donor registry is offering me the chance to pump myself full of hormones, cry for five days, and have my eggs harvested from my ovaries.

It's like they know.

They know *I'll* never be able to use them.

But that's not the worst email in my inbox.

Oh, not by a long shot.

This one is:

REMINDER: HARMONY HILLS HIGH SCHOOL CLASS OF 2009 REUNION! OUR FIRST DECADE!

Huh. Suddenly that egg-donor thing is looking less painful. Even Nigerian princes have more promise. Could I get someone to pay me $6,000 a month to sleep in a lab with a Nigerian prince who extracts my eggs? Because I would totally do that before I'd *ever* go to my high school reunion.

I stare at the date. Ugh. It's still the exact same day as my favorite town festival.

Easy out. Every year, I volunteer at the table for the local Habitat for Humanity chapter, recruiting volunteers. That's way more important than some stupid reunion.

Right?

I'm about to close my laptop when I get a notification. I look at email and to my utter shock, there's a reply for the professional fluffer job.

Hi Marley. You sound like a good fit. What's your number to text?

I blink. What does that mean?

Hi! Thank you. Could you tell me more about the job? What kind of set? I grab a pen and start chewing on the cap.

We're filming today. You know. The standard. Text me 555-444-0001.

The standard. What does this person mean by 'the standard'? Self-doubt floods me. This is some staging lingo I don't know, but I'm clearly *supposed* to know.

Play it cool, I tell myself. *Fake it till you make it. It'll be fine. Remember your bank balance.*

I pull out my phone and start texting.

Right. It sounds very interesting. I am available if you'd like to see my resume and portfolio. It's Mallory, by the way.

Reminding myself that if I don't get the gig, the world doesn't end, I take deep, cleansing breaths that expand my diaphragm.

It's the only diaphragm I use lately, so might as well exercise it.

You have a portfolio? LOL. Wow. That's real professional. Most of our people come to us word of mouth, but a bunch of them quit and went pro, on their own. So we got desperate and listed on Craigslist.

I frown at the phone. Is this person mocking me?

Another text comes through from him. Her? Not sure.

We need someone right away, Mallory. You sound like you know what you're doing. All we really care about is that it gleams in the light and has staying power. It's the focal point, right?

I sit up straight. This is promising. I need to say the right affirming words to make them understand I would be a valuable addition to their team.

Oh, I'll make sure it all stands tall and looks beautiful.

There. Mission accomplished.

Great. You're hired.

"What?" I squeal, shocked and relieved. Finally! Someone values me professionally!

We need it to shine. Bring whatever it takes to really make it shine.

Wow. They obviously care about lighting and art direction.

No problem. With enough spit and polish, anything can shine, I reply.

Spit, huh? I like the way you think. Attagirl.

I'm a little taken aback by *attagirl*. Seems... gendered. Demeaning. I need to show them I'm made of serious stuff.

I'll send you my standard freelance contract shortly. Your ad said cash paid at the end of the day. What is the fee?

The pause before his (her?) next text comes through feels like a kind of soul death. Was I too blunt? Did I blow it? Please tell me I didn't blow it.

Blowing it would suck.

$300. Shouldn't be more than four hours here.

That's a really good hourly rate. My eyebrows go up, my

mouth goes down, and my brain calculates what my bank balance will be if I get three hundred dollars in there.

$293.11. Sad math. Math is always sad, but it's even sadder with dollar figures attached.

My dollars.

And you don't need a contract. Just show up. Be here in an hour and we'll get it done.

I stare at the screen, body flushed with adrenaline.

An hour?

Yeah. We're in Anderhill.

That's where I live. What are the odds? I stare dumbly at the screen. Is this a joke? Or, worse, a trap? What if I'm being lured into some sex-slave human-trafficking thing?

What's the address? I type.

He names it. I quickly map it.

I know where that is. Maplecure Street is where all the super-well-off kids lived when I was in school. I wasn't friends with any of them. They were the country club crowd, the kids who went to Aspen for winter break and Martinique for spring break. I was friendly with the ones in band or theater, but not best friends. Not close enough to be invited to that side of town.

It's not exactly a den of criminal activity.

The only road in town with even more wealth is Concordian Road, and that's where the richie-riches live. Harmony Hills High School combines the towns of Anderhill and Stoneleigh, and while I live in Anderhill, I don't live in this part. I know all about Concordian Road, though. Used to drive past it almost daily in high school.

But I'm not going to think about that.

Especially not when I am so broke.

You still there? the guy asks. I assume it's a guy. Maybe it's a woman. I don't know why I'm assuming it's a man, because most real estate agents I've worked with are women. Something about that *attagirl*.

And yet, beggars can't be choosers. Three hundred bucks cash for four hours and the potential for more work is pretty much a slam dunk.

I'll be there in an hour. Perfect. What's your name?

Spatula.

I laugh out loud, the glow of the small screen casting a surreal feel on the moment.

That's a unique name. What do you do on set?

I'm the creampie specialist.

Oh! A cooking show! Now this is all making so much more sense. I'm about to ask for specifics when Spatula writes back and says:

See you in an hour.

And... I have my first freelance staging job.

Life is good after all.

Chapter Two

On the drive to the new job, I call my best friend. Perky answers immediately.

"What's wrong?"

"Nothing. Why?"

"You're *calling*."

"Yes?" We have this conversation about once a week. Perky is not only all about the new technology, she's remarkably predictable in her complaints about my habits.

"You only call when something is wrong." Smacking noises tell me she's chewing gum. This means it's another Day One of not smoking. Perky–short for Persephone–is in a constant state of trying not to smoke. Patches, filters, special vaping, drugs, gum, crystals, hypnosis, the medical intuitive who was convinced Perky had a brain tumor–you name it, Perky will try it, if it means she quits her nicotine habit.

Inevitably, though, she ends up back at Day One, trying yet again to abstain.

"I can't text and drive. So I'm calling."

"You're driving? You mean you left your apartment and let

sunlight touch your skin? Where are you going? Reese's Cup emergency?" *Smack smack smack.*

"No. Better."

"Better than Reese's Cups? Wow. That's a high bar for you. Has to be big. Job interview?" Before I can answer, she adds, "And plug in your phone. How low is the battery?"

I look. "Six percent. I'm fine." It's actually at two percent, but whatever.

"Oh. My. God. Plug in the damn phone. You do this all the time, Mal, and no one can reach you."

"I do not!" My charger plug is hanging in a half-full cup of old drive-thru coffee. I can't tell her that, of course.

The drive-thru coffee part, I mean. If Perky knew I bought coffee at the National Chain That Shall Not Be Named, she'd kill me.

"Even better. A job!"

"A job job?"

"Yep. A *job* job."

"That was fast! When did you get hired?"

"About forty-five minutes ago."

"And they want you to start *now*? Right now?"

"Yep."

"That's crazy!" *Smack smack smack.* The chewing sounds increase. I've learned to measure her excitement by how annoying the sounds become. Good thing I don't have misophonia, or I'd have to fire Perky from being my bestie.

"I know. But I can't be picky."

"You can *totally* be picky."

"We don't all have trust funds and work fifteen hours a week selling coffee."

"Hey now. I don't sell coffee. I brew it, using artisanal methods from training I received in Italy."

Notice how she's not offended about the trust fund?

9

Perky's family spends a small fortune on an on-staff psychologist in her childhood home. *Home* is a stretch. *Palace* is more like it. And the palace psychologist is there to normalize and to help the family internalize the fact that winning $177 million from a lottery ticket her mom bought one night on a whim while buying smokes is a blessing.

Never, ever a curse.

"You sell coffee, Perk. Don't try to make it sound fancier than it is."

After college, Perky took some of her share of the lottery money and invested it in Bitcoin. Her parents didn't say much. They were too busy adding a private hangar to their new spread in Wyoming. She made a killing buying Bitcoin at $10 and selling at $20.

We don't talk about that one hundred percent return these days.

Let's just say Perky is swimming in cash, and coffee is her fixation. She's so obsessed with it that she changed her name from Persephone to Perky to identify with the coffee. Not legally – that would require forethought and follow-through, neither of which are her strong suit.

"I hand pull and massage perfection that people put in their mouths," she argues.

"Now you make being a barista sound dirty."

"Never underestimate the eroticism of coffee."

Never underestimate Perky's capacity for self-delusional bullshit.

"Congrats on the job!" she chirps. She might be super weird about coffee, but she's also my oldest, most loyal friend. "What is it?"

"Professional fluffer."

The long pause is really, really weird for Perk. She's more

the type to overtalk than go quiet. Finally, she says, "Could you repeat that, Mal? I swear you said 'professional fluffer.'"

"I did! It's an old term for someone who stages houses. I'm guessing the people I'm working with are really uptight. Probably very conservative. I wore a dress, and I have to make sure I don't swear."

"Mallory, are you kidding?" Sharp and increasingly loud at the end, her answer ends with giggles.

"What? No. Not kidding. The guy said the set is—"

"Set? You're going to a *movie* set?" She's reaching high decibels here.

"More like television, I think. I'm not sure."

"Oh, my God, Mallory. This job sounds like it's p—"

My phone dies.

One other thing about Perky: She's always right. I do need to charge my battery.

I love her enthusiasm about my new job, though. I'm *sure* the next word out of her mouth was going to be "perfect."

But I frown at my dead phone.

Hmm. I called Perky to tell her where I'm going. To be my safety net. Every woman knows that you don't go somewhere alone to meet a stranger you communicated with on the internet. That's how people end up chained to basement walls or tucking a fifty-six-year-old man into bed while changing his diaper and feeding him breast milk he bought on eBay from a bottle he trashpicked at the local children's consignment shop.

Don't look at me like that. This exact story was covered in a podcast series and the outcome was just as bad as you think.

But I'll bet even *he* had a date to his high school reunion.

My phone battery's dead, so I can't map the rest of the trip, but I remember the address. 29 Maplecure Street. *Pfft.* As if maple ever cured anything. Maple bacon, maybe.

Maple bacon donuts? Definitely.

Great. Now I want a road trip to Portland to the Holy Donut and to have a date with a box of bacon-crumble-covered maple potato boyfriends. You can't have sex with food (*American Pie* excepted), but it makes for a fine companion when real men aren't in abundant supply.

Speaking of men, as I pull up to 29 Maplecure Street, I see a cluster of them, three in a circle, all smoking. Beards abound. At first glance, I assume they're a moving crew.

But they aren't wearing matching t-shirts with company logos.

Hmm.

As I put the car in park, I take a deep breath and steel myself. Meeting new associates is always nerve wracking. My grey knit dress from Athleta should be just right, the intersection of polished and cool with enough functional stretch for bending and lifting. Real estate agents dress up to look successful; the interior designers I occasionally meet dress up, I think because it's their nature to choose beautiful things.

And they accessorize. I've got big silver hoop earrings and an armful of black beaded bracelets.

"You're fine, Mal," I tell myself as I step out of my car. I am my own cheering section. Running a hand through my curly hair, I briefly wonder if I should have done a sleek ponytail. One of the guys looks up and sees me, saying something to the others. Like a herd of gazelles noticing a large lion nearby, all the heads pop up in unison.

I give a small wave, my fingers like wind chimes.

They look away.

"It's just a four-hour gig," I mutter, my pep fading fast as I sling my black bag over my shoulder and start toward the front door. The wide walkway is laid in a simple pattern of beige stone. *Beige* is such a boring word for the subtle kaleidoscope of color that gives the stone texture and nuance. My mother thinks that beige is as exciting as clipping your toenails, but there are thousands of shades in this world designed to evoke emotion.

And each is important.

Whoever owns this house takes fabulous care of it, little details emerging into a gorgeous, discerning whole. Money makes it easy to maintain a showplace, but cash alone isn't the key.

You have to *care*.

"Hi, there," I say to the bearded trio as they grind out their cigarette butts, carefully rubbing them in the perfectly manicured grass then cupping them in their palms. Their care impresses me. I'm not a fan of smoking, but what really bothers me are smokers who leave their butts everywhere.

One of the guys, blond with a full face and a ZZ Top look, holds the door open for me. "Ladies first," he says in a barrel-chested voice.

The other guys laugh. Being mocked by men isn't new to me—I got plenty of it in high school, for being the band/drama/honors/newspaper geek—but I've learned to ignore it and move on.

"Thank you," I say with grace they don't deserve, walking up the granite steps.

"No, thank *you*," one of them mumbles, giving me a wink and a short, appreciative whistle as I walk up. "Nice ass."

I blush. Wasn't expecting *that*.

The house is extraordinarily designed, open concept with high ceilings, and I should appreciate it more, but my ears are ringing from being sexually objectified by a guy who looks like he's an extra on *Hardcore Pawn*.

I was just turned into a piece of eye candy.

Me.

I'm not sure whether to be flattered or horrified.

After a few seconds, I decide. It's not hard. I am a mature, capable, competent professional with a high degree of emotional self-regulation and a sharp business mind. I know how to handle myself in any given situation. Perceptiveness and the ability to pivot to gain leverage are key in my profession. The answer is clear.

Let's go with flattered.

Down a wide hall and to the right, a giant kitchen beckons. From what I can see, the central island is bigger than most boardroom tables. Aha. This must be where the cooking show takes place. I stand in the foyer, hesitant. A few people are walking around, glancing at me, but no one approaches to introduce themselves.

Asking for "Spatula" seems rather gauche. This is the point where I realize I have no idea what his real name is. I've been hired by a kitchen utensil used to scrape up wet, goopy stuff.

Huh.

Well, I might be a bit intimidated, and I may be out of my element, but there is one thing any good stager can do: arrange a room.

So I begin.

To my left is a sitting room. It's mostly empty, but there is a big ottoman, a red circle made of leather, and a cream-colored sofa. Oddly enough, the sofa—an overstuffed, three-cushion monstrosity with huge arms that looks like something out of a bad QVC television set—is horribly positioned, at an odd angle, as if someone brought it in and just put it down anywhere. Starting to work before I've even met my boss, I try to shove the sofa into better alignment, but it's surprisingly heavy. Instead, I grasp the red ottoman and move it, positioning it in front.

This furniture definitely doesn't match the house it's in.

I scan the room. Metal stands with huge lights are set here and there, with big power packs and heavy cords on the floor nearby. They must be doing the interview with the chef in here. In a corner, I see an aquarium filled with small orange fish. A long, narrow table behind the sofa holds a giant gold bowl, cracked like a mirror mosaic.

It is overflowing with small packets of ibuprofen.

And bottles of coconut oil.

I pause, bent over the red circle, mind roaming. I know coconut oil is all the rage these days, so maybe it's just trendy, but what a weird decoration in the living room. Or maybe it's a cooking ingredient?

My eyes pick up on three red packets that say "Ribbed." Wait a minute. Are those condoms? I stifle a laugh. As a home fluffer, you can never underestimate how quirky some people can be. At my old job, we once fluffed a house full of one-eyed dolls dressed to look like Liberace.

Riding black horses.

But condoms in a bowl are a little bizarre, especially in a group setting. Coconut oil breaks down latex. Is someone here actually stupid enough to combine the two?

And—wait. *Why* would someone here combine the two?

"Hey!" one of the beards shouts at me from across the room, interrupting my thoughts. "Why'd you move that?" He points to the red ottoman.

I crook my finger at him and beckon. My first impulse is to apologize and move everything back, but then some stronger part of me kicks in. I've been hired for my expertise. This client is ignoring me. Some employers want a lap dog. A yes person. Others need you to show them you're in command in order to get respect.

I lift my chin up as I motion for him to come to me. "We need to move this sofa," I declare.

"Why?" The other two beards look at me, as if they are one hive moving in unison.

"Because the energy is all wrong."

"Energy?"

"Look at this," I declare, moving my hands in grand gestures, taking up space before I plant them on my hips. Power pose. Research shows I can increase testosterone levels in my body just by putting my palms on these large-and-in-charge hips.

Large, anyway.

"Look at what?" ZZ Top seems intrigued, his dark sunglasses suddenly lifted up to reveal intelligent blue eyes framed by wrinkles. He's about my dad's age and looks calm and resigned, like men in their fifties sometimes do. He knows himself, and unlike the other two beards, who are poking each other and snickering, he's actually willing to listen to me.

"Feng shui living room principles say you're inviting serious medical harm if you position this furniture the way you have it."

"Medical harm?" ZZ Top says, moving his hand toward the other two guys to shush them.

A small man with a concave chest, wearing a moss-green henley shirt and old, paint-splattered jeans moves swiftly in from the hall. His baseball cap says something about the Red Sox, which is about as common in the Boston suburbs as seeing someone drinking coffee from Dunkin' Donuts.

"Medical harm?" the small man echoes, mouth pursed. Thick wrinkles around his mouth tell me he's a serious smoker. The reek of cigarette smoke that fills the space between us is a tipoff, too.

"If you want to attract prosperity, avoid pain, and keep the energy flowing properly, you need to move the entire room around," I insist.

"But the lighting's all set," ZZ Top says. "Sound checks done. It'll set us back an hour if we have to redo it."

Little Man holds up one finger to the guy, who shuts up instantly. "You're serious?" he asks me, dark brown eyes taking me in, his expression changing quickly to something sexual and not a little creepy. "Wait a minute. You're Mallory."

I sigh with relief and extend my hand for a firm, professional shake. "Yes. Mallory Monahan. Are you Spatula?"

"Yup." He shakes my hand like it's a window sheer.

No one blinks at his name.

"Guys, this is the new fluffer!" he calls out. His eyes roam up and down. "Man, you dressed up. Don't need a dress for this." He looks down at my wedge heels.

Murmurs of appreciation ripple through the room, followed by some laughter. "Want some extra work?" one of the beards calls out, winking at me.

I start to say more to Spatula, but he cuts me off. "What're you saying about how we position the set?" He looks at the red ottoman. "Who moved that? Now Jasmine's gonna complain about her knees."

"I moved it." I point to the beam above. "Did you know that positioning anything you sit on at that angle is—"

"We don't have an extra hour," he declares, cutting me off.

"Do you know how important it is that the qi move properly in this room?" I protest, slapping my hands onto my hips so hard, I stagger a little. "You really don't understand how severe this is. You risk bankruptcy, medical problems, and even loss of reputation!"

"I ain't worried about my reputation, Mal," Spatula cracks, bringing everyone in the room to roiling laughter.

"But surely you want the room to look good and to have good energy. Any show set is about prosperity. Optimizing health and wealth."

A suspicious look comes my way. "Health? What kind of medical problems are you talking about?"

"You name it. If the energy flows too fast or too slow, it can ruin everything."

He nods. "I get that. Happens all the time on set. We have pills and, well," he sniffs, "*you* for that."

I point to the red ottoman. "Red is the color of passion, so you're off to a good start."

"Great!" He shouts to ZZ Top. "Lenny! Get me more red in there. But don't move nothin'. We ain't got an hour to spare." The shrug he throws my way isn't an apology.

It's an order.

"It would be really helpful if you gave me some specs," I snap, deciding I need to be more forceful.

"Specs?"

"Design specs. You know. What's the look you're going for here? How I arrange everything will depend on that."

"The... look?" He has a rat-like face, small eyes set close together, the bill of his baseball cap making them seem like they're peeking out from a dark cave.

"Yes." I wait, suppressing my natural instinct to chatter on. During the last month of my extended unemployment, I've turned to female empowerment books as a way to up my game. The careful pause gives me the upper hand.

As silence stretches between us, I'm starting to think the only hand this is giving me is one with a middle finger poking up out of it. My palms start to sweat as Spatula frowns.

Finally, a dawning look hits him and he says, "We're going for height."

"Height?" Great. Something I can work with. I look up at the twelve-foot ceiling. "The light in here is really good for that. The room could use some color."

"I thought you said red was good."

"It is. But we need more." I tap my fingernail against my front teeth. "Coral. Or, no... how about some soft flesh tones, and maybe a little tan?"

"You like to work with flesh?" he asks, chin set in an admiring way, as if I've passed some test.

"Of course! What pro in this industry doesn't?" I give him a confident grin designed to make it clear I know what I'm doing and we are *definitely* on the same page.

The skeptical look melts off his face as he laughs, a phlegmy sound that matches his reek of cigarette smoke. "You're a hoot, Mal. Can I call you Mal? Or is it Mallory?"

"Either. My friends call me Mal."

"Ok, then. Mal it is. You know, if you work well with Beastman, this could be the first of a lot of gigs."

My pulse picks up, the spot on my neck where I can feel it against my collarbone like a signal. "Seriously?" I don't ask him to repeat the name, but I'm a bit puzzled. Did he say Beastman? No way. Must have been Eastman. Maybe a nickname? I heard it wrong.

Energy shoots through me like a drug. I've hit the jackpot.

These folks have lots of work for me, and the money is excellent.

I rub my palms together and raise my eyebrows, eagerness pumping through me. "My hands are itching to get to work."

He frowns again. "Itching? You're not contagious, are you? Because we don't normally screen fluffers for diseases, but..."

My turn to laugh. "What? No!" I hold out my palms to show him. "It's an expression. You know. It means I'm eager to get down to business and show you how I can make this all come together."

"Beastman is a pro at coming together," Spatula says.

If I were Perky, who has a mind that lives in the gutter with occasional side trips to Decentland, I'd be snickering.

"Sounds like Beastman knows what's he's doing," I say, staying neutral. Professionals don't go looking for sexual innuendos in every work situation. That's for amateurs.

And barista best friends.

He doesn't seem happy about it. "We've told him before about not moving too fast, but it works for the creampie scenes. Makes them really pop on screen."

Some part of me relaxes. Of course. Cooking is all about getting moving parts to work together for a perfectly timed finale. I turn around and look back at the stainless steel kitchen, the Sub-Zero refrigerator, the Bertazzoni range. Oooo, a Bosch built-in coffee maker! Someone knows their kitchen design.

None of the crew is working in there. All the lighting and camera guys are moving down the hallway in this direction. Huh. You'd think the kitchen would be the center of activity at this point.

As I look around, I realize I'm the only woman here. Huh, redux. That's weird.

"Calibrating is hard work," I say, trying to show him I know my stuff as I make eye contact and smile. "Timing is everything."

"Especially when it comes to the payload," Spatula says somberly as he walks me down the long hallway. I must have misheard that, because *payoff*? Sure.

Pay*load*?

He leads me into a small room, where I come face to face with a completely naked man covered in more hair than Sasquatch.

And he's rubbing coconut oil on his decidedly hairless balls.

Chapter Three

"That's a penis," I gasp, pointing at the obvious. If my neck pulse was pounding before, now it's become an angry cat trapped in a tumbling clothes dryer, screaming and clawing to get out.

"Yes."

"A *big* penis!"

The man grins nice and wide. "Sure is."

"Why are you naked?" I've heard of Jamie Oliver, on *Naked Chef*, but he wasn't *actually* naked. Pretty sure, anyway. "Is this some kind of trend in the industry I don't know about?"

Sasquatch laughs. "It's my job."

"It's your *job* to be naked?" What kind of cooking show is this? Aren't there health department regulations about this kind of thing? Beastman looks like a rug with arms and legs. I'm trying to imagine a cream pie made by a shedding bear.

I start to gag.

"Well." He pauses and looks down at himself. "I guess I don't have to be naked until we're filming, but I like to get into character nice and early."

"Beastman is all about method acting," Spatula explains.

"And what method is that?" I squeak, controlling my throat muscles. This is *definitely* not the place to have a gag reflex.

"Not method. Meth head. Get it? Say it fast." Spatula seems inordinately pleased with himself.

"You're a meth head?" I ask Beastman, taking a step back.

"No." Beastman glares at Spatula. "That's just a stupid joke he keeps saying, as if it'll eventually get funny."

"It never will," I say, shock tearing the air out of my lungs.

Beastman snorts. "See? Told you."

Spatula shrugs. "I think it's funny."

"You think trampoline videos of guys bouncing out and cracking their balls on fence posts are funny," Beastman shoots back. He looks at me as if to say, *Can you believe that?*

I can't believe *any* of this. The room starts to spin.

Spatula laughs uncontrollably, reaching into his back pocket for a smartphone. "You seen the newest one I found?"

Beastman looks down at his crotch. "Dude. Not the time. You know those videos make me soft."

Nothing on this hulking man's body is soft. He looks like Jason Momoa crossed with Kingpin from *Spiderverse*.

"Heh." Spatula mercifully puts his phone away. "Fine. After we're done shooting, I'll show you."

"After we're done shooting, my balls will hurt plenty," Beastman says, his half grin somehow sad and proud at the same time. Kind eyes meet mine. "But this new lady will help that."

"Mallory," I gasp. "I'm Mallory."

"Call her Mal," Spatula instructs. "All her friends do."

"Mal?" Beastman gives me side eye. "That means 'bad' in Spanish."

"You know so much trivial crap, Beastman," Spatula says. "You're a walking encyclopedia."

"No, dumbass. I just paid attention in school."

"So did I," Spatula defends himself. "Paid attention to the tramp stamps on the girls in front of me. That's all the education I needed for this industry. That and home ec. We baked some awesome shit in there." He points to Beastman's penis and looks at me. "Here you go. We talked about the look we're going for. We want all the height we can get, Mal."

Beastman cups his balls, his half erection looking about as crestfallen as I feel.

"I can't arrange *that*!"

"Why not?"

"It doesn't fit any of my color palettes!"

What am I saying? Sweat blooms instantly between my breasts, under the soft curve of my overly tight, bound breasts in this too-small bra. I can't stop staring at the half-limp penis resting on the pale inner thigh of a guy in his dressing room on a cooking show set. Undressed.

They should call it an *undressing* room.

"You don't need to arrange it."

"I don't?" Maybe this is an elaborate joke.

"You need to make it look better."

I shake my head slowly, sorrowfully. "No can do. Sorry."

"What do you mean, 'sorry'? It's your job," Spatula growls, his demeanor changing fast. Eyes that were friendly turn cold. "You've got five minutes to make this happen." He looks at his phone. "I've got talent that needs Narcan in another location." The doorbell rings. "He'd better be tight and gleaming when I get back. Jasmine's on her way to film with him, and she likes 'em ready to ride."

"Jasmine?"

"Yeah. The star."

"When is she coming?" I ask.

"On cue," Spatula says with a smoky laugh. "Now get Beastman looking better, like I said."

"Then it's an impossible job. Penises are just plain ugly," I lie, trying to say or do whatever it takes to get out of this surreal moment. "No amount of styling will change that," I call after him, slightly dizzy as all the different parts of me try to put this together into a whole that makes sense.

"Don't call my junk ugly," Beastman protests, looking genuinely hurt. Guilt pours through me, tugging at my heart. "You can't let that get into my psyche. It'll ruin filming. Most of this job is in the mind." He looks down at his member. "Maybe ten percent happens with him."

"Oh, no! I wasn't calling your, uh, member ugly! It's not you! Don't be offended. It's all men. It's a universal truth that all penises in search of visual validation will be disappointed," I blabber on.

"What the hell does that even mean?"

So much for my attempt at a witty Austenism.

"Um, where is the furniture I'm supposed to work with?"

"Furniture? You mean the special wedges?"

"Wedges?"

"Or the Sybian?"

"Isn't that a kind of bread?" I ask, confused. Why bring Middle Eastern baked goods into this conversation?

"You know. Sybian." To my horror, he begins rocking his hips toward me.

Not bread. Okay. Got it.

I feel a little faint now, but I pull it together and ask, "Where is the bedroom? Why don't we start there?" Maybe I can escape through a window.

"Nah. The living room this time. But I like the bedroom, myself. On my other jobs, that's where we always start," he says, nodding as if I'm finally on the same page. "And end. And it's pretty much where the middle happens. Unless we're doing a casting agent thing. Then there's a desk and the girl wears glasses." He squints at me. "Hey. *You're* wearing glasses."

"Yes, I am." I touch one of the arms.

"You sure you're just the fluffer?" His eyes roam up and down my body. "Because with that rack, you could make some serious bucks with pearl necklaces."

From artisanal bread to fine jewelry. This place is about as hipster as you can get.

"I thought this was a cooking show. Not jewelry." I look down at his lap. "Unless you count those as family jewels."

He chuckles, then moves to a small chair where he manspreads. If there were a pageant for naked manspreading, he'd be world champion. I wonder what the crowns for *that* contest would look like?

"You're funny." His grin widens. "So what kind of lube did you bring?" His gaze moves up to my mouth. "Other than spit."

My jaw drops.

"Man, that's freaky," he says as he leans back, his legs spread, and makes it clear what he expects me to arrange. With my tongue.

"Excuse me?"

"The way your mouth just made a big O like that. You look like Kathleen."

"Who's Kathleen?" I squeak.

"The blow-up doll. You know. The AlwaysDoll?" He clears his throat and says, in a radio announcer's voice. "She's always ready for you." His chest puffs up like a peacock. "I did the demo video for that, for the sex-toy company. It went viral."

"I'll bet you're viral, all right," I mutter, my skin on fire as

25

it really sinks in that I've walked into a porn set in an obviously rented house in the fanciest part of town. A *porn set*. Pornography is being made right here, right now, and I'm smack dab in the middle of it.

And I'm expected to elevate the talent. I mean, I believe a rising tide lifts all boats, but this guy has an aircraft carrier between his legs.

Porn set.

A flash of the last day of senior year hits me. My best friends covered my car with streamers and "balloons" made from condoms.

And as a joke, painted the words "Most Likely to Become a Porn Star" on my windshield. It was a joke because I turned out to be valedictorian.

Joke's on me now.

Just then, Spatula walks back in. "Hey! Great! You two are getting along nicely." He thumbs toward me. "She said in the interview she was willing to use spit."

"I said spit and polish!" I protest.

"Even better," Beastman says suggestively, looking at my hands.

"No, no, no. Not literal spit! I'm not spitting all over his–" I gesture toward Beastman's crotch.

"Hey, Mal. You know how it goes. You're a pro. You do whatever it takes to make Beastman perform at peak," Spatula explains, voice going low and dangerous.

"That's not a peak," I say. "That's Mount Everest."

"Any tape residue left on the tip?" he asks Beastman.

"Tape?" I gasp.

"I have to tape it to my leg when I wear jeans," Beastman explains. "Sometimes it messes with the close-up shots."

"Do people comment on that? I mean, are viewers of porn really looking *that* closely?" I blurt out.

"Of course! We get tons of fan mail and reviews."

"Reviews? People *review* porn movies?" I'm imagining Yelp pages for that.

"Sure. All the time. Holds us to higher standards."

Spatula abruptly hands me a small bottle of Goo Gone. "Here. Get rid of the sticky stuff on Beastman's tip." He shakes it, impatient.

I don't touch it.

"I thought the point was for him to *produce* sticky stuff."

"Only for the money shot."

"He... has sex with money? Does he wrap it around his shaft? How does that work?"

Beastman laughs. "She's funny. It's like she's never watched our stuff."

"I–" Sudden shyness overwhelms me. I haven't watched their stuff. I haven't watched *any* stuff. I joke about YouPorn, but it's not like I use it. If I want to get off on something, it's an audiobook of a favorite romance novel. No worries about ass to mouth, no sudden choking.

No unexpected scat play.

An audiobook is dependable. Aural sex is the best.

When you're single, at least.

Or, maybe, when you're *me*.

Unreality has a funny way of announcing itself when your entire way of viewing the world melts into a gooey pile of chaos. All the carefully spread layers of life, each in its place and held apart from the others by psychological forces so mysterious they're almost magic, converge into one big mess.

I have become a Snickers bar left on a car dashboard in July.

"Hey, hey, hold on there," Beastman objects, pointing to the bottle Spatula shoves in my hand. "That shit stings like a mofo. I'm not letting her put that on me. Last time you had to CGI out the red burn spots!"

"Only on close ups," Spatula retorts, minimizing poor Beastman's protests.

"This is a pornography movie set!" I shout. It's obvious, I know, but I have to say it. *Have* to. It's like that moment when someone trips and you shout, "Careful!" afterward.

I mean, what's the *point*? What's done is done. Your words aren't going to make a difference.

But you do it anyhow.

"Sure is," Beastman replies calmly. Spatula moves to the door, his palms flat against it, behind his back. Panic covers his face with an urgency that looks like I feel inside.

"Why are you announcing that? You wearing a wire?" His eyes roam over me, lower teeth biting his upper lip, looking like he's assessing whether he can do a body search.

"You lay one hand on me and I will squash you like a bug, Spatula!" I shout. My hands curl into fists and every self-defense class I ever took–all two of them, that I was dragged to by Perky because she wanted to hit on the instructor–run through my memory bank with one final conclusion:

Drop to the floor and use your legs.

So I do.

Beastman groans. It's a sound of... pleasure?

And sure enough, the tide raises his boat, the mast moving up, up, up, the tip rubbing against the light fixture in the middle of the ceiling.

Or, at least, that's what it looks like from my viewpoint as I bend my knee and rotate my hip for maximum ball kicking. Good thing I'm wearing my Spanx.

Spatula's jaw goes slack, the panic deepening, one hand ripping his baseball cap off to reveal a nearly bald pate covered in newly implanted hair plugs.

Looks like he's in phase one. I've seen old plastic dolls with better patterning.

"I have looked at plenty of penises in my life, mister!" I holler up at the hairy redwood. "Yours isn't so special! I never promised to use spit on you! I just thought I was arranging furniture and getting lighting and accessories to sell it!"

"You are, baby, oh, you are. You are *so* selling it." Beastman is stroking himself. He's, um... definitely fluffed.

Spatula lunges, grabbing Beastman's arm. "No, man! Don't! You're too close to climax. We've got a daily budget we have to meet. No choking your chicken when you're not being filmed. It's in your contract!"

"He's not allowed to masturbate when you're filming a new movie? Not even on his personal time?" I ask, righteously indignant on poor Beastman's behalf. "Masturbation is a basic human right! We need a 28th amendment to the Constitution! The ACLU needs to take this case! How can an employment contract prevent you from self-pleasure? That's just *wrong*. Someone needs to defend the rights of single people. Lonely people. People who aren't willing to settle. People who can't even pick up a guy at speed dating at the library. People who– " I wind down and shut myself up, fast.

People like *me*.

Damn it.

"Nope. No sex with anyone, either. It makes the movies more authentic," Spatula elaborates, peering at me with those beady eyes.

"That's outrageous! He has the right to private pleasure! It's not like masturbation makes hair grow on your hands or anything." I cannot shut up. The words keep rolling out of me, as if that coconut oil is lubing the path from the fear center of my brain to my mouth.

Beastman just shrugs, but then he carefully examines his hairy hands with a dawning look of horror.

Why I am lying on the floor, my leg cocked like a cricket, arguing for Beastman's right to flog his meat is beyond me.

This is all out of the realm of possibility.

I'm dreaming, right? This is a sick dream.

Sounds from the foyer make it clear someone else is having an argument, a man's authoritative baritone booming through the whole first floor.

"He has every right to spank his monkey if he wants to!" I shout.

Spatula pulls the door open, taking a step toward me.

"Naw, man. We did that movie last month. No more monkeys. They bite!" Beastman extends his thigh and points to a small, thin scar, slightly raised and red.

"That was a euphemism!"

"Oh." Beastman frowns. "I played that in my high school marching band. But only for a year. Then they moved me up to tuba."

"Not euphonium! *Euphemism*!"

"What's the difference?"

"About fifty IQ points, apparently!" I shout at him. "And please tell me you didn't have sex with monkeys in a movie?"

"What do you take me for?" he bellows, clearly offended. "I would never fuck a monkey. They were there for the dance sequence only."

While I'm deeply relieved to hear that, I point the toe of my shoe at Spatula. "You come any closer and I'll give your taint an episiotomy!"

"I don't have time to talk about that Episcopal stuff," he whines, impatient. "You're just here to give Beastman a rise."

Beastman moans, making bass sounds so erotic, I'm pretty sure he's Barry White's love child.

Spatula inserts himself between us, spraying Beastman's chest with an oily substance. "Listen here, Mal. You've got him so hard. He could use that thing to cut diamonds. This is great, how you're using his kink to help." He opens the door even further, poking his head out to see what's going on. Voices are louder out there, but it's hard for me to tell. My head has an alarm in it, going off like an air raid siren.

Only this isn't a drill.

"His kink?" I squeak as my eyes scan the small desk that Beastman turned into a makeshift dressing table. I need a weapon. I grab a dog's chew toy from underneath. It's baby blue plastic and about two feet in length, and has increasingly large spheres along the shaft as it progresses. Holding it in front of me, I fling it around, the air making a *whoosh* sound as my strokes turn it into a whip.

"Beastman loves femdom," Spatula explains, leaping out of range of my makeshift defense mechanism. Having a weapon makes me feel bolder. Hopeful. Less terrified.

I am ready to kick some ass and get out of here.

"Femdom?" I look at Beastman, who is watching me with his tongue out, eyes glassy, hand on his, um... beastdom. You know how guys always say they're so big, it's not going to fit? And how it always fits?

This one ain't gonna fit. I am pretty sure Beastman would need a large farm animal to be able to–

Oh. Oh, no. I never thought to ask why he's called Beast-man, did I?

"Yeah. Hey, Mal. You willing to wear a strap-on? Because you could turn old Beastman into the Titanic if you'd do some ass play and–"

"I REFUSE TO WEAR A STRAP-ON! IT IS NOT IN MY CONTRACT!" I shout up at him, waving my magic dog toy in an arc. He curls his belly in before I hit him with it.

Before Spatula can reply, another man interrupts us, clearly stunned by my words.

Someone I know.

Someone I haven't seen in ten years.

Oh. My. God.

Chapter Four

I would know him anywhere.

Will Lotham.

The Will Lotham.

My high school crush.

"You have less than two minutes to get the hell out of my house," he shouts at all of us, my eyes drawn to the way his jaw flexes, how his dark hair brushes against his red, frowning forehead. Still tall, wider and more muscular in the shoulders, Will's face has grown even more handsome with time. Alert, sharp eyes narrow with suspicion, his anger justified and his authority unquestionable.

Looking up at Will Lotham from the carpeted floor with my leg coiled for action, my hand grasping the beaded weapon, I nearly faint.

"And for God's sake, lady," he says to me with a snort. "'Lady.'" He uses finger quotes. "Take your damn strap-on and that anal-bead string and whatever other nasty equipment you're using in my parents' house and don't you ever come back again!"

I drop the dog toy. It falls on my chest and rolls onto the

floor, the biggest bead at the end coming to a final rest on top of my fallen purse.

Anal beads?

Our eyes lock.

His house?

Did he just say *his* house?

I'm fourteen.

In an instant, I'm back to being a freshman. I'm seeing Will Lotham for the first time, in the hallway where we have assigned lockers next to each other. L and M. Lotham and Monahan. Just like that, with a human grizzly bear scrambling into torn jeans and Spatula screaming into his smartphone, I'm frozen, transported back to 2004.

Will Lotham is talking to me. *The* Will Lotham.

Talking to *me*. On a porn set.

In his house.

He bends down and touches me, nudging my shoulder. "Look at you. Glassy eyes. Non-responsive. What are you on?"

"On?" I chirp, finally finding a voice and the will to move, pulling myself up off the ground on legs so numb, I might as well have bathed in Novocaine.

"You're high as a kite." Disgust ripples through his voice, but he stops himself mid-breath, his head cocking slightly. "Wait a minute. You're really familiar."

Beastman turns and interrupts. "You said you didn't do film, Mal. Maybe you lied? This guy's seen you in something?"

"Mal?" Will says, eyes narrowing, mouth firmly set in anger. Then he softens. "*Mallory?*"

Spatula inserts himself between us, Will dropping my shoulder. He waves his phone in Will's face. "I have a signed rental contract. We paid the deposit to rent this place for today and tomorrow, fair and square. It's all done through the online booking agency, and–"

Red and blue lights flash, fast, into the house from outside, the cut-off screech of sirens finally breaking through my awareness.

"Tell it all to the cops," Will growls at him. "You broke *so* many rules."

Oiled up and panting, Beastman stands tall, spine straight. His, uh, *beastdom* stands even straighter. "You got a problem?"

Will Lotham was quarterback for the Harmony Hills Hornets. He's a tall one–six two, one eighty, nothing but muscle and flow. All his stats come streaming back into my brain like I'm a computer program. My eyes cut to Will and I'm guessing he's added twenty pounds of muscle since we graduated, so I have to adjust my Will Lotham database. He is *thicker*.

But Beastman is big and hairy and glistening, and in a match between the two, the odds are ever in favor of the guy who smells like coconut oil and looks like Hagrid's porn twin.

Until Will cocks his arm and decks him.

Beastman goes *down*.

And no, that's not a porn joke.

Because he brings me down with him.

All three hundred or so pounds of slick muscle hit me like a rock slide, shoving the entity that is Mallory Monahan into the floor, the anal-bead string wedged between my ass cheeks as I deeply regret the wrap dress I chose for professional style. All the wind knocks out of me as his oily skin slides against my clothes, my arms, my face, and soon I'm pinned beneath a man who doesn't know the difference between a euphonium and a euphemism, but does know one thing.

"Mal" is another word for bad.

And this, my friends, is the very definition of *bad*.

"Son of a *bitch*," Will swears, shaking his hand out, the air moving as he winces, Beastman toppled on his side, Spatula pressing his hands against his ears.

"Crystal jaw, man," Spatula mourns. "That's why he couldn't keep on with the WWF wrestling." Eyes darting to the window, Spatula looks at me, then Will, then down at Beastman.

Will bends down, offering me his good hand. "You're Mallory Monahan. From Harmony Hills? Class of '09? I knew you were familiar. Jesus, look at you. From valedictorian to *this*."

If I could breathe, I'd answer him.

And I would lie. Wouldn't you?

But I can't breathe, so I just sit there, twitching, Beastman's hairy, oily skin turning my humiliation into a perverted deep-conditioning treatment. I try to rise, but my face is crotch level with Will, mouth open in an O of surprise.

Do I really look like a blow-up sex doll when I do this? Beastman's words flit through me as the room starts to dim, his weight seriously making it impossible to get oxygen in me.

I look up at Spatula, trying to ask for help. All he does is hold up his phone up and press his finger against the glass screen.

"You are *not* taking photos!" Will bellows, dropping my hand and moving toward Spatula, who sprints out of the room. Will's suit jacket flaps as he runs after him.

All the beards race out the front door. Within seconds, two car engines start, tires peeling out as I stand there, arms and legs turning to ice blocks.

My high school crush thinks I'm a porn star.

I am found like this by the cops, seconds later, as Beastman wakes up, hand going to his crotch, crying out, "I'm ready for my close-up!"

And that is when I faint.

Here's the problem with fainting: Sometimes it only lasts a few seconds.

Damn it.

Here's the other problem with fainting: Will is now standing next to the cop, telling him in a firm voice, "I think she needs Narcan. She's high and unresponsive."

I sit up again, surprised I can do it. Beastman is on the other side of the room, hands cuffed behind his back, his jaw an angry red on the left side. Red knuckles attest to Will's aching hand as he talks to the cop in a clear voice, unafraid to be heard.

"I don't need Narcan. I'm not on anything," I protest.

"That's what they all say," the cop mutters, giving Will a raised eyebrow and a look I really resent.

"I am not on drugs. I am not a porn star. I came here because I saw a job on Craigslist for a professional fluffer, and that's what I do for a living."

Blinks. I get blinks. Lots and lots of blinks.

Nothing but blinks.

A female cop joins us and as I look up at her, I realize she's my next-door neighbor's daughter, Karen Minsky.

My mom is going to hear about this in seventeen minutes.

You know how I know?

Because that's how long it took for word to get back to her when we were busted at a house party by–you guessed it– Karen Minsky, when I was a junior in high school.

"You're a fluffer?" Will chokes out. "The valedictorian of my high school class is a *fluffer*?"

"A *house* fluffer!" I say, indignant. "I make everything look better!"

"I'll bet you do," Karen says, pulling out a long zip tie. "Keep your hands where I can see them, Mallory, and we'll do this the easy way."

"You're *arresting* me?"

"We found drugs in the other room, on top of the illegal occupancy and lack of a filming permit for–"

"You can't arrest me! You used to babysit me! You used to bribe me with an extra root beer if I didn't tell my mom your boyfriend came over and watched horror movies while I was asleep!"

"That was then, and by the way," she says, giving me a dark look, "you blabbered about it and got me in trouble."

"You and John Ralston let me watch *Saw 3*! I was six!"

Will is observing me with a calculation that makes my skin crawl, and not just the epidermal layer coated in Beastman's coconut oil. I sniff the back of my hand.

I *hope* that's coconut oil.

"She's not high," Will announces.

"How do you know?" Karen asks.

"Anyone who can bring up a twenty-year-old grudge like *that*," he snaps his fingers, "isn't high."

Karen lets out a long sigh, the kind with an exasperated groan at the end that they must teach in police academy. "Good point." She frowns. "But I kind of want to arrest her anyway."

"For what?" I demand.

"Being a pain in the ass." She turns to Will. "You're the homeowner. We've got all the major characters out there, including some guy who insists his name is Spatula. Spatula Mangucci."

"He's the cream pie expert," I explain, trying to be helpful. More blinks.

"Cream pie?" Will reluctantly asks, a muscle in his jaw pinging. Is he trying not to laugh?.

"You know. For the cooking show..." My voice winds down as I realize what I'm saying. "Wait a minute. This isn't a cooking show. It's porn. It's a porn set." I pinch the bridge of my nose. "So why would he talk about cream pies on a porn set?"

Karen's eyebrows touch the brim of her police uniform hat. "For a valedictorian, you're not very smart."

Laughter twitches at the edges of Will's lips. "But you're funny."

"Huh. Beastman said that, too. Right when he told me I needed to use spit to be a fluffer."

Karen shakes her head and sighs. "Can I arrest you for being too stupid to live?"

"Pretty sure you'd have to arrest half the planet, officer," Will says, frowning deeply at me. "You really don't understand that you took a job on a pornographic movie set? One that's operating illegally in my parent's house?"

"This is *your* house?" My turn to challenge him. "It's not the same house you lived in when we were in high school."

I get a sharp look in return. "How would you know? You've never been to my house."

I can't admit that I made my mother drive past it 8,000 times in ninth and tenth grade, taking a detour through his neighborhood, and then driving myself the last two years of high school.

"Uh, you know. Everyone knows where everyone lives in a small town," I say lamely.

He's not convinced. Here's the thing about Will Lotham: He's a Rhodes Scholar. You know that annoyingly well-rounded person in high school, the National Merit Scholar and football star recruited by a Big 10 school he ended up turning down in favor of an Ivy, the one who got all the Veterans of Foreign Wars accolades and was Order of the Arrow and in Eagle Scouts, too? The one who got the lead in the school play every year, founded a food pantry for people with tree-nut allergies, and who used his ninth-grade science fair project to patent a new technology for turning mud into antibiotics in Eritrea?

Yeah. They annoy the hell out of me, too.

Notice how Will keeps mentioning I was valedictorian of our high school class?

That's because he was salutatorian.

Second best.

To *me*.

Right now, though, would not be the smartest time to mention that, because it appears he is the only thing standing between me and a criminal record.

An aggrieved sigh pours out of him. "My parents bought this place a while ago. Sold the house on Concordian. Mom wanted more land and a pool."

I just nod.

"And then they moved to Florida for half the year after Dad's cancer scare."

My heart pitter-patters with sympathy.

"I'm sorry."

"He's fine. But they dumped this place off on me to manage. The market's still lukewarm in this price range, so we've been renting it through an online clearinghouse." A sour look covers his face. "Why am I telling you all this? Anyhow." He gives me a look that says somehow it's my fault he's spilling his guts. "The neighbors tipped me off to 'unusual activity.' I came here expecting a rowdy house party. Not–" He looks pointedly at the anal beads on the floor. "–this."

"Then that makes two of us," I offer up. "I didn't come here expecting 'this', either." I mimic his finger quotes. "I'm a house fluffer. I fluff pillows. Not penises."

"You're a house stager?"

"Stager. Fluffer. You know."

"And you're pretty sheltered," he adds. "I've never heard the term 'house fluffer' before. Stager, yes. Fluffer, no."

"And I'd never heard of fluffer as a porn term," I say with a rush of heat to my face.

"Fair enough."

"Nothing about today is fair, Will." Saying his name to his face tastes like ice cream with toffee pieces and hot fudge.

"Maybe your friends were right."

"Right?" I peer at him, eyes dry, my mouth parched from stress.

"Remember that day in the parking lot? When they painted your windshield?"

"You remember that?"

He holds his hands up like he's imagining a marquee. "Mallory Monahan. Most Likely to Become a Porn Star."

Oh, God. He *does* remember.

A light laugh comes out of him as he shakes his head, eyes hard. "I assumed that was a joke."

"It was!" I sputter. "A total joke! I'm not — "

Karen returns, fingering the zip-tie cuffs. "Am I taking her in?"

It's tempting to say *yes* right now, to escape this unending humiliation.

But I may be embarrassed, but I'm not *stupid*.

"Please," I say to Will. I'm super close to begging. "Today has been awful, and I just realized I'm not getting paid. There goes three hundred bucks." My shoulders drop in defeat. "And I gave them good feng shui advice about the living room." I look up, troubled by that misaligned furniture. "All that work for nothing."

Karen leads us into the living room as Will huddles with her, their voices just whispers that make me feel even more ashamed and needy. Technically, Will should not have a say in whether the cops arrest me, but in small towns, this is how it works. The wealthy family has pull. Notice how he punched Beastman and no one's talking about charging him with assault?

And I really did rat Karen out twenty-two years ago, so she has a reason to hold a grudge against me. After watching twenty minutes of that horrible horror movie, I peed the bed in fear for a week before telling Mom what happened. I thought she got her payback when Karen busted that house party when I was in eleventh grade, but I guess not.

While Will and Karen chat at the front door, I make myself useful, pushing with my shoulder to move the sofa. They stop talking and watch me as I grunt.

"What are you doing?" Will finally asks.

"I know why you can't sell this house," I blurt out. "It's not the lukewarm market. It's your energy flow."

"Energy flow?" he chokes out, face half amused, one eyebrow up.

"Are you arresting me or not?" I ask Karen. "Either release me and let me go home to lick my wounds, or take me in and make this day suck even more."

"Lick," one of the other officers says with a snicker.

"Suck," Karen snorts.

Great. My permanent record is in the hands of the cop equivalent of Beavis and Butthead.

"I don't want any charges pressed against Mallory," Will declares, giving me a look of kindness that takes me back to my teenage self, when he could have melted my heart with one one-hundredth of that power. "It sounds like this was a case of wrong place, wrong time."

"Wrong industry," I agree.

"I don't want to add another wrong, so let's not read her

her rights," he tells Karen, who tucks the zip-tie handcuffs into her belt and gives me a stern look, as if she's telepathically making sure I understand I'm getting away with something.

"Thank you," I say to him, tears finally emerging, a wave of relief surfacing on the churning ocean inside me.

"You're welcome," he says as I leave, his body a wall I have to pass as he opens the front door. Reflex makes me inhale, his scent similar to high school, yet different. His cologne is more sophisticated, but the essence of Will Lotham is still there.

Still strong.

Still hopelessly out of reach.

I'm halfway to my car when I hear him shout, "Mallory!"

I turn around. He is standing on the top step, his arm pulled back in perfect quarterback form. "Here! Catch!"

The object sails through the air like he plotted out $y = -x^2$ and followed the parabolic curve.

I fumble, but complete the pass.

No. Not *that* kind of pass. I wish.

I take the dog's chew toy—okay, *string of anal beads*—he threw at me back to my car, turn the key in the ignition, and drive away.

With my phone charging this time.

Chapter Five

You know how I know I live in a small town?

When the garbage man shouts through my open window: "Hey, Mallory! Heard you finally found a new job! Nice ass!"

My pillow doesn't act as a good shame silencer, sadly.

The *beep beep beep* of the truck backing up, pivoting to leave the cul-de-sac where I'm renting someone's in-law apartment, adds insult to injury.

I'm up now.

There are only two good things about being unemployed: my time is my own, and I can sleep in.

Tom the Trash Dude just ruined one of those.

Habit makes me pick up my now-charging phone from my bedside table and check notifications.

Seventy-six of them.

I rub my eyes and try to focus. That can't be right. Normally I have four or five, and three of those are links to ketogenic recipes for bread from Perky, who doesn't understand (or care) that gluten-free brownies aren't free carbs that don't count because she has celiac disease.

I open the notifications.

I click the first one, expecting a recipe for some low-carb piece of juicy meat.

And I'm right.

Only it's a picture of Beastman on top of me, shiny and exposed like a bodybuilder, my face squarely in Will's crotch, mouth open like Kathleen the AlwaysDoll.

I close the link.

I bury the phone under my pillow.

And I blink.

I did not see that. That picture does not exist. Nope.

If I tell myself I did not see that, then it didn't happen.

Bzzz.

It's Mom, my mother types in her text that appears on the screen that says MOM at the top.

I know, Mom. I've told you a thousand times, I double thumb back. *You're in my phone as Mom.*

I knew you needed money, honey, but this? she replies, adding a high-five emoji, followed by *Oops!* and a frown.

I sit up so fast, I fall off my own bed, the phone sliding onto the floor, staring up with the blue glow of shame.

What do you mean? I reply.

The picture of you with two men, she answers. *One is very naked.*

What picture? I text back.

The one all over the local news, she says, adding a ghost. Mom really needs to up her emoji game.

"There's a picture of me on the news?" I gasp, scrolling quickly to find the expected text from Perky.

And there it is.

As a photograph, the pic is actually not half bad. You can tell Spatula knows how to frame a scene.

If anyone should, it's him.

On the left, you see nothing but gleaming, oiled-up, tanned skin in bulging rolls of muscle that make Beastman look like a human challah bread that was brushed with egg and butter, then baked.

I'm in the middle. Kinda. Sorta. He's behind me, his crotch on my hip. It was snapped as the dog toy – er, anal beads pushed against my ass, so we're twisted in more ways than one. He's almost on his knees.

My hair looks damn good. Of all the times to have perfect hair.

And I am facing Will Lotham's suit-covered crotch. Will's bent down, his face in an unfortunate freeze frame of intensity that makes him look like he's a Dom ready to go in for the kill.

Perky's text after the pic: *Our high school valedictorian is a porn star. We need to name the new high school swimming pool after you. We'll call it Double Dip Mallory.*

Where did you get that picture? I text her.

Ah, you're up! Got it from Fiona, she replies.

And where did she get it? I start to hyperventilate. Air won't get into my lungs. Tiny white dots appear in my vision. I can't black out. I can't.

Wait. If I black out, I won't have to feel any of this.

Hyperventilation is highly underrated.

I can't believe you didn't tell me about this, I read, and start to reply to Perk.

Until I realize it's from Mom.

I'm sorry. It's a long story, I type, realizing that I use that phrase a lot these days.

I'm sure it is, Mom replies. *Just know that we love you no matter what, sweetie, and we're going to do whatever it takes to cure you.*

Cure me? I text back.

Of your porn addiction. I've spent the last hour online, doing searches. It turns out this is a thing. Mom adds a heart, then a shooting star, to her text.

Mom, I'm not a porn addict, I reply in a blind panic. *Besides, that's not how porn addiction works. It's not about making porn.*

No one ever thinks they are. The first step is admitting you have a problem, sweetie. She adds a poop emoji.

The only problem I have is unemployment, I snap back.

You don't need a job, Mallory. You need help. We can move you back into your old room while you go to twelve-step meetings, she responds.

For what?

Porn addiction! Haven't you been reading? Oh, no, is this part of it, too? Is there some cognitive decline we need to know about? She adds another heart, as if that will somehow make up for her basically suggesting I'm losing my faculties.

There are twelve-step meetings for that? And no, my brain is just fine! Aside from bursting inside my skull at this conversation. *Mom, I swear I am not a porn addict. I'm a house fluffer. I went to a job and it turned out they were filming pornography there*, I try to explain.

A few dots, and then: *Mallory, this is your dad.*

Hi Dad, I reply. My shame is complete.

You're not a porn addict? he types. Bear in mind, my father has his own phone. He could text me separately. But I routinely get texts from Dad on Mom's phone. They also share the same Facebook account. You know the type. Their name is SharonandRoyMonahaninAnderhill.

No, Dad, I am not, I reply, ready to pull out the big guns and use ALL CAPS.

I told Sharon! I tried. She wouldn't listen. I told her you have some perfectly reasonable explanation for being featured in a threesome picture with a naked porn star covered in oil and our old high school quarterback playing with a dog's chew toy, he writes back.

My eyes land on the item in question, sitting on a table by the front door. In the bold light of morning, it looks less like a pet novelty and more like what it is. I can't believe I didn't see it before.

That's what Dad took away from that picture? *That?*

I take it back, Dad. I am a porn star. Mom figured it out, I fake admit. Might as well give in. They've broken me with their earnestness. The CIA could give up waterboarding if they just hired Sharon and Roy Monahan to turn their Earnest Parenting laser beam on prisoners.

I told her you were too shy to do it. You'd sooner eat broken glass than do what it looks like you're doing in that picture. Not my daughter, he adds.

I smash the pillow over my face. Self-smothering is a thing, right?

MAL! Meet us at Beanerino in an hour. Fi and I need to help you through this, Perky's text says.

You mean you want me to give you a blow by blow of what happened, I reply.

YOU BLEW THEM BOTH? she types back.

No, I did not blow them both! I hurriedly reply, clicking Send before realizing I sent that text... to my dad.

If I eat the entire pillow, I can choke to death and be put out of my misery, right?

Uh, thanks for that level of clarity, Mallory. We're glad you feel comfortable sharing with us. This is Mom again. Your father is feeling a bit faint, Mom replies.

Mom, there's a missionary at my door. I need to go talk to him, I lie.

Mormon? she asks. I have no idea why.

Does it matter? Gotta go.

I shut my phone down. All the way. Which means this is bad. Worse than bad. If my mother has seen that picture on social media, it means everyone has.

Everyone. Because once something reaches the Facebook feed of SharonandRoyMonahaninAnderhill, you know it's oversaturated.

All I can do at this point is to do what Perky said. Meet her and Fiona at Beanerino. If anyone can come up with a strategy for managing this, it's Fiona, who is a one-woman anti-shame campaign.

And if anyone can make me feel better about becoming an accidental porn-star-by-proxy, it's Perky.

* * *

"I told you to keep that damn phone charged!" Perky scolds as I sit down with a tray covered in gluten-free pastries and not-disgusting pastries and better-than-orgasmic coffees at our favorite table at Beanerino. This place used to be a fast-food restaurant, so there's none of the hipster ambience of some of the smaller, hand-roasted batch coffee shops that have popped up in the suburbs, but it has clean bathrooms and a drive-thru, two features you can't overlook.

They cater to the SUV-driving mommy crowd who stop between Pilates classes and salt therapy, listening to self-help audiobooks titled *Busy Is Just Another Word for Failure* and *Apply Your MBA to Parenting: Ten Steps to IPO Your Kids and Leverage Their Success.*

With the word *Their* scratched out on the cover and *Your* handwritten in.

"You wouldn't have gotten into this mess if you'd listened to me," Perky pronounces in a sing-songy voice. She has a way of making me feel shame without shaming me. Pretty sure she's secretly my mother.

"It's not my fault!"

"Low battery life is a function of poor planning. Proper planning prevents porny people, Mal."

I pause, mid-sip. "I am holding a one-hundred-forty-degree beverage. Don't test me, Perk."

"How is it? We're using a new Malabar and we're worried weirdos like you will ruin it with your heavy-cream requests."

"I like zero carbs in my coffee. What's wrong with that?"

"Then drink it black. It's *that* good!"

I shudder.

"You ever try to froth heavy cream?" she huffs, as if we're talking about micro cardiac surgery for preemies.

"That barista in Florida on Spring Break did it. Mastered it. Had it down to a science," I taunt.

"She was Norwegian. Pretty sure her technique involved some weird hygge ritual."

But I got under Perky's skin. Always do when this topic rolls around.

"If anyone can do it, you can."

"Quit rubbing my nose in my inadequacies. Let's talk about yours! Turns out you did become a porn star. Fi and I were right back in high school," she says, pulling away before I can hit her.

"Are you two done? Because I'm patiently waiting to look at your porn," Fiona announces as she arrives in a whirlwind of color and essential oils. If a Himalayan salt lamp were a person, it would look like Fiona. All earth tones and soft lighting, she's made a complete reversal of her hardcore butch look back in high school. Her hair is now dyed a pale peachy blonde, long and flowing down her back, all her piercings grown in, tattoos of fairies and stars and butterflies dotting her shoulders.

Big change from the shaved head, bound breasts, flannel, and henna tats all over every surface of her exposed skin, seventh grade through twelfth.

"You're not supposed to like porn, Fiona. You look like a preschool teacher in an ashram," I grumble at her.

"Don't joke. There was an ad for that on Craigslist the other day. I nearly applied."

Perky makes a throat-cutting gesture at Fi. "Now is really not the time to bring up job openings on Craigslist."

Fiona suppresses a laugh and gives me a doe-eyed look. "You seriously applied for a *fluffer* job?"

"I thought it was a *house* fluffer job," I say for the thousandth time, my teeth gritted.

"Only you, Mallory."

"What does that mean?"

"You worked for the Tollesons for all those years, straight out of college. A Mormon couple running a real estate business. You come out and dance and party with us, but you're so goody-two-shoes. You limit yourself to two drinks. You–"

"Only when we're in public," I protest. "If we're hanging at your place or Perky's, I party down."

"Drunk Trivial Pursuit is not exactly living on the wild side."

"You *like* Drunk Trivial Pursuit!"

"I do, I do," she assures me. "But c'mon, Mal. You live in a bubble. Always have."

"Do not! Just because everyone else knew what a fluffer

was on a porn set doesn't make me a weirdo! Plenty of people have no idea what that term means."

Perky stands and walks over to the coffee counter where Raul, the barista for this shift, is cleaning out a frothing pitcher. Long dreadlocks flow down his back, looped together by a multi-colored scrunchy. Raul is the size of a linebacker with the heart of a cuddly teddy bear. When he smiles, those whiskey-colored eyes light up and spread sunshine throughout the coffee shop.

Too bad he's taken.

"Raul!" Perky calls out. "You know what a fluffer is?"

"Perky!" I hiss.

"Is that some kind of sandwich?" Raul asks, genuinely puzzled.

I really love him.

"You know," Perky says, snort-laughing. "Come on."

"No. Really. What's a fluffer?" Raul says without looking at her, wiping down the gleaming Pavoni espresso machine that was imported from Italy. It's big and shiny, glistening as it rises up to make all my fantasies come true.

And now I've triggered memories of Beastman gleaming and, uh, rising up.

"Porn," Perky says, drawing out the word, as if there's a secret code she knows and Raul just needs to hear the right word.

Raul's eyes widen, the whites turning into cue balls. "I know you didn't just say *porn*, right?" His Brazilian accent is light, but when he's surprised or upset, it deepens. His dad, Thiago, opened Beanerino about four years ago, and the coffee is divine.

Raul isn't hard on the eyes, either.

Perky's face goes slack. "Oh, my God. You're serious. You don't know what a fluffer is."

"Remember the conversation we had in sexual harassment training, Perky? How my father told you to stop with the depraved innuendos?"

Fiona and I share a look.

And then we lean closer to them.

"I'm not harassing you!" Perky sputters.

"No, of course not," he says, nose flaring. "You're just starting a casual conversation about pornography with me in a work setting."

"I'm not on shift!" she protests. "And I was just trying to prove a point."

"That you're utterly inappropriate, have no boundaries, and crave constant attention?" Raul replies calmly.

As Perky sputters, Fiona murmurs, "Wow, he figured her out fast."

"And that was just during her first training shift," he mutters, turning back to the machine.

"Never mind," Perky fumes, flouncing.

"See?" I gloat. "Not everyone knows. I'm not a weirdo."

"You're a weirdo, all right. And this proves nothing," Perky insists.

"I think it proves that a certain percentage of our generation knows what these dirty terms mean, and a much larger number has no idea because they aren't addicted to porn."

"You know what, Mal? I love when you showcase your nonjudgmental nature like this." Perky rolls her eyes and takes a sip of her coffee.

"I'm not being judgmental. I'm defending myself. Just because I don't spend my days on Urban Dictionary keeping up on all the newest terms doesn't mean I'm weird."

"You keep saying *weird*. Must mean you have a deep fear of it."

"If that were true, Perk, I wouldn't be your friend."

Perky grabs my laptop and opens it, clicking on a browser window and typing.

"What are you doing?"

"Proving a point."

She taps my screen. "Here we are."

Horror turns the coffee in my mouth to poison.

"We're in *public*!" I hiss. "You can't watch porn in public!"

"Says who?"

"Says everyone! It's indecent! Isn't it illegal, too?"

Fiona shakes her head slowly. "You are really holding onto some outdated notions, Mal."

"I think not watching sex videos in a public place isn't some nineteenth-century ideal. I mean, if they had sex videos then... I just—what if someone sees?"

Perky opens a second window and types "Mallory sex tape Beastman spit." She hits Enter.

"That is a horrible search term!" I practically scream.

But it works. The first link is to the porn-industry gossip blog Spatula sold the picture to.

"Oh, God! My entire social media presence is ruined forever." I swallow my coffee like it's laudanum. I'm single-handedly reviving "the vapors" as a medical condition.

Perky gives me a look and snorts. "Poor baby. That must suck so much, having one picture of you circulating among the thousand people here who give a shit."

"I know it's nothing like what you went through four years ago with Parker, but come on. This sucks, too."

"Until your breasts become a meme that's spread more often than the Ermahgerd girl, just stop." Right after college, Perky fell in love with Parker Campbell, an assistant DA who loved her right back.

Until he leaked sexy pictures of Perky's naked boobs with two dogs humping behind her head and the meme went viral.

No one could prove it was Parker, of course. And it didn't help that Persephone had changed her nickname to Perky in the worst confluence of events *ever*. She dumped him, he begged her to come back and claimed to know nothing about the photo leak, and to this day, she won't admit she still pines for him.

But yeah, what she went through is worse than this photo of what looks like me in a threesome.

With Beastman and Will.

"Anticipatory anxiety is real, Perky. *You* already know what the worst is that can happen. I'm a sitting duck," I sputter. A million thoughts crash through my mind as I look at the article with the picture of the three of us, front and center.

Most of them come down to this: I'll never work again.

"You look like you're in the middle of being spit roasted." Perky tilts her head. "Like the naked guy on top of you is fitting it in before getting up on his knees. What kind of lube did he use?"

"How would I know? We. Did. Not. Have. Sex." My voice goes lower with each word until I'm basically an echo from the Earth's core.

I've resorted to vocal fry as an emotional defense strategy.

Perky frowns. She's deeply disappointed.

"Why is Will Lotham wearing a suit for a porn scene? Is this CEO porn? I love the hot CEO stuff. So dominant," Fiona sighs. A slight blush pinks her cheeks and it hits me.

She's aroused.

"You two are supposed to be my friends! Not get turned on by pictures of me with a naked Beastman and our high school quarterback!"

And what the hell is spit roasting? Are they calling me a pig?

Fiona and Perky share a look that immediately taps into

fourteen years of petty slights that line up in a perfect queue inside my ninth grade self. "We *are* your friends!" Perky assures me, patting my hand sympathetically.

"*And* we can be turned on by your porn," Fiona mutters.

"Stop calling it *my* porn!"

"What was it like, being that close to Will?" Perky asks, eyes all star-crossed and gooey. "Does he smell as good as he did in high school?"

"I wouldn't know. You're the one who stole his jockstrap from his locker in ninth and huffed it every night before bed," I say, giving her my best mean-girls, dagger-filled look. No way will *I* admit to smelling him yesterday.

"Did not!"

"Oh, please. We all know you did," Fiona adds. "If social media had been a thing back then, you'd have been busted. And shamed. And ruined. Your reputation would have been demolished by the giant memory bank that is Google."

"Oh. Gee. How awful," Perky deadpans, giving Fiona a killer look. "Given that already happened, I'm not too worried."

Fiona just laughs in that way you can mock a friend who remembers your Sailor Moon phase, complete with underwear you made using fabric pens.

With every word they say, a piece of me dies. "Oh, God," I groan. "I *am* ruined."

"Huh?" Fiona turns to me. "What do you mean?"

"This *did* happen in the era of social media! Spatula posted those pictures and sold them to some scammy porn-industry gossip site! I am in the great memory bank! The memory bank that never, ever dies!"

"Not a memory bank," Fiona says, avoiding eye contact. "More like a spank bank."

"Success is fleeting," Perky says with a nod, noshing on a piece of gluten-free brownie. "But porn is forever."

"That is not helping."

She shoves the remains of her brownie at me. "Here."

"It's gluten free." I wrinkle my nose.

"So?"

"Yuck."

"You are so picky, Mal."

"I get to be picky when I'm traumatized. That should be a universal human right. Someone needs to add it to the Geneva Convention." I huff. "Along with the right to masturbate."

Fiona twirls a finger around one ear while looking at Perky, who is now busy typing on my laptop.

"You don't have to be silent about it, *Feisty*," I snap, using an ancient nickname for her.

She laughs. "Haven't been called that in a long time."

"Probably because you haven't kickboxed a linebacker into unconsciousness in a long time," Perky reminds her.

"He deserved it! Chris Fletcher was such a jerk."

"He pulled your bra strap. You drop kicked him."

"The only way to deter a bully is to take him on, face to face."

"Which you did."

"Two weeks of detention and a stupid nickname was totally worth it."

"Whatever happened to him?" I ask, curious.

Fiona turns a fiery shade of red, eyes jittery. "Who knows?"

"I know," Perky announces. "I have magic powers!" She presses her fingertips against her temples. "O oracle, bring the essence of Chris Fletcher to me." Yogic breathing comes out of her. She's breathing in for four through the left nostril, out for eight through the right. This is possible only because she broke her nose in tenth grade, and ever since, she's had a deviated septum.

It's not the only part of her that deviates.

"You Googled him," Fiona says flatly.

"I did," Perky admits.

"He owns a gym two towns over," Fiona grunts. "His sister's son is in my class."

"You teach Fletch's nephew?"

"Shut up." Fiona checks Perky with a strong shoulder.

"All this talk of Will and porn stars made me think of Fletch!" Perky mocks.

"That's your trigger? A *porn star* made you think of Fletch?" Fiona is disgusted. So disgusted, she's forced to take another bite of her chocolate chip cookie.

"No, silly. Will Lotham did. The porn-star thing was just extra."

"Let's stop talking about Chris Fletcher and get back to Mallory Monahan, porn star," Fi grouses. Her eyes narrow as she looks at me. "Call me Feisty again and I'll call you Fluffy forever."

"You wouldn't!"

Perky holds her hands up like she's an emcee for some 1930s vaudeville show. "Fluffy!"

I groan. "You guys suck."

I get a self-satisfied smirk from Fiona that turns into compassion quickly as she gets back to business. "Don't worry. My brother Tim is an SEO specialist. He can help us scrub all this."

"Scrub?"

"You know. Online reputation management. That's what he does." Fiona points to Perky. "Remember? Tim helped her and her parents when the two dogs humping mess happened."

"Online reputation? I thought he worked for big companies, making sure their websites float to the top of searches? I didn't know he was still in that business."

"It turns out the real money comes from manipulating the rankings of really embarrassing dirt on people. He makes loads of money on the side now, removing tweets and Facebook posts about indiscretions."

"Indiscretions?"

"Everything from sex tapes to drunk tweeting an old flame. Or the guy who was fifteen and sent naked pictures on Snapchat, but now he's twenty-one and trying to get into law school and those pics are haunting him."

Perky nods. "He got a bunch of melon memes removed by claiming they were causing economic harm to the melon industry, and that melon farmers might sue."

"That's a thing? They believed him?"

"The stupider site owners did, and that's what matters."

"But your boobs are everywhere. I've seen that meme on MySpace, for God's sake."

"I'm less scandalized to hear that my boobs are on MySpace than I am to hear that you still go there, Mal. Why?"

"It was an accident. Came up in some search recently."

"I'm going to ask Tim to get my boobs off MySpace. We didn't even think to go that far back when Mom and Dad hired him to clear my picture off the internet."

"Why bother if no one goes there?"

"I don't know. Just to feel like I'm doing something."

I turn to Fiona. "You're saying Tim could help me if this goes too far? Because I really, REALLY don't want people to be able to type 'Mallory sex tape Beastman spit' into Google and find those pictures. That's who I'll be for the rest of my life!"

"Tim can help. But let's look at old Beastman, first," Perky interrupts before Fi can answer.

"What?" I'm so confused.

She goes into the big porn-video database and types one word: *Beastman.*

"Holy smokes, he's done a lot of movies!" Fiona gasps.

Perky's eyes narrow as she points to one on the page. "He looks familiar." *Click.* "Oh! That's why." She starts laughing.

"Because you watch so much porn, you're on a first-name basis with the stars?" I ask.

"No. Because he's the spokesman for AlwaysDoll."

"Her name is Kathleen," I mutter under my breath.

"How do you know that?"

"He told me I look like her."

Fiona starts coughing uncontrollably.

"When I do this," I explain, making my mouth a perfect O of shock.

Eyes ping-ponging between the laptop screen and my face, Perky gives me an appreciative look. "You do! It's as if they used you as the prototype model."

"I'll take Jobs Mallory Never Wants for a bazillion dollars, Alex."

Fiona pulls herself together and gasps, "You said he looked familiar, Perk? You a Beastman fangirl?"

"No. It was an internet boycott I was part of. The Always-Doll manufacturer was using slave labor to make the dye for the plastic labia."

"Always looking out for consumers, aren't you? You're like the Consumer Product Safety Commission for sex toys," Fiona deadpans.

"Slave labor is heinous, no matter what it's used to make," Perky declares. "And besides, the one-liners wrote themselves." She sighs. "That was back when Twitter was all about brevity and wit. Once they expanded a tweet to 280 characters, it all went downhill."

"Right. *That's* why Twitter lost its shine," I reply, my tongue so far in my cheek that it might as well be coming out my earlobe.

"I do have to give AlwaysDoll credit, though," Perky says. "They have a robotic clitoris as part of it. The guy has to get her aroused to the point of multiple clitoral orgasms before her vaginal walls clench around him while he's pumping away. Social engineering at its finest."

Fiona nods with deep approval. "That's progressive." Pondering for a moment, she then adds, "And extremely practical. It's a public service, even."

"Their entire engineering team is made up of female electrical engineers," Perky continues. "But if you go on enough men's rights forums, you can find the hack code to disable that function."

"Can we get back to my porn problem? I would rather talk about anything but this," I say as I finish my coffee.

"I am so glad you can finally admit you have a problem," Fiona says to me. "It's the first step."

"In what?"

"Healing."

"The only thing I need to heal is my bank account." I stare at the bottom of my empty cup. "And you sound like my mom. Speaking of Mom, I'm about a month away from having to give up my apartment."

"That bad?" Perky's only half paying attention as she clicks on pictures of women on their knees, the videos frozen on still images that make me realize I really, really don't like mayonnaise, but especially when it's all over a woman's face.

"I'm going to have to move back in with my parents."

"No!" Both of my friends have the decency to be horrified by proxy.

"Yep. The scourge of being a millennial."

"I thought avocado toast and not buying cars was the scourge," Fiona says. She holds her coffee aloft. "And buying overpriced coffee."

"We're blamed for everything. I'm jaded. Name a social problem and we're like Six Degrees of Kevin Bacon. We're always one degree from it being our fault."

"We have a lot of power we don't use," Perky mutters as she stares at anuses pulled open by speculums. "Aha!"

I have never, ever been more terrified by a single word.

"What is 'aha!' worthy?" Fiona inquires, looking about as scared as I feel.

"I found the perfect Beastman porn clip."

A hushed silence surrounds us like a crowded elevator after a particularly loud fart that cannot be blamed on any specific person.

Except in this case, Perky's it.

She clicks Play.

Fiona snaps the Mute button.

The movie starts, Beastman completely naked and oiled up on a bed that looks like something out of a set for *The Flintstones*. It's supposed to look like a carved boulder, but instead it looks like a slightly decayed mushroom.

And speaking of mushrooms...

"He's got quite the tip!" Perky admires.

I cover the screen with my palm. "Turn it off!"

"No!" she snatches the laptop away from me, my hand moving down, thumb running deep along a few keys.

Meanwhile, Beastman starts going at it on screen.

"He's mounting her from behind!" I gasp.

"That's called doggie style," Fiona says, as if she's teaching me the names of the continents.

"I know what doggie style is!"

"Well, don't get mad at me. You didn't know what a fluffer is. I thought I was being helpful."

"Oooooh, baby, you're so tight," says a man's voice, deep and intense, choked with sensuality. It sounds like he's speaking from above us, right here in the room. "Yeah, I'm gonna make you scream."

We all look up and toward the door.

No man.

Toward Raul.

He's not speaking.

Toward the laptop.

"You want Daddy to give it to you, huh?" the man says again, the sound now reverberating throughout the entire coffee shop. About ten people, including one woman with a toddler, are looking around the store, puzzled.

Raul's jaw drops.

Funny. He looks just like a male version of an AlwaysDoll.

"Who is saying this?" I screech, looking around wildly. The sound is coming from *everywhere*.

Fiona points to Beastman's mouth. "It's him!"

"I'm impaling you, baby. How's it feel to be impaled?" Panting breaths make it clear he's *super* into being Vlad the Impaler.

Fiona's finger brushes against his moving lips on the laptop screen. "See? His lips are moving in time with the words."

"Perky! Oh my God!" I scream. "What did you do to my computer?"

Smack! Smack! "You like it when I ride this big wet ass, don't you?" Beastman says to his onscreen costar, grabbing her throat from behind.

Raul starts fanning himself with a coffee-drink menu. The woman with a toddler covers his ears and picks him up, rushing for the door. A cluster of teen boys grins and looks around, following the sound like they're on a scavenger hunt.

Beastman pulls out, bends down, and–

"Ewwwwww!" we three whisper in horror.

I peer closer as I frantically push every keyboard button possible. "Is he licking her *there*?"

"Now we know why she has a big wet ass," Fiona marvels.

And then:

"Baby, I wanna taste you," Beastman moans. The woman turns around.

No.

No!

"Not ass to mouth!" Perky hush-screams as Beastman kisses his costar. "Never ass to mouth!"

Two things happen as she says it.

One: Will Lotham walks in the front door.

Two: I successfully turn off whatever weird wireless glitch has patched my laptop's sound system into the coffee shop's Bluetooth stereo speakers.

"Turn that off!" Raul says, snapping my laptop closed as the sound system dies out. "I cannot believe you're watching porn at work, Perky."

"I'm off the clock, so technically it's not 'at work,' even if it's physically at my location of work," Perky says, going pedantic.

Will leans against a support joist and crosses his arms over his chest, listening. Unlike yesterday, he's wearing casual clothes, jeans that mold to his body with just enough looseness to give him freedom of movement, but tight enough to make me all hot and bothered. The knuckles of his right hand are red, a little raw. Must be from punching out Beastman. Ouch.

A simple green button-down shirt, tucked in, finishes the Old New England Money look. His hair is a little messy, the wind outside likely responsible for the dark waves to have gone rogue.

And he's watching us with the practiced eye of a man who is taking in a scene before acting.

"What do you think you're doing?" I challenge him, blushing furiously.

"Learning that you never go ass to mouth." One shoulder goes up in a shrug as he looks at Perky, who has the decency to blush.

"It's a good lesson to internalize," she tells him as she shrugs back.

"Haven't you caused enough damage?" I huff, shoving aside all feelings of shame, which is Sisyphean but I'm a hopeless optimist, so I try.

"Me?"

"Who released that photo of us?" I demand, holding back from calling Spatula by his name.

"I tried to get him to stop! The damn guy was too fast. Cops took him into custody, but he's out now, and I guess he sold it to a porn site."

"So you *do* know about the photo?" Fiona asks him.

"Is there anyone in town our age who doesn't know about it?" Will snorts. Our eyes meet. If I weren't so angry, I'd see a little hint of compassion in those gorgeous, blue-green eyes. "I tried, Mallory. He got away." He holds the stare for a beat longer than he should.

"It's not your fault," I admit, transfixed. "I can't believe this, though. There goes my career."

"I'm not exactly thrilled about my reputation, either," Will declares, eyes moving to the drink board behind the counter. Narrowing his gaze, he seems to stop scanning. I follow his line of sight and guess he's a macchiato man.

"But you're a *guy*," Perky says, her voice tinged with

venom. "A successful one. This will be spun by the media as the up-and-coming real estate business wunderkind putting an end to obscenity in Anderhill. You'll be treated like a crusader, driving out all of the impure influences that threaten our great region."

"What about me?" I ask breathlessly, caught up in Perky's rant.

"Oh, you're a whore now. Forever. You're toast."

"Avocado toast," Fiona says, patting my hand.

Will's eye roll is epic, and strangely powerful, an intoxicating look of dismissal that makes me think all of this might not be so bad after all. "It's a single picture on a cheesy pornography-industry gossip site. It got around to people our age in town. Big deal. It's not like many people are going to see it."

I look at him. "My mother texted me about it. She saw it in her Facebook feed."

He winces. "Damn."

"Yeah. When something goes viral enough for the Gen Xers to see it, it's *over*," Perky adds.

"I don't want to be a meme!" I cry out.

"Because that would be the worst thing ever," Perky says in a flat, sarcastic tone.

"No. Projecting your porn over the sound system of a family-friendly coffee shop is the worst thing ever," Fiona says, ducking behind me, hiding her face with a menu. "I think that mother was one of the parents of a child in my preschool class."

"What are you doing here?" I ask Will, shaken out of my embarrassed stupor, suddenly defensive. It's fine for my friends to make fun of me for accidentally projecting porn all over the coffee shop, but Will isn't my friend.

He doesn't have the privilege.

Hands in his pockets, going casual in a way that makes me tingle from the tops of my ears to the ends of my toes, he says the words I fantasized about hearing for all of my formative adolescence:

"Actually," Will Lotham says, "I'm looking for *you*."

Chapter Six

I love the scent of old movie theaters. They smell like all of the happy people from the past converging in one place to let their imaginations be sparked by a shared experience.

You know what they smell like, though, during the first show of the day?

Old ladies.

The ten a.m. showing at the local second-run cineplex is filled with old women and unemployed losers like me. For three dollars a ticket, we can watch a movie you'll be able to find a month from now on Netflix.

But hey–it's an outing. An escape.

A procrastination technique that supports a small, local business.

I need to procrastinate. *Hard*.

Because I have a job offer I really, really need to refuse.

At the coffee shop yesterday, Will told me to check my email. This is what I found:

I like how you started to re-arrange the living room. That feng shui theory sounded ludicrous, but then again, I'm superstitious enough to bury a statue of St. Joseph when trying to sell a property. I need someone to handle staging for our company. If you're willing to do a one-month trial as a consultant, I've got a gig for you. No coconut oil, and sorry–clothing isn't optional.

The words weren't the problem.

It was the smirk.

And the fact that I'm so desperate for a job, I'm actually considering his offer.

The bastard.

As if it's not enough that I crushed on him for four years, he also had to save me from being arrested, and now he has the power to give me a consulting gig that saves me from eviction.

See? What a jerk.

If I close my eyes and transport myself back to that moment yesterday, I can feel him. Not through touch. That would involve going further back, to the porn incident.

No.

I can feel the essence of Will, the space inside myself I created fourteen years ago, a habitat deep in my core where he lives. Sounds creepy, right? Like I'm lowering a bucket full of lotion to him. But hey, it's my imagination. My brain.

My *heart*.

And having grown-up Will make grown-up Mallory a job offer is the closest thing to teen Mallory being asked to the prom by teen Will.

It will have to do.

Yet–I know I can't say yes.

My career isn't the issue. Even my bank account, as starved and frail as it is, isn't the issue. The issue is remarkably simple: I can't take my personality and turn it back ten to fourteen years. Working for Will Lotham would do that to me.

As the lights dim in the theater, the creaking old seats make an asynchronous melody of their own, the ten or so ticket buyers settling in. I munch happily on my cheap popcorn, heedless of the hydrogenated coconut oil I'm feeding my arteries. If I'm going to have coconut oil in my life, I want it like *this*.

Not smeared all over me by a naked porn star.

The Diet Coke habit I can't shake–only at the movies!–makes me feel like I'm home again. My mouth is happy, at least.

"Home" being a relative term. I have about a dozen different internal settings for home.

One of them, unfortunately, involves Will.

A trailer for a big, sweeping historical drama starts, the quiet classical music setting the tone that this is a serious movie coming our way just as I tune out, the backdrop perfect for self-reflection.

Or maybe self-indulgence.

"Hey! Why are you sighing so loud?" rasps an old lady behind me. "You having an asthma attack?"

Twisting in my seat, I look back to find a helmet of tight curls attached to a half-worried, half-angry old lady holding a barrel of popcorn bigger than her head.

"No," says a familiar voice. I look up to find Fiona at the end of my row, holding a box of Junior Mints and an enormous bottled water. "She's just hiding from the world."

"Ain't we all?" the old woman says with a surprisingly girlish giggle.

"What are you doing here?" I hiss at Fiona, eyeing the candy. I had planned to be good and not sugar binge, but when your friend brings the sugar, it's not your weakness. It's hers.

Therefore, it doesn't count against you, right?

"Looking for you. You turned off your phone and we figured you went into turtle mode."

"Turtle mode?"

"That's what Perky and I call it when you do this."

"I don't do 'this.' There is no *this*. I am availing myself of some of the finest contemporary cinema at a cut-rate price. I am being a careful consumer, but also a well-educated member of society who–"

"This is a movie about male strippers, Mal. Don't push it."

"The score was nominated for a Golden Globe! And male strippers are an under-appreciated sector of society."

"Damn right about that," says the old lady behind me.

I try again. "This movie is a complex social commentary about upward mobility in American society being thwarted for males by–"

"Why haven't you taken Will's job offer?" I can tell by the look on Fiona's face that I can't snow her.

Shoot.

"*Shhhhhhhh!*" the old lady behind me says."You're ruining the movie."

"I'm not spoiling anything," I protest.

"You're trying to turn it into a thinking movie! I didn't come to stare at abs so I could think!" *Creak creak*. The old lady settles her butt in the seat and sniffs.

"Look," Fiona says, dropping her voice. "You need a job. Will offered you one. He also kept you from being arrested. Why not make hay while the sun shines?"

"That saying really doesn't apply here, Fi."

"You know what I mean. Count all your eggs before they're in one basket."

"Stop, Fi. Please." Before I can point out that she's combined two old sayings, she jumps in and says:

"You need to take Will's job offer."

"Why?"

"Because Perky and I decided so."

"That isn't a good enough reason!"

"Since when?"

She's got me there.

I point to the screen and cover my lips with a librarian's finger. For some reason, she actually shuts up. It works, but now the movie is just going to be two hours of me squirming in my seat, knowing I'm in for a lecture when we're done watching oiled-up, naked men's bodies gyrating in fifteen-foot high technicolor.

Okay. So maybe Fiona's lecture isn't why I'll be squirming. Whatever.

Two hours later, I'm proven right. The second the credits start to roll, Fiona chugs the last of her water and says, "Text him now and accept."

"Come on! I'm trying to enjoy the movie score, you fun sucker."

"It's nothing but shouting the word 'bitch' in twenty-seven different languages."

"It's art."

"You're deflecting."

"That is a form of art, too."

"You've certainly elevated it to one," she says to me, bright and smiling. Fiona has this way of staring at people with those big, round eyes that are a little too interested in the world. Most of us have our friendly, outgoing edges filed off brutally in middle school.

Fiona was ahead of her time, emotionally darker than the rest of us at a time when optimism was rewarded with scorn and therefore being cynical was justified, but somehow she reclaimed that attentiveness. A pure spirit.

Maybe the four-year-olds she teaches did it.

What it's created, though, is a deeply dangerous friendship

pit I fall into over and over: she can be blunt without being threatening until it's too late.

Caught.

"Just because you and Perky think I should take this job isn't good enough. Why? I could lose out on a much better job opportunity if I tie myself up in this one."

"Are you tied up by other men right now?"

"Fi! I expect Perky to do the double entendre sex-joke crap all the time, but not you."

"Are you offended?"

"No! If I were offended, I wouldn't be friends with her. I just didn't expect it from *you*." I giggle through an image of being tied up by Will Lotham.

And suddenly, I'm not giggling. I'm a little swoony.

Standing quickly, I hustle Fiona out of our row and up the incline to the exit of the movie theater. The sun is bright and shining, forcing us both to fish around in our handbags for sunglasses. Without any conversation whatsoever, we turn right, then left, and find ourselves in front of SushiMe and a little Mexican restaurant we both love, Taco Taco Taco, known to the locals as Taco Cubed.

Fiona hesitates, leaning toward the sushi place. "So, Mal — "

"Taco special!" I call back as I walk toward the scent of cumin and affordable. Fiona's shoulder's sag. Why is her sigh filled with frustration? Weird. She loves tacos, even if her choices leave much to be desired.

The line is long at Taco Cubed, filled with people who work regular, full-time jobs grabbing whatever bit of hope and luxury they can in their hour respite from being under the thumb of The Man.

That's what I tell myself as I peel off six of my last dollars and buy the dirt-cheap daily taco special.

"Hey," I say to her as we wait for our orders, "it's Monday. Don't you have to teach today?"

"In-service day. We spent two hours talking about new educational standards and agreed to meet back up at five tonight for classroom cleaning."

"I could have been spared the high-pressure sales pitch if it weren't for that?"

"No. You would have had Perky pressure you at some point."

I shudder.

"See? I'm doing you a favor," Fiona says in that smooth, melodic voice. Our two taco specials get shoved up on the serving counter, crispy, cheesy goodness in brown plastic baskets lined with parchment paper, sour cream and guacamole exactly where they should be.

On the side.

There is a perfect ratio of sour cream, guac, and salsa on a shredded chicken tostada. No one can make it happen for you. Many restaurants have tried. All have failed. Only the mouth knows its own pleasure, and calibration like Taco Heaven cannot be mass produced.

It simply cannot.

Taco Heaven is a sensory explosion of flavor that defies logic. First, you have to eye the amount of spiced meat, shredded lettuce, chopped tomatoes, and tomatillos. You must consider the size and crispiness of the shells. Some people–I call them blasphemers–like soft tacos. I am sitting across from Exhibit A.

We won't talk about soft tacos. They don't make it to Taco Heaven. People who eat soft tacos live in Taco Purgatory, never fully understanding their moral failings, repeating the same mistakes again and again for all eternity.

Like Perky and dating.

Once you inventory your meat, lettuce, tomato, and shell quality, the real construction begins. Making your way to Taco Heaven is like a mechanical engineer building a bridge in your mouth. Measurements must be exact. Payloads are all about formulas and precision. One miscalculation and it all fails.

Taco Death is worse than Taco Purgatory, because the only reason for Taco Death is miscalculation.

And that's all on *you*.

"Oh, God," Fiona groans through a mouthful of abomination. "You're doing it, aren't you?"

"Doing what?" I ask primly, knowing damn well what she's talking about.

"You treat eating tacos like you're the star of some *Mythbusters* show."

"Do not."

"Do too."

"Even if I do—and I am *not* conceding the point—it would be a worthwhile venture."

"You are as weird about your tacos as Perky is about her coffee."

"Take it back! I am not that weird."

"You are."

"Am not."

"This is why Perky and I swore we would never come here with you again."

Fiona grabs my guacamole and smears the rounded scoop all over the outside of her soft taco.

I shriek.

"How can you do that?" I gasp, the murder of the perfect ratio a painful, almost palpable blow. The mashed avocado has a death rattle that rings in my ears.

Smug, tight lips give me a grimace. "See? A normal person would shout, 'Hey! That's mine!' but you're more offended that I've desecrated my inferior taco wrapping with the wrong amount of guac."

"Because it's *wrong*."

"You should have gone to MIT, Mal. You need a job that involves nothing but pure math for the sake of calculating stupid shit no one else cares about."

"So glad to know that a preschool teacher holds such high regard for math," I snark back. *And MIT didn't give me the kind of merit aid package I got from Brown*, I don't add.

"Was that supposed to sting?"

She takes the rest of my guacamole, grabs a spoon, and starts eating it straight out of the little white paper scoop container thing.

"How can you do that? It's like people who dip their french fries in mayonnaise." I shudder, standing to get in line to buy more guac.

"*I* dip my french fries in mayo!"

"More evidence of your madness, Fi. Get help now. It may not be too late." I stick my finger in her face. "And by the way, you and Perky talk about my taco habits behind my back? Some friends!" I *hmph* and turn toward the counter.

Pedro sees me coming and slides a side of guac to me. "No charge, Mallory."

"Thanks! What's this about? You guys always charge me." I dig in my pocket for change.

"We saw your picture." He gives me a sympathetic look, which is jarring, given the gang tattoos all over his face. When someone who got tatted up in prison feels sorry for you, you know you're a hopeless case.

"Oh, that," I laugh, trying to pass it off as a joke.

"Hey, no judgment, man. We all gotta make our money however we can." A knowing smile makes him look slightly less threatening.

"No, no, Pedro, I wasn't really working in a porno."

"Sure." *Wink*. The teardrop tat at the corner of his eye folds up. "Sure you weren't."

I take the guac and run away.

"That was fast," Fiona says, her mouth twitching with amusement.

"You heard every word. Don't pretend you didn't. This place has like six tables."

"You didn't get the three hundred dollars the porn guys owed you, but at least you got an eighty-five-cent side of guac out of the whole mess." Fiona gives Pedro an extra look, licking her lips as she does it. Or she's trying to get every drop of my guacamole that she stole. "And I think he's suddenly viewing you in a new light."

"I'm not a porn star!" I hiss, starting over with my taco calculations. My fork becomes a surgeon's scalpel, assembling a little sour cream, some salsa, and just enough guac to smear on the edge of the taco shell to produce gustatorial bliss. One bite.

One bite is all it takes.

As I chew, I close my eyes and sigh, the push of air out my nose helping me to taste the yummy goodness of Pedro's kitchen. I have lived my entire life here in this little town, and before Pedro, his father, Pedro Senior, ran this place. They opened during my senior year of high school, and I've been a regular ever since.

Why leave heaven–especially Taco Heaven–when everything you need surrounds you?

"Done orgasming?" Fiona asks before shoving the last piece of her McTaco into her McMouth.

"Quit joking about porn."

"I meant your crazy taco system. You look like you're coming."

"No, I don't."

"You totally do. All you have to add is an open mouth."

"Why would I do that? It's gross. I'm eating."

"Women eat in porn movies, too."

"If you say the word 'porn' one more time, Feisty, I'm going to hack your social media accounts and find Chris Fletcher and friend him as you."

"You wouldn't dare."

"Try me."

"Fine. I won't say the word po–you know, P-O-R-N, if you promise to take Will's job offer."

"That's the weakest blackmail attempt I've ever heard. I have the power here, Fiona. Not you."

"But I have something more powerful."

"What's that?"

"Concern. I'm worried about you, Mal. We all are."

"All?"

"Me. Perky. Your mom. Hastings is even concerned." Hastings is my older sister. She lives in the Bay Area, where she works for a financial services tech start-up as director of business development and accumulates money the way I collect website hits on images of my humiliation.

You know. Gotta have a hobby.

"Hasty doesn't give a crap about what's happened to me. She's the golden child and always has been. The only time Hasty thinks about me is when she's looking at pictures from our childhood and an unexpected wind makes my hair cover her perfect face in a photo on Cape Cod from 2003," I remind her.

"Your parents don't have a golden child. You're *both* golden. You know you hit the jackpot in the wonderful-parents lottery."

"I did," I admit. "But don't try to claim Hasty cares. That's overplaying your hand."

We eat in silence for a moment.

"Why won't you work for Will?" Fi finally asks softly, serious and concerned.

I assemble another bite and chomp down. Suddenly, Taco Heaven has turned into the second half of *Law & Order*, complete with an interrogation that tastes like cilantro and 2008.

A very unsatisfactory bite gets swallowed. I look her right in the eye and blurt out the truth.

"If I work for him, I'll fall for him again. I can't do that to myself."

"Mal," she says in a compassionate voice. "You're ten years older. So is he. You've moved on."

"He never had anything to move on from. All those years. Lockers next to each other. A handful of conversations. Decoding his every look and move like I was a Navajo code talker. He had no idea. It's–it's humiliating. Maybe even more than the porn pics."

"That's... a lot of humiliation."

"See? That's why I don't want to work for him."

Fiona wipes her mouth, balls up the napkin, and pushes it inside the guac container, eyeing me. "I think you need to do it."

"Need to humiliate myself?"

"No. You need to get over him. For good. It's like scary horror films."

"My crush on Will is as bad as that?"

"Your resistance to taking a job that you desperately need just because you're afraid you'll revert to your high school self kind of is. Not the horror movie itself, but do you remember when I saw *The Ring* when I was thirteen, and it scared the hell out of me?"

"Sure. You were whacked."

"Right. And remember what Dale did?" Dale is one of Fiona's older brothers. We all crushed on him when we were in eighth grade and he was a senior. And by *we*, I mean me, Perky, and every other junior high girl (and probably a few guys) aside from Fiona.

"Dale made you watch it five or six times, right? Over and over."

"Yes. Five. He said it would desensitize me to the fear."

"It worked, didn't it?"

"I threw up on him the fifth time he made me watch the scene where Samara comes out of the TV."

"Are you still afraid of it?"

"Yes. And now Dale refuses to sit near me anytime we watch television."

"Then his advice was a miserable failure."

"Uh huh."

"And you're bringing it up in relation to me and Will and the job because...?"

"Because you need to take the job."

"You're comparing you throwing up on your brother with me taking a job from Will? You're making no sense, Fi."

"And neither are you. So it's a stalemate."

Bzzz.

My phone interrupts. It's a text from Perky.

Listen to Fiona. Take the job. You don't want to move back home. Mostly, we don't want to listen to you bitch about moving back home. So be a good friend and take the job, she writes.

"I am not taking a job just because you two want me to spare you the pain of my existence."

"That's not why. You need the money. Plus, Will is well connected."

I hate that she's right.

"Do a good job for him and he could help you get another job. Full time, with benefits, like you had when you worked for the Tollesons."

"Why did they have to sell the business? And why did they sell it to a heroin dealer?"

"Pretty sure that wasn't intentional, Mal."

"I know. But I really loved my life. And it all got ruined when Sven and Joyce decided to retire and sell off. And then the DEA showed up and took my work computer away. And my Soylent."

Fiona grinds her teeth. "That powdered meal supplement is disgusting. And they took it because they thought it was fentanyl."

"I know. I went through decontamination, remember?" That was also the last time anyone other than my gyn touched my boob. I don't blurt that out.

I have *some* standards.

Besides, Fiona and Perky already know that, so it doesn't matter.

"Think about it this way. You spent all those years wanting something from Will you could never have."

"Uh... thanks? You're really selling it."

"Your crush on him took something out of you."

"And?"

"Maybe getting to know the real Will could help you to reframe. Refocus. And move forward by getting something out of *him*."

"Like what?"

"A permanent job? A lead? Or even just a reclamation."

"You sound like a therapist."

"I'm a preschool teacher. Same thing."

"Fiona..."

"Promise me you'll take it. Email him and say yes. Worst case, you quit on day one. Best case, you end up married with kids and a family real estate business."

"That is one hell of a lot of room between two extremes."

"It's a spectrum. Just go with it."

"If I don't take the job, you two will never, ever get off my back, will you?"

"Have fun watching *Jeopardy* every Tuesday night at 7 p.m. while your dad clips his toenails in the living room on a hand towel, Mal. If you lose your apartment, that's what you're facing."

"Maybe I'll get a roommate."

"You live in a one bedroom apartment. Good luck with that."

"Toenails and Alex Trebek, or Will Lotham."

"I can see how this is such a difficult choice," she says dryly. "You suffer either way."

"I do! I really do."

"Email Will before Perky hacks into your account and sends an acceptance email on your behalf."

"She *wouldn't*."

"You've been friends with her as long as I have, Mal. You seriously think she hasn't already?"

Damn.

I quickly check email.

"Liar!" I accuse.

"Made you open your app. Now it's simple. Find Will's email and reply, "I accept. When do I start?""

I stare at Will's email:

I like how you started to re-arrange the living room. And

that feng shui theory sounded ludicrous, but then again, I'm superstitious enough to bury a statue of St. Joseph when trying to sell a property. I need someone to handle staging for our company. If you're willing to do a one-month trial as a consultant, I've got a gig for you. No coconut oil, and sorry—clothing isn't optional.

I type:

One month. Fully clothed. And I am charging you a 1% commission if the house sells within that month. No negotiation. Take it or leave it.

Fiona's reading over my shoulder and gasps.

"Mal! You're not serious. You—that reads like Perky wrote it!"

I close my eyes and tap the screen.

"You sent it! Oh my *God*, you *sent* that?"

I did.

I did, and before I can even close the app, a notification informs me I have a reply.

"He's replied already!" I choke out.

"Refresh the screen."

"I can't. I'm paralyzed."

Fi takes the phone from me and reads aloud.

One percent commission and no hourly rate. If you think your feng shui is that strong, prove it. :) As for clothing, we can be flexible.

"Oh, ho ho!" Fiona crows. "He's a crafty one, isn't he?"

A surge of adrenaline rips through me.

Deal, I type.

"Mal!" Fi's mouth is open in shock. "You need guaranteed money. You can't control whether a house gets sold or not. One percent of nothing is—"

I hit Send.

"One percent of nothing is nothing to lose," I tell her. "He thinks he's so smart? He thinks he has all the power? I'll show him."

See you tomorrow, he says, giving me his office address.

"I think I have a job," I whisper.

"I think you have a masochistic streak."

"Same thing."

Chapter Seven

I can't quite catch my breath.

It's my first day at my new job working for Will, and I forgot about the fringe benefits. I may not be an employee, technically—just a contractor—but my, my, *my,* does Will look so fine in that suit.

He's on his phone and angled away from me, face turned up to the arched ceilings that soar as high as my pulse right now. It's summer, so he's wearing a lightweight tan suit, the kind that looks really good on models in Nordstrom's ads but horrible on everyone else.

Unless you're Will Lotham.

If Tom Brady became a supermodel like his wife and started doing Ralph Lauren ads, he'd be one tenth as hot as Will right now. White dress shirt open at the neck. No tie. Tan suit, dark brown leather shoes, and patterned socks, a flash of color peeking out from under his pants cuff. A leather belt the same shade as his shoes bisects his body, the flat abs a wall of yummy goodness as he pivots, turning his body to write something down on a notepad.

In a flash, sunlight glints off the pen he's using, a silver pen in a hand that moves gracefully.

"Mmm hmm. Yes. No. Ten percent. Deliverable is fine," he says as I stand there, suddenly awkward. I move, just enough to make a sound so he knows I'm here. Will looks over, waves, and turns back to his call.

No smile. But I'm mature enough to know his lack of a smile has nothing to do with me.

Um, right?

He's wearing reading glasses, perched on the bridge of his nose the way people who haven't worn glasses most of their life balance them. Whoever he's speaking with has his full attention. He doesn't notice that I'm watching him.

Out of the blue, a grin spreads across his face, making him change from a hard-edged business executive to a carefree, sigh-able man. He's all ease and achievement, relaxed and unwaveringly stoked. The energy in the room changes so fast.

And now he's ending the call.

The downtown headquarters of The Lotham Group turns out to be in a former yoga studio. Brass elephants line a very high shelf that runs a few feet below the tall ceilings in a room painted in purple and mustard tones that make my trigeminal nerve do the samba. The place is clearly not finished, giving off the feel of an office in limbo. They've either just moved in or are preparing to move out.

I close my eyes. I let the feeling find me. There it is. The space tells me.

Moving *in*.

"Who is your, um, interior designer?" I ask him, nervous, needing distraction as he approaches me, his eyes hard to read.

"My mother."

"She's in the field?"

"No. She just has opinions." He looks up, eyes scanning as

he takes off the reading glasses and tucks them in a case, a wry grin making his dimples appear.

"So do I."

"And? What do you think of the color scheme?"

"I think your mother loves you and wants you to be in a warm, productive environment."

He smiles wider and looks around.

"Which is why this entire office needs to be remodeled."

His fingertips rub his left eyebrow. "That's not what I hired you for."

"Oh, I know. But I can't come into a room that almost seems designed to suck energy out of its inhabitants and not say something."

"Are you going to be like this in every single physical setting?"

"Yes."

"Then I need to set some limits with you."

"Such as?"

"Don't tell me every single room in my business office needs to be remodeled. I don't have a budget for that. We're straddling two locations right now as we migrate into this space. All my employees are still in the old offices until next week."

"I can tell you what you need to know. Once you *know*, you can prioritize."

"Remodeling is not a priority."

"You don't care about productivity?" I ask, giving him a hard stare.

His double take is so gratifying. "Of course I care about productivity."

"How about profits?"

"I care even *more* about profits." Will goes from mild

annoyance to interested attentiveness. I like being the focus of his attention.

Like it a little too much.

"Then you'd better let me remodel every inch of this place," I declare in a haughty tone that covers my nervousness.

"First of all, no. Second—why would you need to remodel every inch?"

"Intuition."

"I didn't hire you for your intuition. I hired you to reorganize the space and feel of my properties to help them sell. Starting with my parents' house."

"Which means you hired me for my intuition."

"I hired you for your skill."

"Skill plus gut feelings equals intuition. I have a sixth sense when it comes to space."

His attention becomes derision. "Don't tell me you're one of those people who believes in woo."

"Woo?"

Will eyes my purse. "You don't have a smudge stick in there?"

"No."

"Good."

"It's in my car. I pull that out at the end, after we've cleared the energy blocks." I give him a big smile.

"Jesus Christ."

"If you want him involved, you need an ordained minister or priest. I don't specialize in *that* kind of energy clearance."

"You were the valedictorian of our graduating class, and now you burn *sage* for a living?"

"I do way more than burn sage, buddy."

"Don't tell me you use crystals?"

"Crystals? Do I look like an amateur?"

He cracks a grin.

"I do spells," I inform him. It's hard not to smile back when someone so deliciously hot is grinning at me, but I do not. I am resolute.

"Spells?"

"Witchcraft."

"You do not." His chuckle is low and throaty, and it makes me tingle.

"I'm distantly related to Rebecca Nourse, you know. The famous accused witch." We've grown up a short drive from Salem. Every schoolkid in New England knows who Rebecca Nourse is. It must be written into the history curriculum that proper education includes having the crap scared out of you in fifth grade by going to the Salem witchcraft museums.

"We're all distantly related to people from 1690s New England," he shoots back. "Confess, oh, witch, that ye be a liar, ye seductress o' the night."

"You sound like a pirate. Not a Puritan." Oh, how his mouth revels in the word *seductress*.

"Both start with p. Close enough." He laughs easily, with a confidence I remember all too well. Not arrogance. A surety that who he is, how he is in the world, is enough.

"Fine," I admit. "I don't do spells." My voice is breathy. Ethereal. He makes me feel like I'm floating away, barely here, turning into stardust.

Wet, thrumming stardust.

He walks across the room to an unoccupied desk and gestures for me to sit behind it. He takes the visitor's chair.

"My bottom line is this: I need to unload my parents' house. I have a price threshold. If you can get it to sell, you get one percent of the selling price." He slides a folder across the desk to me. I open it. A contract is inside.

"That's the agreement we had in our email. What's in

here?" Pulling all the loose pieces of myself together and focusing on business is harder than it should be.

"Standard legalese. Plus your budget."

I almost blurt out, *I have a budget?* but I stop myself. Instead, I pretend to be a wise, edgy business woman and read the legalese.

"There isn't a line item for dandelion root in here," I joke.

His eyes narrow. "Where did you go to college again?" he asks. A part of me is hurt he doesn't remember, but my cool, sophisticated grown-up parts hand her a Lisa Frank journal and some glitter pens so she'll be distracted.

"Brown."

Eyebrows shoot up. "That's right. They taught you the woo at Brown?"

"I taught *them* the woo at Brown." I bat my eyelashes as he chuckles. Hearing him laugh is its own reward. "And quit talking to me while I'm reviewing a contract. It's bad business."

"It's good negotiation."

"Are we negotiating? I thought the terms were set."

"Contracts are never set. They're just set *for now*," Will says, but then he goes quiet.

Two and a half pages later, I'm happy but troubled. Happy because the contract is fine.

Troubled because Will seems to think I shouldn't be happy. Shouldn't settle for what he's offered.

His expectation that I will negotiate is the only reason I am *going* to negotiate.

"I want to add to the budget."

"What do you want to add? Dandelion root?"

"A live elephant."

"An elephant."

"And nine ounces of platypus milk."

FLUFFY

"Really? What does that do to the energy of my parents' house?"

"You ride the elephant around the outside of the house while drinking the milk."

"And that does what?"

"It makes me laugh. And when I laugh, it gives a space good energy."

"You really went to an Ivy League school and this is the result?"

"It's okay, Will. You don't have to understand. Not everyone does." I give him a pitying smile, calculated to be condescending. "And if you're having second thoughts because you know you'll lose–"

"No second thoughts."

I sign the contract. "Great. Done. Now get me some platypus milk."

"You didn't attach an addendum."

"Damn." I look around the office, which is atrociously claustrophobic in spite of the fact that it's about five thousand square feet of tall-ceilinged warehouse space. "I'll have to find one of the critters and milk her myself."

"You are a woman of many skills, Mallory."

"Or I'm easily distracted. You pick."

"My pick is for you to go back to my parents' house with me and get started on the fluffing."

"Excuse me?" I pretend to be offended, but my blood is supercharged. The mental image Will's joke conjures....

Rich laughter fills my ears. "*House* fluffing. Did you really answer that Craigslist ad and not know what a fluffer was?"

And... here we go.

"Not all of us spend more time reading *Urban Dictionary* than *The Atlantic*."

"It doesn't take being well educated to know what a fluffer is, Mallory."

"Survey any ten random strangers on the street and I'll bet you three of them have no idea the term fluffer is for porn. In New England, I'll bet half will think you're talking about fluffernutters."

"Is that what you call an insane fluffer?"

"You're about to get a stapler to the nose, Lotham."

"Wouldn't be the first time my nose took a hit." He pinches the bridge of it. "But it would be the first time a woman threw something at me in anger."

"I highly doubt that."

"I tend to date nonviolent women."

"Or ones who are exceedingly patient."

As the words come out of my mouth, I feel his breath hitch. The air between us changes. I don't know why he offered me this job. I also don't know why I look up and catch his eye.

But I'm glad I do.

Because that half smile on his face is the best.

Will leans across the desk and taps the stapler. "You don't have a license to wield a deadly weapon, Mallory. And I didn't hire you to fling inanimate objects at my face."

I wonder about *animate* objects I can fling at his face.

Wait. No. Halt. Ahhhhh! Stop thinking that. I wince, which makes him frown.

"Are you okay?" he asks, looking at me intently, making this so much worse.

"I'm fine."

"You look like you're in pain."

"It's my contact lens."

He stands up and steps close to me, so I stand, too. "Why

are you wearing these when you have contacts?" he asks, touching the arm of my glasses.

"That totally explains the pain!" I gasp. Whew. An excuse.

His thumbs and index fingers delicately grasp the edges of my glasses, pulling them forward, giving me time for a deep breath that fills me with the scent of Will. Instantly, he's in soft focus. He seems more solid, the sharp edges blurred, making it easier for me to quell the growing storm inside me.

"Better?" he asks.

"Much," I lie.

"Good." I can't really see his face, but I can read his body language. Hear his breath. Smell his aftershave and the soapy scent of a man who showered an hour ago, lime and mint mixing with something earthy, something cotton. He's close enough to smell coffee on his breath, and I have to stop moving, stop inhaling, stop the world because it's spinning faster than I can think.

Slower than I can feel.

His head tilts. "You look different without them."

"Most people do."

"I can't decide which I like better."

My heart stops beating.

"Which do *you* prefer?" he asks me, handing the glasses over, his fingers grazing mine.

I can't answer until I find my heart again. It's wandered off into 2009 somewhere. Every inch of skin, however, is firmly in the present.

"I prefer to see clearly," I announce in that haughty tone again, the one I use whenever I'm covering for the fact that I am only pretending to be a functional adult who knows what the hell she is doing with her emotions.

"Don't we all?" he asks in a tone that says there's more to that statement.

"Yes," I say slowly, unable to look away. "Yes, I think we do."

I didn't know you could live for nine thousand years and not blink.

Somehow, that actually happens to me, standing in front of my new desk on my first day as Will Lotham's contract employee.

And then his phone rings.

Spell broken.

In a rush to answer it, he grabs the phone out of his pocket, losing his grip. For a former quarterback, he's remarkably clumsy as it flips and flops in his hands, falling in one big arc–

Straight into my cleavage.

Quarterbacks have a physical precision that moves beyond exceptional eye-hand coordination and well into the realm of sheer magic. It's more than alchemy. More than discipline and practice. It takes muscle memory and endurance and raises them a level–one that Will demonstrates as he stops his hand, fingertips mere millimeters from diving between my breasts to grab his phone.

Magic, though, *bleeds*.

You cannot conjure the divine and ask it to do a simple task. Once unleashed, it seeks a challenge. It does not respect boundaries. Spells are notorious for breaking the laws of physics. Why would a power source stay within the confines of lines drawn by others who fear a world they cannot see or understand?

Will's body is pure magic. Reflexes like that don't come from following rules.

They come from playing with fire.

The cold metal case with a glass face makes the soft, warm

valley of my boobs feel impersonal, like a speculum in the wrong place. A simple error, born of a fumble.

No big deal, right?

His eyes are glued to my chest, the phone vibrating between my girls in an insanely, embarrassingly pleasurable hum, his jacket lapels moving up and down, wide and narrow as he breathes, so close to me that I feel his warmth. With a steady hand I reach into my shirt, pull out his phone, and start laughing.

Hard.

Everything is a blur at normal distance, but it comes into sharper focus when I look at him this close. I'm nearsighted. You have to be an inch or two from my face before I can see all your edges, all the lines that separate you from the rest of the world. Objects blur until the perfect range makes them distinct.

That range is different for everyone.

But we all have a focal point for clarity.

Finding yours is a life journey.

"Nice catch," Will says as I hand him his now-warm phone. It stops ringing. Is it my imagination or does his hand linger for a few seconds longer than is socially polite?

"*That* is as athletic as I get. Good to see them finally do something constructive," I say, looking down at my breasts. "They've been nothing but a source of agony for most of my life."

"Agony? I think you mean pleasure."

His phone rings again.

Literally saved by the bell.

"Conference call," he whispers, turning his back to me, a move designed to help him keep his conversation private but that serves better as a way for me to watch his ass without being observed.

I have been working with Will Lotham for a grand total of fifteen minutes and all I can think about is his mouth and his ass.

I am doomed.

I am *so* doomed.

When someone is this doomed, there is only one sane response.

I leave.

Packing up my purse, phone, and keys, I wave to Will as he talks on his boob-warmed phone. I get a flicker of acknowledgment from him that reminds me of the high school hallway.

Enough to say *Hey, I know you*.

But not enough to say *Hey, you're important*.

Chapter Eight

The drive to 29 Maplecure Street takes exactly three minutes. I don't even have time to decompress from that conversation with Will before I'm smacked in the face with more Will. This isn't his childhood home. That address I've memorized and will know until the day I die.

I'll be on my deathbed, overtaken by dementia, and while I won't know the name of the current president, by God, I'll know the exact time on Tuesday afternoons that Will had to mow the front lawn when they lived on Concordian Road and I got Mom to drive me past his house on the way to the mall. (2:30 p.m., before his lacrosse practice).

I pull up to 29 Maplecure Street and look at the house through new eyes.

Without a porn crew bustling about, it's got a different feel.

Imposing. Manicured. Polished and sophisticated, this is the home of someone significant. This is a showplace, designed to send signals. Financial signals.

Power signals.

Most people buy a home because it's what they can afford,

or for a specific school district or neighborhood. Most people settle into an environment out of a desire for comfort. We use adjectives and phrases that actually contain the word *home* to describe emotions:

Homey
Make yourself at home
It's like coming home
Home is where the heart is

But houses like 29 Maplecure Street aren't about comfort.

They're about prestige.

Homes talk. They might not be able to speak directly, but if you're fluent in Space like I am, you can pick up what they're putting down. When I came here last week for the fluffer job, I thought I was staging a television show set. I wasn't looking at the house through the eyes of a space professional working on selling this place.

Now I am.

I grin.

Will Lotham is going to give up that one percent so, so soon.

At the thought of Will, my body tingles, heat pouring into my arms, legs, chest at the instant memory recall programmed into me. See, this is the problem with Will being back in my world: I've spent ten years chasing him out of my head.

I evicted him.

Turns out he's been squatting in my heart.

Who knew?

Okay, okay–Perky and Fiona knew. But that's because

they're jerks who think they know me better than I know myself.

But they are wrong—

Shoot.

They're *right*.

Will's parents' house, on careful examination, is more than a showplace. Quiet beige dominates the stonework, but it's done with such fine taste and superb craftsmanship that it commands attention. Together, the architectural designer and the mason elevated the simplest scheme to an artisanal visual feast, with the stonework itself at the center. If you've ever been caught off guard by beauty, you know what I mean. I could look at the walls, the steps, the intersection of paths for hours and never be bored.

And that's just the beginning.

When I arrived here last week for the fluffer job, I was in a different head space. Head space matters. We think of reality as one monolithic state, but it's actually a prism. Twist in another direction by a millimeter and the world you thought you knew disappears, replaced by a charmingly different–yet disturbingly familiar–state.

The Mallory who walked up this stone path last week is one twist away from the Mallory I am now.

I like the *now* better.

Combining an appealing, comfortable feel with an eye for power display is tough to manage. The Lothams have done it. Will said his mother managed interior design for the company, and while her own ideas at the office made me cringe, as I punch the key code into the lock and open the front door, I have to retract my doubts. She obviously hired the best to do this house.

It is, simply put, damn near perfect.

Gone is the garish red ottoman. Gone is the strange sofa.

In their place, I see neutrals in tones that someone has assembled with a delicacy that is intriguing. Meant to blend in, the layers are all different shades and textures, with occasional soft blues and greens to bring the outside in. The New Zealand wool carpet isn't there just for show. It's meant for bare feet to walk on, for the indulgence of treating your sore tootsies after a long day, for allowing everyday pleasure to be factored into design.

Isn't that supposed to be the point?

Yet only the best design does that, and few people look for it.

Except me.

And, apparently, whoever designed this home.

I said *damn near* perfect, mind you. The energy is still off, the unused, stagnant spaces making it pool into frustrated ponds of lifeless potential. This house was not meant to be even partly empty. Energy matters. Just like people.

Just like Will.

I move down the hall to the kitchen on the right, and stop dead in my tracks.

There, on the counter, are three items.

A jar of marshmallow Fluff.

A jar of creamy peanut butter.

A loaf of bread.

A note, with an envelope embossed with the initials WJL (*William Joshua Lotham*, my mind recites, pulling up data I shouldn't be able to retrieve so quickly but do), is propped against the Fluff.

Ha.

Ha.

With an eagerness I don't want to admit, I open the envelope and run my fingertips along the slanted handwriting. In high school, Will wanted to be an architect. His penmanship has a draftsman's quality to it, almost font-like in its squared uniformity.

In case you have a sudden craving.

W

There's a house brochure on the honed marble counter behind me, printed on heavy paper with gorgeous, full-color photos. It makes a useful fan. I wave it in front of my face, staring up at the beamed ceiling, willing my pulse to re-center itself where it belongs, at my throat.

And not between my legs.

Bright, natural light bounces off the whitewashed cross-beams in the kitchen, the big, antique iron and glass lanterns over the center island creating an interesting focal point that grounds me. Inhaling deeply, I smell clary sage and cinnamon, which tells me more than I learned about this house during my brief time as an accidental porn-set fluffer.

Will's mother, or her interior designer, was going for the whole environment.

For the next hour, I consider relationships—of objects, not humans. People think that the stuff is what matters, and they're right.

But only half right.

It's also about the space. The relationship *between* objects, some complementary, some contradictory. How they exist relative to each other, and how we move between and around them. How we find our place in the world is dictated by arrangements.

Arrangements of items, people, and time.

I want my one percent, I text him, attaching pictures when I'm done.

Nice! he texts back.

Of course it is!

When it sells, he replies.

Get your checkbook ready, buddy, because this place will be under contract in a week, I text back, thumbs flying so fast, doubt can't creep in.

If this place is under contract in a week at full price, I'll up that commission to one point two five and throw in a case of Fluff.

Deal! But you can keep the Fluff.

No deal. You have to take the Fluff or else.

Or else what?

No deal.

You're forcing me to accept an entire case of Fluff because of a double entendre?

Yes.

That moves the joke out of the funny category into the stupid category. Why are you making me?

Because I already bought the case and have no desire to be stuck with it.

Too bad. You'll have to find something to do with all that Fluff. Think of it as a timesaver.

Timesaver?

Now you know what your lunches are for the next year.

I hate fluffernutter sandwiches.

Really? So do I. I thought I was the only kid in Massachusetts who didn't like them, I text back.

Admitting you hate fluffernutter sandwiches when you live in New England is like saying you're a Yankees fan.

You're entitled to your opinion as long as you never, ever express it.

Yet another thing we have in common, Mal.

What else do we have in common?

We both want to sell my parents' house.

Yes. But no Fluff for me.

Then the entire deal is off.

You can't do that! We have a contract.
You want that extra .25 percent? Take the Fluff.
I'll donate it to a food bank. If they'll take it.
That's fine.

My phone rings and I jump. *Unknown*, the caller ID says, but it's a local number, and I know it's Will.

"Fluffers Anonymous," I answer without thinking.

"I'm looking for an anonymous fluffer," he says. I close my eyes and conjure him in the office, jacket off, the tuft of chest hair at the V of his open shirt, the corded muscle of his forearms.

"Then you've come to the right place. How can I help you?"

"I need a professional fluffer to help me take care of a problem," he says, voice dropping at the end.

"How big is the problem?"

"Twelve."

I gulp. "Twelve, uh, what?" *Inches?*

"You really don't like fluffernutters?" he asks, his voice smooth and inviting. I'm not expecting the question, so my mind goes blank.

"Uh." I open the jar of Fluff and search the drawers for a spoon. "I'm really not a fan."

Twelve inches? I want to ask. What did he mean by *twelve*?

"I've got a case of the stuff, twelve jars," he says as I find a spoon and use it to dig into the creamy marshmallow goodness. "And besides," he says slowly, sensually, his voice taking on new character. "If you don't like fluffernutters, why are you licking that spoon like it's your last meal?"

I freeze. "Licking what? I'm not licking anything." My tongue peeks out to catch a smear of fluff at the corner of my mouth.

"You are definitely licking something, Mallory. You wouldn't lie to me, would you?"

"How would you—wait a minute!" I look up and stare directly at a glass eye shining from a corner of the ceiling. Bingo!

Camera.

"You have *cameras* in here?" I put the spoon down and yank at the hem of my shirt, as if that alone will make my muffin top disappear.

"Yes. They're new. I was calling to let you know, because I realized we hadn't warned you. It was part of how we figured out the porn situation."

"You said a neighbor told you!"

"She did. Then we checked the surveillance cameras and confirmed it."

"You have cameras inside the house? Are they in the bathrooms? The bedrooms?"

"What? No. That's illegal. We only installed them in the living room and the kitchen, and can legally turn them on to monitor under really specific conditions. The house is only being rented to corporations for daytime business activities."

"Daytime what?"

"Focus group testing. Kitchen demonstrations. Small corporate training retreats. Not overnight, not vacationers. So the privacy element is a little different. If that idiot Spatula had read the rental contract, he'd have known," he informs me, his voice a little too soothing, like a kid who got caught with his hand in the cookie jar, but before he took a bite.

"What if I had been undressing?"

"Then I would have been extra glad I'd installed them," he says with a short sigh at the end, voice husky.

"What if I—" I halt. Back up. Those words he just said... Is—is Will Lotham *flirting* with me?

He laughs. "Besides, why would you undress in a client's living room?" He pauses. "Unless you really *are* a porn actress?"

I choke.

"What? No!" I cough out. "What if I'd needed to adjust the girls?"

"The girls?"

"You know." If he's watching, might as well. I reach in with my non-Fluff hand and adjust my headlights, if you know what I mean.

He goes dead silent.

"That's a thing?"

"What's a thing?"

"Adjusting—women reach inside their bra cups and *do* that?"

"Of course we do! Haven't you ever had a girlfriend? Or a live-in lover?"

"Lover? Who uses the word lover? That's like calling pants slacks. And yes, I've had plenty of girlfriends. No live-ins."

"Wife?" I ask before I can stop myself.

"No. Look, Mallory, I've had plenty of girlfriends and none of them are secret girl adjusters."

"That makes me sound like a guard in a women's prison."

He laughs again, then makes a sound of consideration. "It makes sense, when I think about it."

OMIGOD WILL LOTHAM IS THINKING ABOUT MY GIRLS.

"Guys adjust, too," Will adds, his voice casual.

"Guys adjust... what? Unless you magically sprouted moobs in the half hour since I last saw you, Will, you have nothing of importance to adjust."

"You know." He clears his throat meaningfully.

"Oh! Those!" I gasp.

"Last time I checked, I still had those. No girlfriend or lover has stamped 'property of' just yet." Pause. A strange breath. "Yep. Still here. Just checked."

"You... touched your... *those* while talking to *me*?" I squeak.

"Seems fair. You touched your breasts. Now we're even." His voice sounds like every cranberry cosmo I've had in a bar, all while waiting for transformation in the form of That Guy. You know. The guy who miraculously picks me out of a crowd, one out of a million, and tells me I'm the answer to all his questions.

That Guy.

Will sure sounds like That Guy, if That Guy ever actually existed. But he doesn't, because he's a fantasy I've conjured in my starved imagination.

But I'm not imagining it. He really said that.

Am I having phone sex with Will Lotham and I don't even realize it?

"This is, without a doubt, the strangest client conversation I've ever had," I blurt out. Innuendo dies when exposed to bluntness.

"TMZ has photos to prove that's not true," he counters. "I cannot imagine that your interactions with Spatula and Beastman weren't worse."

"You have a point."

Laughter booms through the phone, along with a sigh, then a swallow that goes straight to my bloodstream. "How's the house?"

"It's beautiful." Now we're on firmer ground.

Firm.

No, Mallory! No! Stop thinking about firm and twelve inches and Will touching his balls while you touch your breasts and—

"It is. Why isn't it selling?" Will's voice is rich and complex. It reminds me of college radio, when you're listening late on a Saturday night while everyone else is out on their third drinking binge of the week and you just want to catch up on political philosophy and introductory Spanish. The quirky, smart guy with the whiskey voice who plays a mix of Depeche Mode, Thermal and a Quarter, and college bands that are going to break out five years later and be called an overnight sensation but you'll know better.

You and your local college DJ with that voice that lights up your limbic system and melts your panties.

"Why isn't this house selling? Because you have a secret porn production company running out of the house?" I choke out, trying to lean casually against the cool marble counter with panties that are in flames.

"Ah, so you figured it out," he says in a conspirator's voice, amusement tinging his words. "You're a smart woman. I should have known you'd put the pieces together."

"You mean there was no rental? This house really was a movie set? You're actually Spatula and Beastman's boss? I knew it. Will Lotham—former Harmony Hills quarterback, Rhodes Scholar, and king of the creampie scene."

I didn't know you could feel a spit take through the phone.

"For someone who claims she had no idea what a fluffer was, you've got a dirty mouth, Mallory." He makes a sound, deep and amused, that connects to every red blood cell in my body, setting it aglow. "A dirty, filthy mouth."

My dirty mouth goes dry.

Other filthy parts of me get very, very wet.

I breathe. I know I breathe because I don't pass out, and generally speaking, that's a good indicator of consciousness.

Silence fills the air between us, no one making a sound. Nothing but the heavy rasp of breath.

As seconds tick by, I become more turned on, the outrageous cocoon of this surreal conversation spinning me into a hyper-aware state. He's not even in the room with me. Not within my visual zone. We're miles apart, connected only by jokes and innuendos.

And yet, what he does to my body.

And oh, what this man does to light up my mind.

"I—"

I have no idea what I'm about to say, but whatever it is, I'm sure I'll humiliate myself.

And just then, my phone dies.

Chapter Nine

"You still have the best apartment of all of us, Mal, so if you ever can't make rent, you know we'll take this place off your hands," Perky announces as she walks in with bags of Indian food in her arms and plunks them down on the big, reclaimed barnwood counter. She looks up at the ceiling, wide bead-board painted a soft, glossy white. No common plaster here.

This is the real deal, all finishes considered.

"Will Lotham is going to make it so I never have to worry about where to live again," I inform her. It's evening after my first crazy day working for Will and I need curry therapy. Perk and Fiona are here to administer it by mouth.

Perky pauses. "Because he's proposed and you two are moving in together and getting married and having adorable babies with your perfect auburn curls and thick-lashed eyes?"

"Don't forget the dimpled chins and Perfect Taco Ratio Radar," Fiona chimes in.

"What? No! Where on Earth did you come up with that?" Hope—a strange and fleeting feeling born of fantasy and subconscious wishes—makes my heart skip a beat and rush to catch up.

I also touch my hair involuntarily, because thanks for the unsolicited compliment, Perk.

"Ninth grade. Probably during a football game while we sat in the band bleachers. You told me that. And then you repeated it pretty regularly for the next four years."

"I was fourteen!"

"You were still saying it at eighteen."

"That was ten years ago!"

"But I'll bet your fantasy factory is still working that Will angle really hard."

Damn her. "How did we get from talking about my awesome apartment to Will Lotham?"

"Because you can't have a conversation without mentioning him, Mal. It's like high school all over again, only with more debt and no one's a virgin." Perky's grasping a container of mint sauce like she's holding it hostage.

"*Pfft.* The only one of us in high school who was still a virgin was Mal," Fiona says.

"Uh, thanks? I guess?" I lean across the counter and start opening white take-out containers to find my order.

"I want to learn more about Will Lotham and how he loves your dirty, filthy mouth," Fiona announces, hands under her chin, giving me a wide-eyed ingenue look that is better than any truth serum. "He said that? And then you let your phone die?"

"I didn't *let* my phone die," I argue.

Perky and Fiona glare at me.

"I didn't! It wasn't *intentional*."

"It's never intentional," Perky snaps back. "But look at the trouble it causes. First, you end up on a porn set with pictures of you all over the internet and almost get arrested because your phone died before I could explain what a fluffer really is. Then you lose out on some great aural sex with Will!"

"What? Oral sex? How the hell did you get from phone sex to oral sex with Will Lotham? We weren't having oral sex! He only touched his balls and I only touched my boobs!"

"A-U-R-A-L sex," Perky says slowly, spelling it out. "You know. Phone sex."

"Will was not trying to have phone sex with me!"

"He totally was. Boobs? Balls?" Perky takes two vegetable pakoras out of the aluminum foil wrap and holds them in her hands suggestively.

"Was not!"

"Mal, when was the last time a client told you over the phone that you had a dirty, filthy mouth?" she asks, dropping the pakoras and tearing off a piece of naan bread, chewing while waiting.

"And touched his junk while talking about your tits," Fiona adds.

"Stop saying that word," Perky says, turning her attention to Fi. "You know I hate that word."

"Tits!" Fiona says, because we're frozen in time at age fourteen.

"Tits," I add, because. Just... because. See above.

"I hate you both." Perky dips a pakora in the mint sauce, taking a big bite. It looks like she's teabagging Shrek's ball.

"You can't hate me," Fiona declares. "Because I am in charge of the honey-raisin naan." Holding up the warm, foil-wrapped treat, she grins, triumphant. Every time we eat Indian, we overstuff ourselves at the end with the sweet bread. It's tradition.

She who holds the honey-raisin naan rules the world.

"You're right. I love you, Feisty," Perky mumbles around her mouthful of Shrek.

"Don't call me that, Tits."

"Did he call you back?" Perky asks, changing the subject

away from anything that draws attention to her breasts, which have been viewed more times than unboxing videos of Elsa dolls on YouTube.

"If he did, I wouldn't know. My phone died and then I just came home." I spread my arms out as if I've invited them on a house tour.

"So that's it? You left each other hanging? Because when I have phone sex, I always have to take care of business." Fiona clears her throat like she's being suggestive but she just sounds like an actress in a post-nasal-drip medicine commercial.

"I did take care of business. I arranged Will's parents' house and got rid of the bad chi. I put the peanut butter and the Fluff and bread away in the cupboard, cleaned up, and—"

"Not *that* business." Fiona makes another sound like she's clearing pebbles out of her throat with a bubble wand. "You know. *Business.*"

"You have got to be kidding me."

"I never joke about *business.*"

"You can say the word *masturbation*, Feisty," Perk informs her. "You don't need to use euphemisms. We're modern women."

"Right. No more euphemisms," Fiona says pointedly. "Like saying *bosom* instead of *tits.*"

Perky is biting into a green-covered pakora and makes a face.

"Bad pakora?" I ask.

"Bad friend." Eyes narrowing, she glares so hard at Fiona. Doesn't work. When you're a preschool teacher with a class of four-year-olds, your skin becomes Teflon for angry stares from immature beings.

"We shouldn't be arguing," Fiona says softly, in that soothing tone she uses for correcting little kids. And Perky.

"We have a common goal: to get Mallory to tell us why she didn't let Will go all the way."

"All the *what*?" My brain shouldn't have to work this hard to understand them.

"Phone sex. You know. Why didn't you let Will give you some relief?"

"Why do I tell you people anything?"

"Because you're a masochist. I thought we established that a long time ago," Fiona says, carefully spreading aloo gobi all over a plate covered with a thin layer of rice.

"Speaking of enjoying self-abusive behaviors, are either of you actually going to our high school reunion? Ten years, can you believe it? I got invitations by email, Facebook messenger, a direct message on Twitter, another one on Instagram, and some kind of text alert I know I didn't sign up for." Perky's casual drop of this question sets my skin to Creepy-Dude-in-Back-Alley mode.

"I've been ignoring them all for months," I say brightly, plastering a smile on my face.

"I downloaded the app," Fiona cheerfully says.

"Our high school reunion has an *app*?" I choke out. As my mouth takes in the yummy curry I'm finally eating, my mind tries to parse what Perky's up to, and my body keeps hijacking my heart.

"Everyone has an app," Perky says with a hand wave.

"I don't have an app!" I protest.

"You can't keep your smartphone charged above six percent at any given time, Mallory. You don't deserve an app."

"That's not— " Fiona shoves a piece of pakora in my mouth before I can finish.

"I'm going!" Fiona announces, and my stomach craters. Herds move as one unit, but choosing directions takes a tipping point.

One person saying yes is one third. Two is—

"I'm going, too!" Perky declares.

A disaster.

"I can't," I inform them with an officiousness that peels my fingernails off. "I have to man the table at the Dance and Dairy festival for Habitat for Humanity."

Check.

"No. You don't. I already talked to Mrs. Kormatillo. She said they can find someone else," Perky says.

Checkmate.

"Please," I groan. "Please don't make me go."

"Why wouldn't you want to go? You were valedictorian! You went to an Ivy League school! You came home and got a job with benefits and— "

"I am the overachiever who never left and now I'm unemployed and fat."

"Whoa! Who took Mallory and replaced her with her sister's voice?" Fiona asks, shocked. "You just morphed into Hastings for a minute there. She was drunk the night she said that crap to you, Mallory. That was four years ago! Don't internalize it."

"And you are not fat." Perky shuts one eye and examines me. "In fact, I'll bet you're within five pounds of high school weight."

"I am." I'm actually two pounds lighter, but I don't say that aloud, because that's just begging for the universe to throw three pounds my way.

"Stop calling yourself fat. You are an overachiever, however," Perky notes.

"She is not!" Fiona jumps in. "Quit insulting poor Mal."

"Overachiever is an insult?"

"It implies she's pushed beyond her natural abilities. Like it's some kind of psychological problem."

"You have a very negative view of the world for a preschool teacher, Fi," Perky shoots back.

"Says the woman who hates everyone."

"Not everyone. Just people who say the word *tits*."

We settle in with our rice and curries and deep-fried chickpea flour concoctions and for five minutes, we shut up about the stupid reunion.

Five minutes.

That's the outer limit of how long Perky can stay silent.

"So," she says, exactly three hundred and one seconds later (yes, I clock watched), "Now that Will is back in town and the reunion is coming up—"

I start gagging uncontrollably on a piece of spiced cauliflower. Coriander *burns* when it coats your uvula.

Massive side eye gets thrown my way by my two friends. "You're going, Mal," Perky declares. "Plus, remember Rayelyn Boyle? She checked 'Going' on the reunion app."

"Rayelyn's going?"

"Your nerd friend," Fiona says casually.

"Uh, she was just my *friend*. We were in all the academic curriculars together."

"Right. Nerd friend."

"If she was my nerd friend, what were you two?"

"Your hip friends," Perky interrupts.

"Ha!"

"You live here. All three of us do. If we don't go, everyone will assume we're losers," Perky argues.

"Or maybe they'll assume we're mature women who don't need to go back to some stupid high school nostalgic gathering where the popular kids relive their importance and the rest of us try to pretend we're not still traumatized by the social dynamics of an oppressive system where people with underdeveloped frontal lobes were forced to operate by survival of the fittest!"

They stare at me.

"Wow, Mal. Baggage," Fiona says, clearing her throat as I chug water to clear that nasty taste out of my mouth.

The taste of the past rising up.

My sigh comes out with more anger than even I expect. "I don't have baggage. I *didn't*. I didn't until Will Lotham waltzed back into town and re-entered my life. I take a lot of crap from people for deciding to come back after Brown and live in my hometown. You both know that."

Perky shrugs. "I don't."

Fiona smiles serenely. "I know what you mean. Our high school was so competitive. Leaving town was a sign of being serious about going out into the world and conquering."

"But you're a preschool teacher, Fi. You're collaborative. Not competitive," I point out.

A flash of emotion fires up in her eyes, tamped down quickly by some other part of her. "I used to be. I've mastered that competitive part."

"Your kickass kickboxer part?"

"Right. She's still inside me. Waiting. Watching. But that kind of anger and worry isn't good to carry around. I let it go a long time ago."

"You can't," Perky declares flatly. "You can't let it go entirely. We carry *alllllll* our crap around with us on some level. I can decide to let go of my anger at Parker for turning our sexting into a worldwide meme about my boobs and two dogs screwing, but it's always there."

"Like Will Lotham," I mutter.

"Exactly," Perk says, grabbing her tablet. "Which is why you need to find an FWB."

"No–she needs an ONS." Fiona huddles heads with Perky.

The conversation has clearly shifted, but I don't know in which direction. Like a sewage plant spill, the direction *matters*.

"What are you two talking about? ONS?"

"One night stand," Fiona says slowly.

"You need a date," Perk says.

An image of Will in his suit takes over my mind.

"Do not! I hate dating."

"Which is why you need it. When was the last time you got laid?"

I go quiet.

"Knew it! It's been a long time, hasn't it?" Perky's tapping on her glass screen. The sound of fingers thumping reminds me of cantaloupes falling off a kitchen counter onto an area rug.

"The reunion is two weeks away," Fiona starts, her voice making it clear she's about to prove a point.

A point involving *me*.

"Yes?"

"So that's two weeks to find a date."

"Or two weeks to avoid, avoid, avoid and come down with strep throat at the last minute so I have an excuse not to go."

"This isn't debate finals, Mal. That's not going to work this time."

Tap tap tap.

"In!" Perky announces. "I've logged into your online dating profile," she informs me.

"What? After that weird guy who bragged about how he scales his own teeth with a nine-dollar kit from DebtSlavesNo-More.com and showed me his DIY-dental channel on YouTube, you know I swore off online dating."

JULIA KENT

"His videos were impressive," Perky says. "I didn't know gums could bleed like that and still heal."

Fiona and I share a shudder that rates a 3.2 on the Richter scale.

"I am not so desperate that I need to find a high school reunion date on an online matchmaking website."

Fiona and Perky look at each other.

"Come on!"

They turn their attention to the dating site.

"I'm just going to flip you to Available," Perky announces, her fingertip slowly swiping. She peers at the screen. "When did they add Desperate as an option? Huh."

"You have to field the dick pics," I inform her. "No way am I sorting through those again."

"Why do guys think that's a good idea? Do we send them pictures of our labia?"

"Only when they ask," Perky mumbles.

"You do not!"

"No. I don't. I send back a picture of a huge cock and say, 'Mine is bigger than yours.'"

"Bet that shuts them up," Fi calls out.

"No." Perky frowns. "Not all of them." A thousand-mile stare settles on her face.

"I don't want to talk about this," I tell them seriously. "You know, and I know, that I'll suck it up and go to the reunion. Between my mom finding out about it, the onslaught of everyone from our class coming into town for it, and my own eternal optimist curse, I'll go. Just don't make a big deal about it, okay? It's hard enough having my past thrown in my face every day now that Will's back."

"That bad?" Fiona asks softly.

"That good." I set my fork down and just go for the sweet

118

naan. "He's even better. Ten years has made my freaking high school crush even *more appealing*."

"I'm sorry," Perky commiserates. "What an asshole."

"He's an asshole for turning out to be an even better human being as an adult?"

"Yes."

"That makes no sense, Perk."

"It does according to Friend Code." She snatches the naan from me before I eat it all.

"You both know how it is. I love living here. I love our town. The downtown is where I belong. There is nothing about our area that isn't perfect for me. I went to Brown and loved Providence, too, but it wasn't home. This is home. I want a house here. A husband. Kids in Little League and Boy and Girl Scouts. I want to take them to Fenway Park and ride the Swan Boats and avoid Salem every October. I want to take them to the Dance and Dairy festival every August and gorge on funnel cakes and fried Twinkies. I am hooked. I was born in the just-right place." I sigh. "But when people who left come back to visit, there's always that sneer. Like they're better or smarter or *whatever* for leaving."

"Does Will have it?" Fiona asks.

I think about him in that suit this morning. Our conversations. The phone call.

Oh, that call.

"I don't know."

"Don't invent it," Perky warns me. "It would be easy to find something negative in Will that isn't really there."

"Why would I invent it?"

Another look passes between Fi and Perk. "Because, Mal," Fiona says, the self-appointed speaker of truths we hide from ourselves, "you spent all those years in high school inventing reasons why you couldn't take a risk and see if he liked you, too. Don't make that mistake again."

I start to protest.

I stop.

I remember the one deep conversation I ever had with Will. The one time I thought maybe, just *maybe*, he was interested in me.

I stuff my mouth with sweet naan as my phone's notifications start to ping from the dating app.

I was wrong then, and I'm wrong now.

But this is my life.

And Will Lotham's back in it. Like it or not.

Problem is, I *do* like it.

I like it too much.

Chapter Ten

I have to go back to the office, like it or not, because Will is my client.

A client who made sexually suggestive conversation with me yesterday before my phone died.

A client who certainly seems to have been flirting with me.

A client who... isn't here today.

I've tried to avoid coming to The Lotham Group, but I can't. I need to see him for approval on renting a few antique pieces to fill in at the house. I also need an orange lacquered urn his mother has in the worst possible place in the office, but that will be perfect for a pop of color in her front entry hall.

So.

Driven to overcome my own uncertain humiliation, my perfectionistic design tendencies get in the way. You would think I'd be relieved to come into the office, grab the urn, and run off, not needing to face Will.

Disappointment, though, seeps into my pores.

And then I check my email.

My pulse leaps when I see his name in my inbox.

Out of the office for the week as we migrate from old location to new. Agents showing house. Be ready.

That's the entire email from Will.

What's the opposite of a pulse leap? A coma? That sounds restful.

Perky and Fiona were wrong. He wasn't hinting at more. If anything, this is a measured, cool, all-business approach.

The lacquered urn feels heavy, stupid, trivial in my arms as I walk out of The Lotham Group's office and into the bright summer sunshine.

Okay, this is a reprieve. A break. A breather from the sudden whirlwind of having Will re-appear in my life.

This week is a chance.

A chance to prove I'm worth that stager's commission.

And a chance to get Will out of my life by getting the house under contract as fast as possible.

The drive to his parents' house is a blur. It's not just a blur because unexpected tears come, but also because it's a small town. Five minutes, tops, anywhere, unless it's rush hour or parade day.

I get there and storm up the Perfect Path to the Perfect Door and enter the Perfect Home.

In tears.

Why?

Why am I crying?

Setting the urn down on the table in the hall, I walk in, close the front door, and make a beeline for the bedrooms. My mission is clear:

Learn more about this family.

Staging a space involves personality. My approach is the exact opposite of all those real estate advice articles about making a house as neutral as possible so potential buyers and renters can project themselves into it.

Personality *matters*.

People are more pliable and open than we think.

When a potential buyer or renter enters a home, yes, their headspace is all about them. Imaginations are quirky when it comes to space. We have to live in the past, the now, and the future, all at the same time. People do need to be able to imagine themselves living in a new home, but it doesn't have to be a blank space. It can be aspirational, a place to grow, change a little, maybe live a little better.

Will we be able to let go of our current space and all the joy and disappointment attached to it? Can we appreciate what we're seeing in front of our face without bringing too much emotional baggage along?

Television shows and modern media about home living focus on that third layer: the future.

But it's the past that really propels us into that unknown.

The house is ice cold. Somewhere in the AC system, a piece of machinery must have malfunctioned. Before I forget, I pull out my phone and send the office manager a quick email requesting repair service, cc'ing Will. I shiver and forge ahead.

I walk up the stairs, headed for the first group of bedrooms. Bedrooms are windows into people's souls.

Bzz. Bzzz. Bzzzzzzz. My stupid phone (86% charged, thank you very much) is going nuts in my pocket. All day, I've been plagued with offers to screw.

Yes. That's right. No one has asked me out on an actual date yet. They just want to fill every hole except my mouth.

Er, actually... that one, too. A few guys are really, really specific about what they want. Including pictures, and one enterprising soul even sent a flow chart.

Last time I checked, semen didn't qualify as a dinner date.

But for some of these guys, those calories *count*.

Opening the app, I swipe *Hell no* over and over until one of the offers catches my eye.

Do you like to dance? No screwing required.

Clever pickup line. Spelled correctly, with–bonus!–punctuation. My bar is *so* low right now. I open the message.

Hi Deco91, he starts.

No, my username isn't original, but that's the point. Anonymity requires a certain blandness. If I wanted creepy stalkers to be able to find me for a good old-fashioned kidnapping, I'd call Beastman and Spatula.

I am trying to find a way to be clever and different from the troglodytes on these dating apps...

Troglodyte? Five points to the guy for using an SAT word correctly.

I'm branching out and trying something new. Would you be interested in a really different first date? A dance lesson? I'm tired of coffee-shop speed dating and I have two left feet (full disclosure). Want to meet up for some fun? David. His username is NiceGuysFinish.

Huh.

David's photo shows a vague, generic image of a broad-shouldered guy with muscular arms wearing a tight t-shirt, jeans, flip flops, and a baseball cap, walking a golden retriever on the beach. I do a reverse image search. Nope. Not a stock photo or stolen from anywhere in the photo database. Doesn't come up as a profile picture for any public social media account. Hmmm.

What? You don't reverse image everyone? I might be naïve about pornography film sets, but I'm savvy when it comes to sex scammers on the internet. Especially scammers I might sleep with. Bad sex is bad enough. Bad sex with someone who pretends to be someone they're not is so much worse.

Because then you feel like you slept with someone other than the person you agreed to sleep with.

Not that I would know.

Ask poor Perky all about it, though.

My phone buzzes with a text. It's Fiona.

Go for Dance Guy! she says.

I do a double take.

How do you know about Dance Guy? I ask, groaning internally. Once we name these people, they become more real, and how can I say no to someone we've named? It's like feeding a stray cat in your neighborhood. Do it once and it's yours forever.

Perk and I downloaded the app and are monitoring your account. We knew you'd ignore it, so we're doing this for your own good.

Of course they are.

You asshole, I text back.

Except... I accidentally type that in the message box in the dating app, hitting Send before I realize my mistake.

I get an immediate reply, even before blood flow has been restored to my brain.

Normally I don't get called names until the date's over. This is refreshing :) , David replies.

Mortified laughter pours out of me as I hover over the reply bar, wondering what to type.

I finally decide on: *I'm branching out and trying something new, too.*

If you're looking for a guy who's a sub and into being degraded, sorry. Not my kink, he responds.

Bummer, I type back. *Have to give you the boot.*

Is that a dancing boot? If so, say yes. Come on. Try me. I promise I'm a nice guy.

They all say that.

I know we all say that, but the odds are that some of us are telling the truth, he adds, as if reading my mind.

Bzzzz.

My phone makes it impossible to ignore the text. I flip over to read:

Are you flirting with Dance Guy in the app? Fiona texts.

Leave me alone. I accidentally called him an asshole because of you, I reply.

Me? I didn't do anything!

You and Perky are assholes. I called him one instead of you.

So you blew it?

No. He still wants to go out with me.

Masochist?

Hey!

Sorry. Then again, not sure which one of you is the masochist, but go on the date! Dance with him. Then you can press against him and see what he's packing.

I start to reply something about guns and then groan.

You want me to dance with a guy on the first date so I can use my thighs and belly to figure out how big his erection is?

I hit Send, then panic. Did I send that to David?

Closing texts, I go back to the app. Whew. Nope.

Sure, I type into the app's messaging system. *When and where?*

Tonight? Seven? At Bailargo?

That's the dance studio one town over.

It's a date, I type back. *My name is Mallory, by the way.*

I was looking forward to calling you Deco91. Like a Star Trek *character.*

I figured I'd help a nice guy finish, I reply before I realize that's a big old no-no.

I get a smile in reply.

Bzzzz.

We're Googling David. Found his LinkedIn profile. Works as a conversion consultant.

Did you hack his DNA test results to determine his percentage of Neanderthal genes? I joke.

No, but Perky says that's a great idea!

"From erections to Neanderthal genetic material. Come on. When did finding someone to have sex with become so complicated?" I mumble, coming back to reality here in Will's boyhood bedroom.

"I don't know, Mallory. You tell me," says a deep voice behind me, the sound of a live human's vocal cords shattering every speck of composure I possess.

Right behind me. He's right behind me. The primitive part of my brain signals to me that I'm about to be eaten by a velociraptor. I grab the nearest object I can, lifting a crystal football trophy over my head as I step forward, impulses set to *away*.

Screaming at the top of my lungs, I jump on the bed, knees unlocked and thighs ready to lunge. I inventory my situation with lightning speed:

I am alone.
In an empty house.
No one knows I'm here.
A man is threatening me.

So I do what any sane woman would do.

Hurl the trophy at his head.

SCORE! Heavy lead crystal and sheer panic combine really well when it comes to weaponizing them to stay alive.

Unless you're Will Lotham.

"OW!" he shouts, arms up to defend against his own Most Valuable Player trophy attacking him. You know how in movies a moment like this is captured in slow motion, as if the victim lives through it on a time delay?

The exact opposite happens to my adrenaline-filled blood-stream. Time speeds up.

Blood runs pretty damn fast, too.

"Jesus, Mallory, what the hell?" he grunts out, holding his right hand against a spot on his scalp above his ear. Our eyes meet. His are outraged, full of pain, and instantly, I feel awful.

But still very, very pissed.

"Don't ever come up behind me like that! You scared the hell out of me!" My knees go weak. I'm standing on the bed, the mattress soft enough to make it hard to balance as stress hormones turn my joints into silly putty.

"You didn't have to give me a concussion!" He winces.

"I thought you were a velociraptor!"

"Do I look like an eighty-million-year-old beast with light-ning-fast reflexes that loves to tear flesh off people?"

"How would I know? I haven't seen you for ten years!"

"What are you doing in my bedroom? Turning my inani-mate objects against me?"

"I'm–I'm–" Of course, I can't tell the truth about why I'm in here. I pivot and move close to him, worried about the blood dripping down his jaw line, staining his shirt. "I need to look at that."

"You are not touching me. You've done enough damage." He flinches, but doesn't step back. I'm close enough to smell his cologne, the scent mingling with fresh blood, my nose filled with my own adrenaline-fueled fear that is winding down.

"Will, you need a first aid kit. Where is it?"

"Bathroom. Through that door."

Skittering over to the next room, I rummage through drawers until I find the kit, part of my brain admiring the exquisite vanity from Waterworks. Finding a washcloth, I wet it with cool water and return to find Will sitting on the edge of his bed, glaring at the trophy like it was all the crystal football's fault.

"At least she didn't drop to the floor and kick me in the balls," I hear him mutter to himself as I enter the room.

"If I had, you'd have deserved it," I tell him matter of factly, bending before him and looking up at his face. "I'm sorry."

"You're telling me I deserved it but you are also sorry in the same sentence?"

"Complexity is the hallmark of being a mature human being." I carefully dab the cut with the wet washcloth as he winces.

"Then you're the most mature person I know, Mallory, because you're exceptionally complex. Always have been."

My heart has been pounding like crazy from fear, but as Will's words wash over me, it picks up the beat, dancing a new set of steps that are unfamiliar, exhilarating.

Always have been. That implies he's paid attention to me across time.

What does that mean?

Carefully, I reach for his hand, the one pressed to the head wound I created, and as our fingers touch, he sucks in a deep breath. I assume it's from pain, and make a sound of compassion. He lets his hand drop, and I quickly press a big square of gauze to the cut.

"I am truly sorry," I whisper, wincing as I look at his split flesh. I did that to him. Adrenaline rushes through my blood again, like a sugar high after eating baklava at my favorite local

Greek restaurant, Athena's Delite, and as much as I'm still crazy upset by what I thought was an attack, I'm starting to realize how much I really hurt him.

"It's okay," he says through gritted teeth, but he doesn't pull away from my touch. Being allowed to atone for what I've done to him takes some of the sting out of my sense of horrified remorse.

"It's not okay." With my spare hand, I get an antiseptic swab ready.

He sighs, green-blue eyes twin gemstones that shift in the sunlight. "At least you know how to defend yourself when some strange man attacks you in his own home."

I laugh, a bubbly sound that surprises me.

"That's some arm you've got," he adds, Adam's apple bobbing as it's obvious he's fighting pain.

"I'll take that as a compliment, coming from a quarterback." His hair is dark and thick, falling in handsome waves against his scalp and ear. Being this close to him means I see all his edges clearly. The collar of his shirt against his neck, the small whorl of hair that spirals behind his ear. The way his cologne has faded since he last showered, the scent mingling with a very human scent, skin and oil and pheromones all blending to make a warm, tingly sensation begin between my legs, traveling up to my nipples, which tighten in response.

I swallow, hard. If *I* had an Adam's apple, it would look like a slot machine lever in a casino.

"The wound," I say, clearing my throat, as if that will do anything to stop the bass drum between my legs, "is small. Looks like I hit you with the corner of the base." The cut is L-shaped and deceptively tiny. So much blood from such a small tear. His hair follicles are clean and even, as if he were genetically engineered. As I peer at his scalp, I move in closer, standing up slightly.

"Uh, Mal?" His voice is strangely muffled. "Can't breathe."

I look down and realize he's half an inch from being smothered to death by the girls.

"Sorry!" I jump back, dropping the gauze in his lap, heart pounding.

A lazy smile turns his mouth into a weapon of mass destruction, if by *mass* you mean my sense of propriety. "I can think of worse ways to die."

Bzzzz.

My phone startles me. Will rescues the gauze and presses it back against his head while I fumble for the phone. It falls at his feet. He picks it up, the text stream right there on the screen.

"Erections have no correlation with Neanderthal genes," he reads slowly, wincing as I try to grab the phone, brushing against his ribs and shoulders, his warmth driving me nuts.

"Give that to me!"

He looks down at his crotch. "Never thought about caveman genes and my junk before."

"Junk? You call it your... junk?"

"What else should I call it?"

"Penis. That's what it is."

My fourteen-year-old self has her hand in the air, jumping in her ninth-grade desk chair, begging to be called on because *omigod* I am in Will Lotham's bedroom and my boobs almost smothered him and we're talking about his penis.

"Do you use the proper terms for everything, Mallory?" He makes an inarticulate sound as I peel the gauze off the cut, wiping gently. "You call your pretty place a vulva, right? And you use the word vagina."

"*'Pretty place'*?"

He shrugs.

"And yes, I do. Vulva and vagina. And then there's the clitoris," I say primly.

"What's that?"

"What's what?"

"A clitoris. Never heard of it."

I freeze and look down at him. Bright eyes meet mine. Is he serious?

"The clitoris is a nerve cluster above the opening to the vagina," I begin, taking a breath to continue my impromptu human sexuality lecture, because when a man tells you they don't know what a clitoris is, you educate them immediately.

For the sisterhood. All the women Will is going to sleep with from here on out will thank me later.

He starts to laugh. I'm so tempted to pour the small bottle of isopropyl alcohol directly on his wound, but I'm a kind, compassionate woman, so instead I dab it on with a swab.

"OW!" he bellows.

"Sorry."

"You're not sorry at all."

"I'm sorry for your sex partners that you have no idea what a clitoris is, Will."

"I know what it is. And my tongue knows how to find one. Blindfolded."

"Why would you blindfold your tongue?"

Bzzz.

This time, it's *his* phone. Turning away, I resist the urge to fan myself. Lord have mercy.

"Huh. Wedding." I can't help but notice the knuckles on his right hand, the bruising from his brawl with Beastman still evident. Then I realize what he's just said.

"You're getting married?" I choke out, appalled.

He laughs. "That would be pretty bizarre, given I'm not dating anyone."

I file that bit of information in the THANK GOD folder in my brain.

"Don't underestimate how quickly those internet mail-order brides can be delivered, Will."

"I'm not the groom." His eyes dim a bit as he says that. "I'm in the wedding party. I've got a–" He frowns. "A thing I have to do."

"You want antibiotic cream?"

He shakes his head. "I'm good."

"The risk of infection from being hit with a ten-year-old statue is probably small."

Squinting, he looks at me, hair disheveled, drops of blood on his collar. He's never been more attractive. Maybe I was a vampire in another life.

Wait. That's not technically possible. Vampires are immortal, so how could I have been one in another life when they get one, eternal life?

Never mind. Will's staring at me staring at his collar. I lick my lips.

"You're really invested in getting this house under contract. We should talk more about it," he says, his eyes on me.

On my *mouth*.

"We should?" Where's this coming from suddenly?

"In a location where you do not have access to weapons."

I cross my arms over the girls and lift my eyebrows. "Don't startle women when they're vulnerable and alone, and–"

"Are you free for dinner tonight?"

Chapter Eleven

Words catch in my throat. I just stare and blink, until finally he asks, "Mallory?"

"Dinner?"

"A business dinner," he says, suddenly looking away. There's a wet spot where I hit him, the hair darker than the rest, slightly matted. Regret kicks in and I feel about two feet tall. "Talk about design trends, real estate, you know."

I nod. Right. "I can't tonight. I have a date," I blurt out, remembering David. The app. The asshole who isn't an asshole.

Yet. I haven't met him, so that judgment remains withheld.

"A date?"

"Yes. A date. You know, that thing where you go out with someone who has no intention of really getting to know you and you spend the entire time eating bread that doesn't taste as good as your date claims and trying to decide whether to initiate rescue-text sequences with your mom."

"That's your idea of a date?"

"That is my actual *experience* of every date I've had since college."

"You're dating the wrong guys." He holds my gaze for just a little too long. I look away.

"I have to keep fishing in the pond if I ever want to catch a different one."

"If that's the way you talk to your dates, I am beginning to understand why they all turn out so badly."

"Hey!"

"What?"

"Don't accuse me of being a bad date. I'm a great date! I Google the guy in advance and read his LinkedIn profile. I make sure I don't wear super-tall heels in case he lied about his height on his dating profile. I pretend to care about all his hobbies and don't reveal that I'm secretly tallying all the micro-aggressions he's sending my way during appetizers and wine. And if he makes it to dessert, well–" I falter.

"You never make it to dessert, do you?" Will asks, eyebrows up. He drops them quickly, wincing.

"I–well–it's not that *I* don't. *He* doesn't!"

"He ditches you?"

"No! No! It's just that he always has a thing."

"A thing?"

"A work emergency. Or a dog with a twisted bowel. Or a grandma in the ER."

"How many guys used the twisted-canine-intestine thing?"

"Three." I sit down and sag against his teenage desk, elbows sliding forward, fingers deep in my hair. "I looked it up. There's an entire subreddit devoted to inventive ways to get out of a bad date."

"And yet here you are." He leans against the edge of his desk. "Trying again."

"I'm a masochist."

His eyes gleam. "Maybe you should start your dates with

that line. 'Hi. I'm Mallory Monahan. I'm a masochist.' You'd definitely make it to dessert."

"I'd make it into the headlines, too. 'Woman found in cage, collar attached to washing machine after online date goes wrong. News at eleven.'"

I stand and grab my purse while Will laughs.

"Good luck," he says, voice a little quiet. "I hope this one works out."

"Why should it? None of the other ones do."

"Why not?"

I shrug. "I wish I knew." Sigh. "Perky thinks it's because I won't make myself smaller."

Appreciative eyes look at my body. "You don't need to be smaller. You're... great."

Did Will Lotham just size me up?

"No, no, not this," I say, patting my hips. "Not my body. I mean me. My mind. My way of talking."

"Way of talking?"

"I don't... hide it."

"Hide what?"

"The fact that I'm smart." There. I said it.

"Why would you hide the fact that you're smart from a guy?"

Laughter, fourteen years of it, all bottled up and fizzy, comes shooting out of me like I'm Diet Coke and his words are Mentos.

"Are you kidding me? *You* of all people are asking me why I would need to play dumb?"

"What makes me so special?"

Talk about a loaded question.

Nodding toward the door, he motions for me to follow him. We walk down the hallway and into the kitchen, where he grabs something to drink from the mostly empty fridge.

"What do you mean?"

"What do *you* mean? You just said *you* in a way that was loaded with some hidden meaning." Opening a soda, he raises his eyebrows, then flinches. "Want a drink?"

"No, thank you," I choke out.

We move over to the breakfast area and sit at the antique pedestal table, beautifully scarred from generations of use. I think briefly about all the important conversations that must have taken place around it, before this one.

He really doesn't know. Really, *really* doesn't know. I knew I was shy. I knew I was also careful. But to sit here ten years after graduation and realize I spent four years of my emerging adulthood hiding my feelings about this guy and being extremely successful at it makes a part of me feel so stupid.

Mostly the teenage part.

A mature, worldly woman would admit it. Make it a joke. Turn the past into a whimsical *ha ha*, a shared laugh that would display how far she'd come since high school graduation. A mature, worldly woman would invite Will out for drinks, talk over martinis, and wax nostalgic about those care-free years.

I, unfortunately, am neither mature nor worldly.

"I just mean, you know."

"No. I don't."

"Remember ninth grade? When we had to debate in English class?"

"You mean the debate about animal rights in laboratory research to cure cancer?"

"Yes."

"What about it?"

"You said, in front of the entire class, that I couldn't

137

possibly make a reasoned argument because I was emotionally attached to the animals."

"You were!"

"You then made the broad generalization that *all* girls were impossibly biased."

He's halfway through a swallow of soda and starts choking. "*I* said that?"

"You did."

"I don't remember that!"

"Maybe the memory is buried by the sound of all your football buddies laughing their asses off."

"Oh." He frowns. "I guess I do remember that."

"So." I cross my arms over my chest. Point made.

"So?"

I shrug with one shoulder.

"That proves nothing. You took that away from some cocky comment I made while I was trying to win a debate and get a better grade? You didn't have to dumb yourself down. "

"Didn't I?"

"Why would you take *that* lesson away from some random comment a dumbass fourteen-year-old boy made? I wasn't exactly enlightened. That was half our lives ago! I used to think all kinds of bullshit."

"Because I was a supersensitive fourteen-year-old girl, Will."

"How could something I barely remember hurt you so much?"

"I didn't say it hurt. Just that it made me dumb myself down."

"No. No way. There's no way one comment like that did it."

"I—"

He's watching me in a way that makes it clear he's

studying me. Figuring me out. This isn't about his being right. It's about Will trying to find the truth.

Dear God. He's more dangerous than I thought.

My heart starts to pound hard, the drumbeat moving up under my collarbone as I wait him out. He's patient, but he's far less practiced. I have a treasure trove from four years of turning Will Lotham into my unofficial honors class, an independent-study project that no teacher supervised. If you could earn an A+ in Will, I'd have that shiny grade on my high school transcript.

But never, ever, did I imagine he'd study me right back.

"Mal." His frown is miles deep. "What else?"

"It was your friends."

"Which ones?"

"The big, hulking ones."

"You'll have to be more specific."

"Ramini. Osgood. Fletch." A mental image of them in their football jerseys, one of them half sitting on the edge of my rickety desk, makes my stomach sour.

"What about them?"

"After the debate. They... said stuff. Did stuff."

He goes tense. "Did stuff? To you?"

"No, not like that."

"Then like what?"

"They told me you were right. Later on, in the hallway as we walked to lunch. They said a girl couldn't beat Will Lotham. Said I was being stupid for even trying. They told me I talked too much in class."

"You didn't."

"Does it matter? They said I did. And then they told me to give them copies of my study guides."

"What?" Real outrage flashes in his eyes. "I assume you said no."

JULIA KENT

"Of course." I look over at the pine server, where a pile of Zen stacking stones sits with great anticipation. The expectation of stress release is mocking me, telling me I'm derelict in not doing what I need to relax. Pressured by Zen.

Classic Mallory.

"And?"

"And they got mad."

"And...?" This time, the word is drawn out in that way people say it when they're really listening. He's caught up in my story, half participant, half observer. I'm connecting him to behind-the-scenes events when all he has is the center stage. What's in front of the backdrop is all Will's memory has.

"One of them called me a name. It starts with c."

Will growls.

"He told me I would regret it. He looked at his own hand and curled it into a fist."

Will's eyes go wide with astonishment, a small, incredulous laugh slipping out of him. But it's a low sound, protective, and it's invoking something dormant in me, a feeling that I can't fight even if I try.

Leaning closer to me, as if entering my space to keep me safe, Will asks, "He threatened you?"

"It was implied."

"Did you do anything about it?"

"Like what? Punch a two-hundred-pound freshman football player in the face?"

"No, like tell a teacher."

"Tell her what? That he looked at his fist? Of course not. Really good bullies know how to skirt the line. He was *gifted*. If Harmony Hills had a gifted and talented class for bullying, Ramini would have been the teacher's pet. Osgood could have been an extra on *The Sopranos*. And Fletch looked like the high school equivalent of a bouncer."

140

"So it was Ramini? He could be a jerk sometimes."

"He could be a jerk *all* the time, to some of us. But I'm not telling you which one it was."

"It was Ramini, Osgood, or Fletch, though."

I shrug.

"I–" Will deflates slightly, a hopelessly confused look on his face. "I'm sorry."

"Why are *you* sorry?"

"I know I didn't do it, but it feels like someone should tell that sensitive fourteen-year-old girl 'I'm sorry.'"

"I didn't bring this up to have a pity party." I stand, thoroughly reeling, turning to leave.

"Mallory," he says, grabbing my arm, making me stay. He has no idea what he is doing to my pulse. "I don't think you're doing that."

"I know I'm not."

"I want to make sure you know *I* know you're not."

We freeze. I'm wearing a short-sleeved wrap shirt, and his fingers curl around my elbow, the touch firm but respectful. His palm is soft, the kind of skin men have when they don't use their hands to work for a living. He has long fingers, elegant and tapered. I should know. I'm staring at his hand.

Breathing together becomes an end in itself, our chests rising and falling as if choreographed. I'm looking at his hand and he's looking at me. My face can feel it, the intensity palpable, the ache of my past self turning quickly into a very different ache in lower parts of my body. The woman I am becoming is deeply appreciative of this extraordinarily handsome man standing before me, breathing with me.

And touching me.

"The minute I came home, the past came rushing forward, like it had been waiting this whole time, impatient and fidgety. Waiting for its turn," Will says as his fingers open and drop, one by one, from my arm. As the brush of his thumb removes our connection, I feel hollow.

I didn't know how full I felt just from that touch.

"Were you running away from the past?"

"No. Running toward my future. The past wasn't fast enough to catch up."

"You sound like most of our graduating class."

"That's because most of us left. But you didn't."

"No." I look him in the eye and have no reaction. I've cultivated this response. He's not original in his topic. Most people wonder why the class valedictorian stayed so close to home. Brown was only ninety minutes away. My job with the Tollesons was here. My apartment, my friends–the continuity in my life is strong.

Tilting his head just so, for a brief second Will's eyes flicker with questions I can tell he thinks he doesn't have a right to ask. *Not yet*, those eyes say.

But soon.

What do you do when you can't read another person as well as you want to?

You divert.

"Wait a minute." I bite *my* lower lip and activate the movie reel of memory in my mind. "That day on the porn set, here at your parents' house."

"What about it?" His head shake tells me my distraction technique is working a little too well.

"I have a question."

"I have lots of questions about that day, too." Crossing his arms, Will cocks one eyebrow, winces, and goes into interrogative mode.

"Let me ask mine first."

"Shoot."

"You told me to leave with my anal beads." I hold up one finger and hastily add, "That were most definitely not mine."

"I did."

"That means you know what anal beads are."

"You didn't?" Oh, his body language.

"I thought it was a dog's chew toy," I admit.

"Sex toys for dogs? You think there are *kinky dogs* out there? The whole pet-pampering industry has gone way over the edge, but I don't think it's gone that far, Mal. What's next? *Fifty Shades of Rover*?" He cracks the knuckles on his left hand, starting with the index finger and working his way down.

"You're changing the subject."

"How do you know that's what I'm doing?"

"Because you have this thing you do when you get nervous. You did it in high school and you're doing it now."

"What's that?"

"You start cracking your knuckles. One by one."

He halts mid-crack on his ring finger. His bare ring finger.

Will looks down. A slow smile pulls at his lips. "You're right. I do." Our eyes meet. "How did you know?"

"I sat behind you in nearly every honors class, Will. I've watched you answer countless questions from teachers. And every time you didn't know the answer, you cracked your knuckles. One"–I crack my index finger–"by"–I crack my middle finger–"one." My ring finger won't snap.

He waits.

"You spent a lot of time paying attention to me, Mallory."

"I sat behind you. It's not like I could stare at your ass all day. I had to have something else to look at."

"You stared at my ass?"

"It was two feet in front of me! Four classes a day!" I start to sweat. The memory of him in football uniform pants. Oh, sweet ice cream fairy, deliver me from evil.

"You okay? You look," he says, stepping closer, "a little disturbed."

"I'm fine."

"Hot, even." The rise and fall of his chest pauses after those words, as if he's holding his breath, too.

"I am fine! You just need to turn on the air conditioning."

"It's sixty-two in here. Remember? You emailed about getting the HVAC company to come fix it because it's stuck."

We remember to breathe, over and over, magically living through the seconds of some unverbalized emotion I can't name, but can only feel.

Does he feel it, too?

"Have fun on your date tonight, Mal," he says softly, biting his lower lip as he smiles at me and turns away, the break in eye contact making me long for a past that just happened. "I hope it goes well."

"Thanks," I say, the words so different from what my heart is screaming.

But *thanks* has to be enough.

Chapter Twelve

Bailargo is impossible to miss. Years ago, some town council got money to renovate an old Victorian home, which is now a painted lady.

Painted red.

None of the muted jewel tones you see on old Victorians are anywhere near the Bailargo building. Oh, no. Red, white, and black dominate, with murals. The original ballroom in the house became the main dance-lesson venue. If you have to learn to dance for a wedding, prom, bar mitzvah, Purim ball, cotillion, or any other purpose, this is the place to go.

And to be *seen*.

Like every Pilates studio on the planet, Bailargo's dance-lesson clients are there to impress. To have others notice their presence. To take selfies and perfectly positioned Instagram photos, and to be giddy and excited about dance.

I have not danced since college, where arms in the air, foot shuffles, and the requisite booty shake were my repertoire.

Pretty much every college student's alcohol-infused dance set.

JULIA KENT

I'm sitting in my car, texting with Perky, five minutes early, when I look up and gape.

Will is walking into the Bailargo building.

Given that there are no other businesses in this building, this can mean only one thing:

I must enter the witness protection program.

Will just went into Bailargo! I text Perky.

Her instant reply: *Don't call him Will, Mal. His name is David. Do you shout out the wrong name when you come during sex, too? Geez.*

I do not! I reply, incensed. *And Will really did just walk in!*

Didn't you decapitate him earlier? How is he walking? That sounds unnatural. Maybe he's a zombie.

I gave him a small scalp wound, I correct her. *Barely a scratch.*

You're lucky he didn't have you arrested for assault. That's twice he's saved you from your emerging criminal tendencies.

Focus. Focus on the now, Perky. What am I going to do? Will is in the same building where I'm having a first date with Dance Guy.

What if Will IS Dance Guy????? Perky texts back. I can feel her hot breath and shaky jadedness through the phone.

Before I can answer, I get a notification on the dating app. I open it.

Ready to have some fun? David asks in the message section.

Sure am! I type back. *Where are you?*

Already inside, waiting for you. :)

Damn it.

K. Be there in a minute, I reply, sliding my phone away before realizing I've left Perk hanging.

David texted me. He's inside already. This is crazy, I tell her.

She texts back a popcorn-munching emoji.

So much for friends.

The rearview mirror reflects a vision of my better self. Auburn hair in waves that are so close to curls, the humidity doing its thing. My makeup is crisp, eyeliner perfect, eyes no longer red from doing that eyelid-flip trick Perky swears by. With my pulse tap dancing in my veins, I climb out of the car.

I'm not sure whether I'm more nervous about meeting David or running into Will.

No. Actually, I am sure.

It's Will.

The studio smells like linseed oil and geranium, a weird combination that works surprisingly well. Gleaming, polished wood floors go on for what seem like miles, rolling on and on until I start to wonder if my depth perception has been altered by panic.

"Mallory?" Will's over to the left, next to a water fountain, wearing a navy blue polo shirt, jeans, and a confused smile. My eyes dart to the spot where I hit him.

No bandage.

No blood on his collar, either.

"Will!" I feign surprise. "What are you doing here?"

"I was about to ask the same question."

"This is my date."

He looks behind me. "Where is he?"

"Oh, hahaha, I mean this is where I'm having my date. With David. David, our first date," I ramble. If this were a flamenco-dancing studio, could I snap myself to death with castanets and end this misery?

"What are the odds?" Will crosses his arms over his chest, the move making his biceps bulge. There's not an ounce of fat on him, all of him contoured, strong, and tan.

I narrow my eyes. Was that a dig? Does he think I'm

following him? Does he think I have no life and all I do is stalk him to find ways to "accidentally" run into him at the farmer's market or his lacrosse games or when we shared the same orthodontist freshman year and I figured out his schedule?

Because that is *sooooo* fourteen years ago.

Okay. Fine.

Ten.

"What are you doing here?" I ask him, quirking one eyebrow. Maybe Perky and Fiona are right? Maybe Will is Dance Guy, and this is all an elaborate scheme to get me to go out with him?

Wait. That's the entire plot of one of my ninth-grade fantasies, with the addition of the app.

Never mind.

"The wedding."

"Wedding?"

"Remember? I'm a groomsman in a wedding. The bride requires us to take dancing lessons."

"Hah. You got a zilla."

"A zilla?"

"Bridezilla."

"It's not that bad." Shrug.

"I'll bet she's an over-controlling, pedantic, neurotic freak who has a high need for perfection and she thinks objects are more important than people."

"She's my sister, Mallory."

Foot, mouth, insert. Awkward.

I try to recover. "Actually, that was *my* sister that I just described."

His head tilts, like he's trying to understand me, as if that shift will somehow give him more power. "That's right. You have an older sister, too. Hayley? Holly? Hannah?"

"Hastings. She's four years older than us."

"My sister is four years older, too. Bet they knew each other in school."

I don't know what to say to that, because I know Hasty hated Will's sister with a burning passion she once compared to a raging yeast infection, so I just ask, "How's your head?"

"Better. Some ibuprofen, emergency brain surgery, and an ice pack later, I'm good as new."

I laugh, but I'm suddenly filled with remorse. "Seriously, I'm sorry I hurt you."

His eyes soften, attention deeper. "Thanks."

"But if you ever creep up on me like that again, I'll do the same."

"What are the odds that I'll surprise you in my bedroom a second time?" He smiles, mouth closed, dimples emerging, his eyes filled with mirth. It's as if he actually wants me to quote him a number.

May the odds be ever in your favor.

And why am I recalling *Hunger Games* when it comes to thinking about being alone with Will in his bedroom?

Because my entire dating life has been nothing but a post-apocalyptic race to the bottom.

Nerves get the better of me and I look down at my phone, wondering where David is so I can move from one awkward conversation to another.

"Uh, excuse me," I say, wishing my skin didn't feel like a tingling war zone. "My, uh, date is texting me."

I'm going to hell for that lie, but whatever.

Will takes the cue and crosses the room to a table with lemonade and store-bought cookies, pouring himself a cup as I will my date to say something.

What are you wearing? I type into the app message system.

Nothing.

JULIA KENT

Two full, sweaty minutes roll by as I wait for a guy to answer the easiest double entendre ever. One hundred twenty seconds of sheer hell pass as I watch a blonde woman talk up Will like she wants to take him home and turn him into her evening protein shake. She's wearing lululemon tights and Jimmy Choos, an unusual combination that seems to indicate she's ready for anything.

Clap clap! A man in a tight, black Lycra shirt, grey fitted slacks, and the most beautiful Italian leather shoes I have ever seen glides like melting cheese on a raclette into the center of the ballroom.

"Hello, hello! My name is Philippe, and I am your instructor tonight. Welcome! Two more minutes for refreshments, and then we DANCE!" The word DANCE comes out of his mouth in capital letters.

Philippe heads straight toward me, eyes meeting mine, his dark, wavy hair slicked off his face with curls escaping at the nape of the neck, a perfectly manscaped moustache adding to his rakish look.

"And you are?" he asks, the words a demand to reveal my soul.

"Uh, Mallory."

"Uh, Mallory, it is nice to meet you."

"It's just Mallory."

"Are you Uh, Mallory, or Just Mallory?" he asks, mouth pursing with amusement.

I cannot tell whether I like him or hate him.

"Mallory."

Eyeing me up and down, his expression changes to approval when he sees my shoes. "You have come prepared."

Will chooses that exact moment to walk over, a lemonade in each hand, and offer me one. I smile a thank you as Philippe

150

watches us like he's judging a couple on *So You Think You Can Dance*.

"You are here together?" he asks.

"OH, NO!" I call out, as if it's the word DANCE. "I'm waiting for my date."

"Date?"

"First date, actually. I don't know what he looks like, but..."

"Was his name David, by any chance?" Philippe asks, mouth twisted with disgust.

"Yes!"

"Corporate," he hisses. "Again!"

Will exchanges a confused look with me, then takes a sip of his lemonade, choosing to stay out of this. One hand goes to his hip as he politely looks away, drinking like it's his job. I can see his profile out of the corner of my eye.

"Excuse me?" I ask Philippe.

"Did you meet him–this *David*–on an online dating service?"

"Yes."

Philippe takes my hand as if I'm a mourning widow at her beloved husband's wake. "Then I am sorry to inform you, Mallory, that David is not coming."

"Why not?"

"Because David is a salesman."

"No, he's not! He's a conversion consultant."

Will's mouth tightens as if he knows something.

"Mallory," Philippe says sadly, "David works for the corporation that owns Bailargo. He is one of their best sales-men." Anger flashes in his eyes. "Because he toys with women's emotions and sets them up for this."

"This?"

Gesturing at me, he says, "This. You. The poor, lonely single woman looking for love on apps."

"HEY!"

Are Will's shoulders shaking?

"Watch," Philippe says, clapping twice again. "Are any women here for a date with David? First date?"

Two hands go up.

"Oh, God," I mutter, my hands flying to cover my burning hot, deeply embarrassed face. "What does this mean?"

"David has developed a new technique. He goes to dating apps and pretends to be original, asking women to have a first date at a dance lesson. He is charming and funny and–"

A feral sound comes out of my mouth.

"Sound familiar?" Will asks, reaching up to run a hand through his hair, looking really sympathetic on my behalf.

Which makes me feel even stupider.

"And then the women come here, there is no David, but some of them stay for class," Philippe finishes.

"You're telling me your corporate headquarters is hiring a guy who goes on dating sites and convinces single women to come to a dance class with him, then ghosts on them? On the chance that a certain percentage of us will sign up for dance lessons and convert to paying customers?" My voice goes higher and higher, until I start sounding like Mariah Carey the second everyone finishes Thanksgiving dinner and it's time for her songs to start on the radio again.

"Yes."

"That's *horrible*!" I cry.

"That's ingenious," Will says. My glare makes him add quickly, "And completely unethical, of course. Some men are disgusting pigs." His brow drops, eyes troubled with vicarious empathy, but they move in patterns that tell me he's processing this information and finds David's business acumen to be worthy of note.

"If you will excuse me, I need to find some tissues for those two women who are, like you, expecting a date with the charming David. Since he started doing this four months ago, sales have increased eleven percent, but my operating supplies have gone up 286 percent with all the tissues!" Philippe glides across the floor and approaches the two women, who are whispering and comparing phone screens.

Bet mine makes us triplets.

I take mine out and open the message app, livid.

You asshole, I type, hitting Send.

I told you women normally say that after the date :) he responds immediately.

There is no date. And no, I'm not buying dance lessons because you lured me here, I add. *I'm complaining about you to corporate!*

Come on. I'm sure dance lessons will lift your mood.

I hold the camera up to my left hand, middle finger flying high. I text that back with the message: *This is the only thing I'm lifting when it comes to you.*

And then I delete the damn app.

Will appears again, this time with more lemonade and a box of tissues under his arm. "Here," he says, holding out the cup.

"I don't need to be patronized." But I take it anyhow and drink some, wishing it had vodka in it.

"Need these?" He offers the tissues.

"NO!" I'm not letting that weasel ruin my night. Who cries over someone with a username like NiceGuysFinish?

Wincing, Will gives me a look that says he's judging me. I agree. I'm totally judging myself now.

The door is to my right. Without another word, I head for it.

"Mallory!" Philippe calls out as the other two David victims stroll along the room's perimeter, talking about getting dinner at the new Mongolian barbeque in town. "Please don't leave!"

"Are you kidding me? I'm not converting to a paid customer so David the Asshole can meet his quota!"

"No, no, no! Tonight's lesson is one hundred percent free for you, Mallory! It's just," he says, looking around the group of dance students with eyes that dart as he clearly counts heads, "even including me, we have an odd number." One super-old dude with an impressive *Duck Dynasty* beard appears to be comforting a crying older woman in a Chanel-style suit.

Is that going to be me in thirty years?

"So?" I challenge Philippe.

He looks at Will, then me. "It would be a much richer experience for everyone if we can pair up properly."

"Do you have any idea what my day has been like, Philippe?" I start, winding up inside, ready to unleash a verbal whip that cracks with emotion. "It's been kinda long. And very full."

Will reaches up to gingerly touch the wound I gave him.

Philippe takes my hands in his again, an earnest expression on his face wearing me down. Exhaustion fills me, emotional and physical. My calves ache along with my heart.

"Do not let David win. Let your pain step aside and your soul take over, Mallory," he says with a dramatic flourish, looking just over my shoulder as if the horizon beckons him to take a journey to the divine.

"Is that a corporate slogan for some advertising campaign, Philippe?"

"Just because it's a commercial does not mean it isn't good."

I laugh in spite of myself. Will steps closer to me.

"C'mon, Mal. Stay." His eyes watch me, face filled with expectation and, dare I think it–hope?

"You really want to be in a class with a woman who threw a football trophy at your head today?" I ask him.

Philippe jolts. "You two are married?"

"What? No," Will says, frowning. "Why would you think that?"

"Only someone with years of great passion for another would fight like that!"

"It wasn't–"

"That's not–"

Will looks at me with a seriousness behind his mirth-filled eyes.

Two claps drown out our protests as Philippe turns to everyone else and says, "It is settled. Now we will start!"

"He doesn't take no for an answer, does he?" I murmur to Will, who keeps looking at me.

"If my sister weren't already marrying someone, I'd set them up. They'd make the perfect couple." Finally breaking the gaze, he blinks, giving Philippe his full attention.

Setting my purse down on a chair, in a line with all the other purses, I take a few deep breaths, facing away from the class. Am I crazy? There is no date. David was a sleazy salesman at best, a con man at worst. I have nothing else to do tonight, and I did bash Will's head in earlier.

Might as well stay and make the best of it.

"YOU! Uh, Mallory!" Philippe calls out. "It is time to DANCE! Find a partner and hold each other's hands, facing one another."

Five women start walking toward Will.

"Mal?" Shyness infuses his question, sending chills up and down my arms and legs. They settle at the base of my neck, riding shotgun next to the arousal centers of my nervous system. He's adorable, one hand out to me, eyebrows slightly up, blue-green eyes asking to dance with me but hinting at more.

Or... am I inventing that part?

"Sure," I say, instantly regretting my answer. Does it sound grudging? He doesn't seem to think so as I take his hand and stand before him, tall in my high heels but he's even taller. Looking at him from this height makes him even more human, more masculine, more real.

My heart skips a beat.

But the music sure doesn't.

"Now, the 'man,'" Philippe starts, using finger quotes because there are several female-only couples in the class, "puts one hand on the woman's waist. The right hand."

Will complies.

It's like sticking my finger in a light socket and orgasming at the same time.

His left hand takes my right hand and he holds it, strong and firm, smiling at me with a boyish grin that makes me feel instant remorse for hurting him today.

"I'm sorry I bashed your head in," I whisper, moving near his ear, our mouths inches apart.

"You don't have to keep apologizing." His breath warms my cheek.

There is a gap between us. My lungs live there, in that space. They breathe. I don't make a move. My autonomic nervous system works without intention. If it didn't, I'd die.

Because I would hold my breath forever in Will's arms.

Philippe is moving from couple to couple, adjusting positions, commenting and correcting.

"Closer," Philippe says right behind me, the press of his firm palm against my lower back a shock as he pushes me into Will, closing that gap.

My autonomic nervous system gives up entirely.

"Look into each other's eyes," Philippe commands, his accent making this even sexier. "When you dance, you show your love with your hips, your eyes, your languid grace. You are making love in public with your bodies, fully clothed."

Is Will holding his breath, too?

"Your hand goes here, Mallory," the teacher says, taking my left hand and putting it on Will's shoulder. My breasts brush against his chest, our breathing ragged. I try to look away, but we're too close. All I can do is look at his eyes or his mouth, and right now, both are so, so tempting.

No one else in the room exists. The light that bounces off the polished floors is ours. The murmurs and giggles in the background are ours. The way he breathes my air and I inhale him is ours, too. We're touching, my thigh against his, and every warm part of Will Lotham's front half that is decent to display in public is rubbing against me.

Except his lips.

"Now, take one step forward," Philippe says. "Together."

Will steps on my foot. Hard.

I make a very unfeminine sound and start to pitch backwards. Tightening his grip on my waist, his hand sliding, open and splayed across the small of my back, he saves me from a complete wipeout.

But that save has its costs.

In an instant, all traces of that teenage girl in me are gone, disintegrating, turned to stardust that sweeps off me like a fine spring breeze. I am all woman now, mature and wanting.

All I want is this. Now. The man before me, his arms warm and assured, grasp confident and bold.

And very much wanting me back.

His desire is evident, in physical form as my thighs meet his, our eyes locked, the fringe of his dark lashes around those intense eyes making me ache to spend hours cataloguing him. Each detail on his face becomes part of an extraordinary whole, emotion inserting itself into each pore, every curl of muscle, the sleek press of skin on bone as he watches me back.

Breathless.

I'm breathing, my body pulling oxygen in as the rest of me orbits us, gravity turning into lust, pulling us closer.

We can't break free.

We don't want to.

"Mallory," he says, his voice low and serious, the kind of vibration a grown, sophisticated man uses when he's talking to his equal. Desire pulls me closer, our faces inches apart, the edges of Will disappearing.

Clap clap!

We both jolt, Philippe grinning as he looks around the class. "Change partners! Time to learn from variety!"

As if scalded, I leap out of Will's arms, his hands holding me for a few seconds longer than propriety would dictate, as if he doesn't want to let me go.

But he does.

The strong hand that was on the small of my back slides through his thick, dark hair, fingers spread like he's about to grasp a football. Dipping his chin, he looks up at me and smiles. With his free hand, he gestures, as if to say, *by all means.*

Meanwhile, my heart is screaming, *by all means necessary.*

"Oh ho ho! My lucky day!" says an old gentleman who looks like an exact replica of a garden gnome, minus the red hat and suspenders. I look down a good half foot into a radiant face framed with wrinkles, a white beard, and so much good cheer I have to smile back.

Unable to form words quite yet, I just let the man take me in his arms, his feet so graceful that I finally choke out, "You're a wonderful dancer!" I feel like room-temperature butter in his hands, molded with a fine touch, not too much or I'll melt, not too little or I'll go cold and hard.

"Thank you. Dancy's the name. And you?"

"Mallory."

"You single, Mallory?" he asks as he passes Will, who makes a sound of amusement. He obviously heard.

"Yes, I am, Dancy," I say loud enough for Will to hear.

"Too bad you're not ten years younger," Dancy says with mock sadness. "You're a bit ripe for me." Wink.

"Missed opportunity." I chuckle as he moves me across the room like a short, bald Gene Kelly impersonating Santa Claus.

"What's wrong with him?" Dancy thumbs toward Will. "He taken?"

"No."

"Gay?"

My heart jumps in my throat. "Not that I know of."

"Then he's just stupid, eh? Not dating you, I mean."

I know what he means, all right.

"Are you Canadian, Dancy?"

"Matter of fact I am. Did the 'eh' give it away?"

"No. Your common sense did."

His turn to laugh. "Hmm, how old are you?"

"Twenty-eight."

"Ah. Much too old for me."

Philippe calls out instructions from the other side of the dance floor but Dancy ignores him. "Wait a minute," I ask as the world blurs along, like I'm a spinning top in the arms of a toymaster. "Dancy isn't your real name, is it? Dance lessons, Dancy."

"It actually is. My parents were cruel people who gave a newborn a name that would get my arse beaten many times in school."

"British, is it?"

"How'd you guess? Do I look like the queen?"

Clap clap! Philippe moves toward us like he has wheels for toes. "Dancy? Again? If you're going to pick up women, please go for the ones David the Asshole lied to."

"That's me," I sigh, remembering.

Dancy drops his hand from my waist and makes a deep, solemn bow.

"And while you're great for business, you never, ever do any of *my* dance moves," Philippe chides.

"Because your choreography is a crime."

Philippe sniffs and looks the old man up and down. This is clearly an old conversation on an infinite jest loop. "Your suit is a crime."

"You know what's really a crime?" Dancy says as Will wanders over, closely followed by two chattering old women. I hear the words *granddaughter* and *crossfit* and *good cook*.

"What?" Philippe asks, playing along.

He points at Will and narrows his eyes. "That he," Dancy says with a flourish, finger now pointing skyward as if getting God Almighty's attention, "hasn't asked the beautiful Mallory out on a date."

I die.

I die right there.

Chapter Thirteen

My legs work unbelievably well for someone who is dead.

I flee. This day is too much.

Even *I* have a limit.

My purse is conveniently on a chair by the door, and in a gazelle-like feat of grace, I loop my arm through the handle and crash through the doors to the outside, hearing Dancy shout, "Was it something I said?" in the distance.

The parking lot is a blur. My electronic key won't work. I stare at it, dumb, with a head full of buzzing bees all trying to find their way out through my corneas, until I realize I've unlocked the trunk twenty times. I walk to the back, slam it shut, and successfully press the right button to open the driver's door.

"Mallory." Will's at my side as the lock clicks open, his hand on my shoulder, his scent unmistakable.

"Yes?" I can't look up. Looking into his eyes means he'll see my need. It's like the parking lot at the high school ten years ago. I can't relive that.

Especially not *now*.

"Don't go home. Not yet. Come with me."

"To the office? For that meeting? You want me to work *now*?"

"No, not there."

"I already ate dinner before the dance lesson, Will, and I'm feeling really embarrassed, truth be told. Being stood up on a date is bad enough. Being used as a conversion target to meet someone's sales metrics feels even dirtier." I'm about to add all the Dancy stuff when he interrupts me.

"You don't deserve to feel dirty." His voice drops. "Unless you want to."

My eyebrows shoot up and I can't stop myself from turning around and looking up at him. "What do you want, Will?" I ask, the words inadequate but better than waffling on the inside, over-interpreting and analyzing every word out of his mouth.

His warm, sensual, alluring mouth.

"Something sweet." Grasping my hand, he pulls me back to the sidewalk. In order to get my attention, that simple tug would be enough. From a utilitarian standpoint, he should let go of my hand now.

Now.

Definitely *now*.

He doesn't let go.

We're walking hand in hand down the sidewalk, in public, downtown, on our way to–

"Where are we going?" I ask, my hand starting to sweat, every bit of skin on fire.

He makes a left turn toward a little nook of shops, squeezing once.

"You'll see."

Lovers entwine their fingers. We're palm in palm, which means nothing, right? Like kids, like siblings. He's just holding my hand so he can guide me down the remarkably well-lit streets of this neighboring town, streets and sidewalks I know like the back of my hand.

A hand that Will Lotham has commandeered.

Stop it, Mal! I shout in my head, willing my inner fourteen-year-old to shut up. If I could give her a box of Oreos, that would do the trick.

We stop in front of a small hipster restaurant known for avocados and saffron and maple, sometimes in the same dish. It's the kind of place filled with exposed brick walls, painted ductwork, and an open kitchen where you can sit at a counter and watch your food being made.

Will leads me in.

Within a minute, we're seated at a table and I look at him, deeply confused.

"What are we doing here?"

A very chipper waitress comes over, hands us menus, and begins listing what sounds like every food banned by paleo diets around the world. I'm pretty sure half the internet diet forums view this place as Ground Zero in the PUFA Wars.

"And we have espresso-based drinks with any liquor you want. Can I get you a macchiato?" she asks me. "Decaf?"

"A triple. I'll take a triple regular macchiato made with heavy cream."

Her satisfied grin says she upsold me nicely. "And the regular for you?" she asks Will, who just nods.

"Bring us a sampler," he adds as she leaves. She flashes him a saucy grin that is either flirting or teasing him for being here on a date.

Which this isn't.

Which means she's flirting.

Which suddenly pisses me off.

"Sampler?" I ask.

"It's a small plate of every dessert on the menu."

Could he be any more perfect? What man orders *that*?

"Why dessert?" I snap at him, torn between being pissed and falling deeper in love.

"You told me you never make it to dessert on your dates. I wanted to change your luck."

Silence fills the space between us, heavy like air before a rainstorm, what happened back at Bailargo hovering like dark clouds.

"Here you go!" The server—whose name tag I refuse to read because in my mind that makes her important and gives her energy to flirt more with Will and I'm not handing out my energy like that, thank you very much—sets my triple macchiato next to me, and a caramel-colored soda with two slices of lime on the rim in front of Will. She returns quickly with a small platter of pastries and chocolate that looks so delicious. I need to find the chef and offer up an ovary or something.

She leaves.

I moan.

Chocolate ganache in little cups made of solid dark chocolate with burnt marshmallows on top, tiny sailboats made of graham cracker poking out of the center. Tiramisu bites. Miniature pistachio cannoli. Rock candy in jewel tones stacked across burnt-sugar canoes filled with some kind of extraordinary candy-cane-speckled ice cream.

"You act like you've never seen dessert before," he says, laughing.

"I haven't. Remember?" I swallow the words *Not on a date, at least,* before they escape.

I choose this moment to sip half my macchiato. Why I'm drinking three shots of coffee at nine p.m. is beyond me. Must be channeling Perky.

He picks up his Coke and squeezes the lime, then drinks a few swallows, closing his eyes. I sneak a long peek at him.

Dancy's words ring in my ears.

The press of Will's hand around mine burns my skin.

I put out the fire with the coldest thing in reach: peppermint ice cream.

He smiles and reaches for a chocolate ganache cup.

"This is amazing," I say through a mouthful of yum. "How have I not discovered this place before?" I evaluate the platter, picking up an individual dessert with my fork.

"New management. And it's for an older crowd. Lots of grey hairs here."

I look around. He's right. This is exactly the kind of place my parents would adore, though if you call my mom a grey hair, she'll beat you to death with her box of Madison Reed Amaretto Red.

"It's a great place to bring a date," he adds.

There it is.

I pause, fork with salted-caramel macadamia nut cheesecake bite in midair, and make eye contact. "Is that what this is? A date?"

Before Will can answer, someone behind him cries out, "Mallory! What a coincidence!"

It's my mother.

Small towns. What can I say?

"Are you two here on a date?" Mom adds, pushing the envelope, hope spilling across her face like nighttime moisturizer. I can smell the jojoba and lavender from here.

Dad takes a seat as if we invited him, reaching to shake Will's hand with two manly pumps and a grip competition. Roy Monahan is proving he can open more pickle jars than any other guy on the planet.

Mom stands there for a few awkward seconds until Will's

manners kick in and he jumps to his feet, pulling out the chair next to him.

I died once tonight already, back at Bailargo.

Too bad it didn't take.

Will and my dad raise their hands at the exact same time, exact same head twist, exact same movement to get the server's attention. It simultaneously thrills me and makes me a little sick to my stomach. Dad laughs and claps Will on the shoulder as he says to the woman, "A bottle of Rosso di Montalcino." She nods and this time skitters away without flirting.

Funny how that works.

Mom resumes her topic. "So, you two kids are having a–"

"Business meeting," I say firmly as the server returns with wine glasses and a green bottle, the label a blur in the dim light.

Will's mouth twitches with amusement. Dad pours the wine, waving the server off. Mom shakes her head no. Three glasses appear before Dad, Will, and me. I drink it.

I'd suck it out of the bottle directly if I thought I could get away with that.

"Coffee and wine at the same time?" Mom asks, eyebrows up.

"Life is a merry-go-round of moods, Mom."

I chug the coffee, then turn to my wine.

"We're just so glad you don't think poorly of Mallory after that whole incident at your house." Mom's eyes go shifty. "You know. The porn," she whispers. Her voice goes back to normal. "Because the last thing my Mallory would ever do is have sex before marriage!"

Wine sprays in an admirable arc. Will looks down at himself, my mouthful all over his front.

"Jesus!" I shout.

"You're close. You drew blood earlier. Now it's wine. Just

get some nails, thorns, and two thick beams and let's recreate that scene from the Bible," he quips as he blots himself with his napkin and stands. His eyes, amused as hell but full of a pained confusion that makes my heart squeeze, dart from Mom to Dad to me.

"This was nice, Mallory. Glad to get those work details hammered out. I've got a call in fifteen minutes with some investors from China, so if you'll all excuse me," Will says with a polished, smooth tone that has a finality to it. The lie comes out easily, a social nicety that gets a pass. It's a tone you take when you're in command.

Or when you're just *done*.

A nod to Mom and Dad each, and Will walks away. I see him stop at the counter and take out his credit card, gesturing in our direction. Then he's gone.

Taking my guts with him.

"That was abrupt," Mom says, taking in the half-empty dessert plates, my coffee, Will's half-finished wine glass, and his unfolded napkin like a little white mountain on the tabletop. Dad picks up the wine bottle and pours the rest of the bottle into his glass. He catches the server's eye and gestures for the check, but she shakes her head and smiles, pointing to the door that Will just went through.

"He has a lot of ground to cover. With the Chinese investors, I mean," I grind out, grabbing my purse and turning toward the door.

"We didn't end your date, did we?" Mom asks, alarmed, as I walk in front of her and Dad, assuming they're on my heels.

"It was just a business meeting."

"Oh."

We get outside and I realize I'm parked back near Bailargo.

"Sharon, you're driving," Dad declares, handing her the keys. They're a well-oiled machine, aren't they?

I feel like a rusted-out Yugo left at a nuclear accident site for the last twenty-eight years.

Hugs all around and Mom and Dad go in the opposite direction of me, their hands seeking each other reflexively, fingers threading. When two people have been together for decades, is that how it works? Their bodies just know what to do, the muscle memory so wired for connection?

I sigh, my throat tightening as I watch them fade into the darkness.

I want that.

The parking lot at Bailargo is down to two cars, mine and Philippe's. I know it's his because he comes out of the building, locks the front door with a keypad code, and turns around, hands on hips, staring at me.

"You!"

"Just Mallory!" I call back, a bit cheeky.

"You like the DANCE?" he asks, walking toward me, his car three spots away from mine.

"I do." A little embarrassed, but mostly just tired, I give him an apologetic look. "Sorry for disappearing like that. Long, weird night."

"You didn't disappear, Just Mallory. You were like a rocket." He makes a hand gesture for emphasis, one hand clapping against the other and skyrocketing to the moon.

"Thanks for the visual."

"Listen," he says. "David is a jerk. Call corporate tomorrow and complain about him, okay?"

"Sure."

"You and your man were good dancers."

"My what?"

"Your man. His eyes. His love for you shows in his eyes."

"He's not my man," I insist as Philippe unlocks his car, climbs in, lowers the window, and turns on the engine. Pulling forward, he's facing me in his driver's seat. I bend down to peer in the open window. As I exhale, I smell coffee and wine, sugar and unfulfilled expectations on my breath. I'm safe to drive home because I sprayed my wine all over Will.

I'm dangerous to drive home because I'll wallow in self-pity.

Philippe laughs at me. "He is absolutely your man."

"No, he's not." Stepping back, I take him in, the desolate lot, the glare of streetlights on faded asphalt. It's too bright, too dark, too empty, too full.

Too *everything*.

Eyebrows up, he points at me and simply says, "Not yet."

Chapter Fourteen

"It looks like my parents' house might be going under contract today," Will announces as I stand in the coffee room on Monday morning, making an Americano. Free coffee at work? Are you kidding?

I'm totally taking advantage. It's this or go to Perky's coffee shop, and I'm avoiding her right now.

I spent all morning trying to figure out what to say to him after my mom and dad and the Bailargo mess, but he just made is super easy.

"SQUEEEEE!!!" I scream.

He winces. "You need to warn people about that air raid drill that lives in your throat, Mallory."

"Sorry. It's just–that's AMAZING!" I grab him and hug him as I jump up and down. His laugh feels like his chest is jumping, too. As his belt buckle grazes the space beneath my navel I pause, remembering the last time we were so close.

Funny. His hands are resting in the exact positions for tango. The dance where you make love standing up, fully clothed. He keeps his hands there, the smile between us turning intense.

"Whatever you did, it was magic," he tells me.

"Not magic. Energy."

"Same thing. Call it whatever you want, it worked. And now you get your commission."

"How much did it sell for?"

"Two point three."

"Asking price?"

"Yes."

"Then I make..." I do the math. Good thing his hands are on me, because I nearly fall over.

"You're good at this."

Being in his arms? Yes. If there's a gold medal for enjoying being in Will Lotham's arms, get me on the Olympic team. Stat.

"Have you thought about staging homes for a living?"

"No, Will. I was going back to porn."

"Better benefits?"

"Free condoms and coconut oil. All the dog toys I can sterilize after a shoot. Can't get much better fringe benefits than that." My eyes cut to the right, and down. He's still holding my waist. We're breathing in each other's warm air. One step closer and–

He takes it.

"I can think of lots of benefits I can offer you, Mal. Stay."

His breath warms my nose. I look up, my hands moving along the fine, hard lines of his arms, over the business shirt he's wearing, the cotton weave like sandpaper and silk all at the same time. I close my eyes, his breath so close, I can taste his morning coffee, and then we lean into each other and–

"Anyone here?"

Is that my *mother*? AGAIN?

"Mallory?"

With my *dad*?

"Do they have some kind of radar for moments like this?" Will mumbles as he pulls away.

Moments like this? So I wasn't imagining Friday night was a date? That Will is interested in me? Because there's no imagining this.

And there's no imagining the horror of my mother's bangle bracelets jingling the death march of a kiss as she waves at us.

"We thought we'd stop by and see Mallory's office!" Mom chirps as Will shakes Dad's hand, then leans against his desk.

And cracks his knuckles.

"How's that China deal?" Dad asks Will. "The one you left dinner for on Friday?"

"Fine. Big real estate acquisition company buying up some of our West Coast properties." Will's voice is crisp and flat at the same time.

Dad lets out a conspirator's whistle. "Sounds like a solid business deal."

"Speaking of which," Will says, smiling at me with pride. "Your timing couldn't be more perfect."

"*What?*" I croak.

"Mallory just clinched another deal. Helped get my parents' house under contract at full price. Took her less than a week. That house sat on the market for five months. It took her extraordinary eye to make someone see how special it really was."

He's talking to my parents, but he's looking at me.

Will's phone rings. He grabs it. "Tony! I was just talking about the Maplecure house. What's that? Great!"

Dad beams at me. "Congratulations, Mallory! I was skeptical when you took this little job, but you turned it into a gem. Maybe Will can find a more permanent position for you?"

In bed, I think to myself.

Doesn't *your* mind go to silly Chinese-fortune-cookie jokes like that when you're under stress?

Or just, you know, want someone so much that every word out of everyone's mouth is a double entendre, even your own father's?

No? Just me?

Will moves away from us, his voice a string of business jargon that makes it clear he's just getting started.

"I, uh–we need to get back to–"

The kiss, I think.

"WORK!" I shout over my own mind, as if I can drown it out. *Pfft.*

It floats.

"You don't have to be so adamant about it, dear," Mom says, smoothing a spiral lock of hair off my face.

Dad leans in and asks, "How much you making?"

"One point two five percent."

His whistle is appreciative. Nice to hear it directed at my accomplishments for once.

"No worries about living in our basement with that kind of deal," he says, beaming. "Good for you, kid. Beats that porn gig you tried."

"Dad!"

"Roy!"

"Am I wrong?" He snorts, then looks at Mom. "Let's get outta here. Looks like they're busy."

No kidding.

They start toward the door and I walk along.

"So much for lunch," Mom sighs.

"You were going to invite me out for lunch?"

Mom's eyes flit back to Will.

"Mommmmm," I groan. "Dad, you too? Quit trying to make Will happen. It's not happening."

Especially when you keep interrupting us.

"We're just, you know..."

"Interfering meddlers?"

"Concerned parents."

Same thing.

"Got it," Dad says as he hugs me. "No lunch. No more dropping in on you two. You can just acquire cats and live alone with your Netflix and your bananas dipped in Nutella."

"Sounds heavenly."

Mom gives me a fast hug as Dad drags her away, muttering "One point two five, huh?" as they leave.

I return to my desk, heart racing, my skin ready to pack up and move to Sweden and practice hygge with cozy, oversized sweaters and big mugs of elderberry tea in lopsided stoneware. Can I just hide from the world right now?

Or at least, from my parents?

"They're really intrusive, aren't they?" Will asks from behind me, making me squeak with surprise.

"Yes."

"Downside of living at home."

"I don't live at home. I have my own apartment." *Want to see it?* I think to myself.

His eyes reflect that thought right back at me.

But his words don't.

"I mean living in our hometown."

I bristle. Here we go. "Nothing wrong with staying in a place I love."

"Do you? Really?"

The way he adds that *really* makes me turn and face him, taking a deep breath to prepare myself.

"Love this place? Of course. How can you not love a place

174

that has a town festival called the Dance and Dairy? I can't wait for Saturday! Hesserman's Dairy will be there with the ice cream VW bus!"

He looks at his phone, then slides it into his front pants pocket. "Are you going to the reunion?"

All this air is trapped in my lungs, ready to form into words that eviscerate him, and he asks me *that*?

"What?"

"The high school reunion. Class of 2009, Harmony Hills, the whole bit. Just got a reminder text about it. It's Saturday, in fact. You going?"

"I–I don't think so. I have to help with the Habitat for Humanity tent at the D&D."

"D&D? You play that?"

"What? No. Not Dungeons & Dragons. Dance and Dairy. You know — the summer festival?"

"That dinky little thing?"

"It's fun!" I protest. "And I wouldn't want to miss the fried-pickle ice cream sundae. This is my one chance for the whole year."

Surprise crosses his face, eyes narrowing as he steps closer to me, into resume-the-kiss territory.

"That must be some sundae."

"No kidding. The combo of their creamy ice cream–"

He interrupts, one eyebrow arched. "I don't think this is about the festival."

"You don't?" I huff. "You've obviously never experienced the culinary orgasm of a fried pickle drenched in caramel and dark chocolate fudge."

His pupils dilate when I say *orgasm*. As Will opens his mouth, I wonder if that kiss is still in play.

Or maybe I need to make the next move.

And then he says:

"You're afraid to be seen at the reunion. For people to question your choices."

"What choices?"

"Staying. It's weird, Mallory. You never left. Were you afraid?"

"Afraid of what?"

"Being a small fish in a big pond. Not being able to cut it in corporate life."

"You're making some pretty big assumptions about me based on knowing only one variable!"

"Sometimes the simplest explanation is the answer."

"It's not about fear. It's not like there's something wrong with me. Why does the fact that I make choices that don't conform to *yours* mean that I'm the deviant?"

Intensity level notched up by a few increments, the swiftly moving conversation has me *charged*.

Or maybe it's the almost kiss.

All I get is a steady gaze in response. Is he actually listening? Of all the reactions I'd expected from Will, this is the one I never anticipated.

"Explain."

"I don't have to explain any part of who I am to you, Will."

"No. You don't have to. But I want you to."

"Because you're going to find a way to tell me I'm wrong?"

"Because this is the most authentic conversation I've had with anyone since..." One corner of his mouth goes up in a wry smile that shows emotion. "Since that time our senior year."

My mind goes blank. I thought we were closing the gap for a kiss. Not dissecting my choices and certainly not... *this*. Will goes from shallow to infinite depth in seconds, an intellectual and emotional whiplash I find myself enjoying, but it's so strange.

Strange to find someone else who does it. That kind of pivoting comes naturally to me. I've had to tamp it down with family and friends.

But no tamping needed here.

"You had an authentic conversation with someone in twelfth grade, and that's your benchmark? And you've gone an entire decade since without authenticity?" I challenge him, the words out before I can stop them.

"I had that conversation with *you*, Mallory."

My mind buzzes as memory races to catch up to what he's saying. "Me... what?"

"You don't remember." He's perplexed.

More emotion than I have any right to evoke in him comes out in a long sigh, one weighed down by something inside him I can't even begin to understand.

"I don't," I confess. For the longest time, I stored every single interaction with Will Lotham in a hard drive in my head and heart, but time faded some of those memories slowly, like the tides rushing in and out, steady and strong, wearing away at every inch of me until all that was left were smooth fragments of shells.

"Last day of finals senior year," he starts. A sigh lingers in the air between us as my heart stops. "You had bangs back then." He looks at me and smiles. "They were auburn, like a shelf across the top of your eyebrows. And you were at your car."

My emotional foot hits the brake pedal in my memory bank as the conversation he's describing comes into full, blooming relief in my mind.

"When we went outside? To get textbooks out of our cars for the government final?" Plaintive and soft, he's practically pleading with me to remember, as if the tables are turned and we're in high school but *he* is trying to impress *me*.

I remember thinking it was a strange coincidence, that Will left his book in his car, too, and walked down the long vocational education wing with me, his voice so serious, his conversation almost existential.

"Yeah. When your friends decorated your car."

"The 'Most Likely to Become a Porn Star' glitter paint on my windshield was the most authentic conversation in your life?" I goggle.

A sound of mocking comes out of him, self-deprecating and sheepish. He looks at his palms. "That magenta glitter crap was all over my hands for days. My friends and parents gave me so much shit for it." He looks at me. "Not that, though," he says, suddenly terse. "The rest."

And then I know.

I know.

I know why he's bringing that moment from ten years ago into our *now*.

"You asked me about Brown."

His eyes light up. "Yes."

"And why I'd reject Harvard for *that*." I say the words verbatim. Teen Will's revulsion came out loud and clear back then: Why would you reject Harvard for *that?*

"I didn't understand."

"No kidding. I felt like your eyes were burning me. You were so disgusted."

"You thought that?"

"I *felt* that. Words are connected to emotional states for most of us, Will. What you said back then mattered."

Still does.

"Ooof. I'm sorry."

"And you considered that conversation to be the most authentic interaction you'd ever had?"

"You were the most authentic person I'd met."

"Me?"

"Don't you get it? You rejected Harvard. *Harvard*, Mallory. You said *no* to the top school in the country."

I know what he's really saying. He didn't get into Harvard. I did.

"Dartmouth wasn't exactly a bottom-tier school, Will."

"I've done fine. Dartmouth, Rhodes Scholar, the whole bit. I succeeded on the hamster wheel of academic success."

Here it comes.

"But you made your decisions based on what *you* wanted. Not based on what other people told you you should do."

Blink.

Blink.

Blink.

"That's right," I finally choke out. "I did."

"You did back then, you do now. No one does that, Mallory. Especially not eighteen-year-olds who are nothing more than chess pieces for adults to play in a game of status strategy."

My eyes drift to the door Mom and Dad just went through. "That's not who I am."

"I know. That's not who you were ten years ago, either."

"Do you make your decisions based on what other people expect?" I ask him, head tilting as though it will help me understand his answer.

Step. We're three feet apart as he moves closer. "Not anymore."

Bzzzz.

My phone goes crazy in my pocket. I can't ignore it. Breaking the spell between us, I step back and look. Four texts, the reminder about the reunion in one, the other three from Mom, Perky, Fiona.

The usual suspects.

"Go with me," he says, bringing the magic back. But it feels like there's a wall between us, one that shimmers with transparency but still separates us.

"Where?"

"To the reunion."

"*Me?*" It comes out as a sonic boom of surprise.

"All my friends are married or have dates. I need to save face." The words are joking. Tone is light. But those eyes, oh, those eyes are making offers I can't believe are true.

Are they?

"I'm the *last* person you bring to a ten-year reunion if you're trying to improve your reputation, buddy."

"Why would you say that?"

"Look at me."

"I am."

"Isn't it obvious?"

"It's obvious you don't see yourself the way I see you. I don't understand why you would say that. You're gorgeous. And smart. And funny. You're the whole package." He breathes, the sound making all the hair on my body tingle, moving like waves of grass on a windy day, drawn to him. "I was too stupid to see it ten years ago. I'm not quite as stupid now."

"You're pretty close."

"Is that a no?"

"No. But look," I say with a tiny, huffy laugh, "this isn't some John Hughes movie from the '80s where the popular guy plucks the shy, brainy girl from the crowd and kisses her over a birthday cake on a table and they live happily ever after."

"What's a John Hughes movie?"

"You–I–you've never seen *Sixteen Candles*?"

"No."

"*Pretty in Pink*?"

"Is that a Barbie princess movie? Because I used to hate it when my sister watched that kind of stuff." He frowns. "Besides, why would you watch movies from the 1980s? We weren't even born then."

"They're classics. My mom watched them with me." And, I can't admit to him, they were emotional sanctuaries where, for once, the shy, nobody girl *did* get the hot, popular guy.

Fantasy, right?

"I'll have to watch them someday."

"What did you watch when we were in high school?"

"*Saw* movies. *The Ring*. You know."

"Eww!"

"Don't judge it until you've seen them."

"I am totally judging *Saw* movies, sight unseen. Or not unseen. Karen the overly officious cop made me watch fifteen minutes of *Saw 3* when I was six and it warped me for life."

"Not very open minded of you."

"I embrace my intolerance for gore. I own my judgment on this one. Call me Miss Judgment."

"I misjudged *you*, all right."

Something in his voice makes my breath hitch.

"Say yes."

"What?"

"Say yes, Mallory. Be my date. Let's show those assholes that we're adults. We've matured."

"We have? Speak for yourself. I still can't watch horror movies without a blanket to throw over my head and I have no idea how to change the oil in my car."

"That's your measure of adulthood? If so, I've been an adult since I was eleven."

"I'm a late bloomer."

His eyes graze over my body. "You definitely bloomed well."

"What? What are you saying?"

"I'm saying you need a date. I need a date. We both have needs. Let's meet each other's needs."

There is a point in conversations with people you could sleep with where you find yourself in a demilitarized zone of language. This is one of them. Is Will flirting? Joking? Being ingenuous? Mocking me? I can't read his words right now. The most reasonable interpretation is the one I can't bring myself to believe possible:

He's sexually attracted to me and is making his intentions known.

Occam's razor says this is the most likely, and best, interpretation.

Murphy's law trumps Occam's razor, though.

Anything that can go wrong–will.

Will.

If I'm wrong, I lose Will. Lose the friendship, lose my not-quite-a-job, lose the tenuous sense that maybe all those hopes and dreams and fantasies from years ago weren't in vain.

So I can't.

I can't be bold.

I can't be mature and direct.

I can't hand him my heart with my palm outstretched and the dependable organ beating for him.

I wish I could.

But if I could do that, I wouldn't be me.

I decide to be me.

"If I go to the reunion with you," I say, holding one finger up in protest as his face breaks into a delicious grin of victory, "you have to promise me one thing."

"I promise."

"I haven't even asked yet! Why would you agree to terms you don't know?"

"Because I trust you."

"Because you don't think I'm hardass enough to screw you over."

"With you, Mallory, it's the same thing."

"And with you, Will, it's another sign that you underestimate me."

"Then surprise me."

"By screwing you over?"

"By making me promise something challenging. You just got a blanket promise from me. Use it to your advantage."

"If you just handed me a blanket promise, then I don't want to waste it. I'll hold onto it for future use."

"Wait a minute. I thought this was a promise involving the reunion!"

"I never said that. Not explicitly."

He pauses, thinking it through. "You're right. You didn't."

"I am the queen of delayed gratification, Will. I am holding onto this promise of yours for a good, long time."

"You play a long game?"

Fourteen years run through my mind in a long, long thread. I smile. He smiles back, a little bemused, as I inform him:

"You have no idea."

Chapter Fifteen

Have you ever walked into a mixer at a high school reunion?

It looks like every standard corporate networking event, but with a mild odor of desperation, the occasional whiff of panic, and a general sense of poor life choices catching up to people who realized too late that actions have consequences.

Which isn't really all that different from corporate networking, now that I think about it.

"Mallory Monahan! I heard you're a porn star. Is it true? Because that is so great. I think being fat positive is wonderfully liberating!" says Alisha Buonacelli, complete with hair flip and all.

Nice extensions, I think but don't say, because what's the point? Match her pettiness with my own? Seems like a losing proposition. Alisha was a cheerleader (of course) and the girlfriend of Michael Osgood, one of the football players who threatened me when I wouldn't give them my notes in ninth grade.

Alisha and I are Facebook friends now. She sells makeup and special probiotics for a living.

Facebook friends who become MLM sellers are like

vegans: you never, ever have to ask them about it because you damn well *know*.

Will's body tenses with her words. So it's not just me. He squeezes my shoulder with a possessiveness that makes me want to cry tears of joy. "Actually, she works for me. Head designer," he says, amusement tinging his words, his low rumble making me relax. He finds her stupid, too.

Good.

"You design heads? For what?" She does a double take at my date. "Wait–is that you? WILL!" she squeals, flinging herself at him like he's a river and she's on a bridge, attached to a bungee cord harness. Kissing his cheek with an audible smack designed to make people look, she leaves a bright red mark on him.

Like she's claiming territory.

He moves away from her and wraps his arm around my waist. I find the ever-present pack of tissues in my purse and hand him one. It takes everything in me not to give her a wolf smile.

"Hi, Allison," he says, wiping his face.

Her eyes widen. At least, as much as they can. Are we really doing Botox at twenty-eight now?

"It's Alisha."

"Oh. Right." Carefully cultivated social skills I do not possess fill the space between the three of us, Will obviously a master at whatever strange game we're all playing.

Perfect eyes with long eyelashes too beautiful to be natural bounce between us, her gaze resting on Will's hand on my hip. "You two?" If her eyebrows could lift, they would.

He grins. It's so natural. A shrug and a tighter squeeze are his entire answer.

Alisha's fingers twitch, moving for her purse, like she

needs to text. As if texting about the unreal experience of seeing Will with me is her oxygen.

"I can't believe it!"

Neither can I.

"Wow! After that whole porn thing? Really, Will?" Punctuating her words, she points to her phone screen, which has the picture of me, Beastman and Will the Dom on it.

No, really, that's the caption: *Beastman and Unnamed Dom Spit Roasting*.

Reproach fills her voice, but I know it has nothing to do with the porn-set misunderstanding. Will's not breaking any social codes there.

It's me.

I'm the violation.

Will kisses my temple and looks at her with a smile.

"Who would have ever guessed Little Miss Perfect and Will would end up together?" she says, deflating me on the spot.

There's that name again. *Little Miss Perfect*. The past comes roaring back.

His hold on me tightens. One of my eyebrows is practically on Mars as I tip my head up for an explanation.

Which is interrupted.

"MALLORY AND WILL! OMIGOD!" screams Perky, running across the country club's event space in high heels like toothpicks, dressed in a sleek red cocktail dress that makes her look even perkier than she really is while pulling off an intoxicating sophistication that makes my classic little black dress seem like a nun's habit.

"Persephone," I gasp, knowing she'll appreciate the use of her full name.

Exuding excitement, she gives me a hug, jumping up and down as she whispers, "Screw them all, Mallory. You're here with Will Lotham and they don't know what to do with that fact inside their little minds made of tiny boxes."

"You are the best," I murmur into her coconut-scented, overly styled hair. There's so much product in there I'm pretty sure it doubles as a hamster habitrail.

"Can I get you a drink?" Will asks me, then looks at Perky with an expectation that she'll cough up an answer, too.

"Cocktails?" Perky asks, impressed.

He shrugs. "Whatever they have at the bar."

"I'll have a Little Miss Perfect, Will," I say dryly. "But refresh my memory: what, exactly, is in one of those?"

"Remorse, vodka, and a lot of forgiveness begging?" he replies.

"You forgot the heaping dose of bitters and two olives on a stick big enough to beat egos to death."

Leaning in, he whispers, "It was a stupid name one of the guys made up for you. I'm sorry. I should have apologized a long time ago. I thought we were all long past that."

I look at Alisha. "We are. She isn't."

"Then let's ignore her and let me get you a drink." A firm touch from him, his hand territorial in a way I like very much, punctuates his words.

"Surprise me!" I say, impulse driving me to loosen up, to be spontaneous. I'm here as Will's date, so what other people think doesn't matter. I get to be me.

Maybe this *is* me.

One side of his mouth goes up, the grin appreciative. Squeezing my arm gently, he fades into the crowd, stopped instantly by a guy who looks like a much more muscular version of Vin Diesel, only twenty years younger and blended with the top two Bollywood actors.

Sameer.

The two do a guy hug. I groan.

Perky leans in and whispers, "Sameer bulked up nice and big. Look at those biceps." She licks her lips. "The whole package is mighty fine."

"The whole package is tainted by memories of what an asshole he was."

"That's not enough to taint," she argues back.

"Asshole behavior is like mold on bread."

"What?"

"You have to throw the whole loaf out once you see even a single spot."

"Why not just cut off the mold spot? That's what my grandma does."

"Because spores don't work like that, Perk. They bore into the–"

"You are not seriously giving a lecture on fungi at our high school reunion, are you, Mallory Monahan?"

"What? No. I was just–"

Over Perky's shoulder, I see Fiona float in, wearing a gauzy dress that a woodland sprite probably hand spun with silk from her wings. She's every shade of lilac and cream and peach. Hair, too. Big glasses, like Elton John started a crystal company, adorn her face. Most people don't recognize her.

Only the ones who stayed, like me.

Fiona spots us and points to the bar. She gets lost in a crowd, which isn't easy when you're basically a cloud from *Avatar* in human form.

Perky snorts. "You and your biology lectures. Because you pulled that shit on prom night and it was stupid then, too, only that one was about spirochetes and syphilis."

"Speaking of people who haven't changed since high school," I sniff.

"People change, Mal. You're not going to last an hour at this shindig if you can't see that."

"Shindig?" I look her over. "Where did my BFF Perky go? Who are you in your sleek red dress, ogling Sameer Ramini?"

"I am Persephone Tsongas." She fluffs her hair, which really doesn't work given the sheer amount of product in it. Her fingers brush against the strands like she's testing out a bed of nails. "And Sameer Ramini would be damn lucky to get between my legs," she says dramatically, like a 1940s glamour actress.

"Is that an invitation or a dare?" says a man from behind me. His voice is smooth and suave, but it comes across as unctuous and cringe-y, too.

Fiona appears, and nudges me as he finishes.

"Gross," she murmurs into her drink.

Perky gives Sameer a very obvious once over. "You've changed in ten years."

"Same." His mouth quirks up on one side and he holds his arms slightly away from his body, as if to show them off. "You look like you need a drink, Perky."

"You look like you need a date, Sameer."

"Got one already."

"Oh?"

He thumbs behind him. "My wife." Is that Amy Whitman he's pointing to? Backstage drama person who loved poetry slams? Whitman Construction, pretty much the richest girl in town? Okay, I'm remembering now. I heard they got married a few years ago. They live in Atlanta, I think.

"Oh!" Perky titters at him, eyeing his ring finger the way she studies her phone when she's recovering her password to a new dating site. "I didn't see a wedding ring. My bad."

He holds up a naked left hand. "Not wearing one." The way he waggles his eyebrows makes it clear he takes his wedding vows about as seriously as he took the football team honor code when he tried to force me to help him cheat.

Once a cheater, always a cheater.

I grab Perky's arm and drag her away, Fiona following in our wake. Will is in the middle of the room, looking for us. The man has magic hands.

No, really. Who balances three cosmos and a beer like that without spilling a drop?

He's a wizard.

He's a wizard because he magically knew my favorite drink, too.

"Here," he says, handing the drinks around to all the intended recipients. Fiona chugs her existing drink, taking the new one with gratitude and placing her empty on a table corner.

Perk, Fiona, and I suck our drinks down like they're medication.

Will grins at me before taking a swig of beer. I watch him out of the corner of my eye, noticing how many people are noticing him, the impending crush of older versions of all the archetypes from my teen years making my heart go into palpitation mode.

Or maybe that's because Will's hand settles on the small of my back as we stand there, drinking and scanning the crowd. It finds its place, the palm sturdy, fingers resting like they're positioned on piano keys. He's playing music on my spine, ready to compose, his touch a melody.

The move is possessive. Instinct makes me lean closer, just a few centimeters, my body responding before I can make a conscious choice.

His grip shifts. He smiles as Chris Fletcher comes over, big and boisterous, arms out for a bro hug.

But Will doesn't move that hand until he has no choice.

"DICKHEAD!" Fletch bellows, grabbing Will like he's a baby goat, lifting him a good two feet in the air.

"Some people haven't changed one bit," Fiona says, mouth like a tightened purse string before she opens it to down the rest of her drink.

Fletch and Fiona have a past.

"Perky says you'll never have fun with that attitude," I snark at both of them.

Fiona turns to Perky and says, "Fuck you."

"Nice mouth for a preschool teacher!" Fletch says with mock horror. "You shape young minds!"

"You want her to drop kick you again? Because she totally could," Perky goads as Fiona takes big mouthfuls of her drink.

"Try me, baby. Try me," he calls out, face red with a combination of alcohol, mild embarrassment, and *joy*.

I never had a problem with Fletch in particular, other than the fact that he was one of the crowd of guys who felt entitled to tease anyone with an IQ even one point above average.

That, and pushing Fiona to drop kick him in seventh grade.

"Let's not stain our tenth reunion with violent rehashings of our pasts," I strongly suggest.

"No kidding," Fletch mutters, eyeing me with the fresh gaze of a man shark who has discovered a bleeding seal pup. "How about we talk about your porn career instead?"

Will makes a growling sound in the back of his throat that forces Fletch look at him and instantly, nonverbally, back off. His body leans away from me, a primally obvious sequence of small muscle shifts I feel rather than see.

"Kick him, Feisty," Perky growls in her ear. "Kick him hard."

"Feisty!" Fletch shouts, tipping his head to the sky, hands on hips like a superhero movie villain without the costume. "Haven't heard that in years. You missed your calling. You'd make a great roller derby player."

JULIA KENT

"You know I'm a preschool teacher. Your nephew is in my class."

"He's not that far off. Preschool teacher, roller derby," Perky says under her breath. "Some of those hellions Fiona's in charge of are brutal little fu–"

"Preschool teacher, huh? Good for you. You'll be paying off those student loans forever," says Alisha, who appears double-fisted, two drinks with pineapple in them. She sips one and gives Fiona a nasty look. "I always thought you'd go into something more violent."

"Like being your Brazilian waxing technician?" Fi says, blinking sweetly.

"What?" Alisha doesn't get it. Fletch rolls his eyes. A pang of something close to guilt hits me. She *really* doesn't get it.

This is when I hate myself the most. When I overthink. My conscience is too large, grossly over-inflated like some people's egos. But then my brain kicks in and analyzes and I short circuit, turning to alcohol, food, and Dance and Dairy festivals for comfort.

I look at the clock on the wall. Too late for the festival. Damn.

Will finishes his beer in one long series of gulps as Fletch asks, "Heard you're using your parents' home for porn production. That pay well? My grandparents have a property up in Rowley and–"

The playful punch Will delivers to his meaty shoulder makes me settle down. They're kidding. They weren't before, when Will made him stand down, but they are now. The familiarity between them says they've hung out recently. They're friends who reconnected.

My stomach drops.

Is this just a replay of high school? Five-year reunions are

192

nothing but repeats. But *ten*? Ten years is long enough to grow and change.

Right?

Fletch's eyes narrow as he looks at me. "You're the valedictorian. Mallory."

"And a porn star," Alisha gushes, eyes taking me in from toe to head, her gaze entitled, like she has a right to document my failings so publicly. "Was it for the chubby chaser section of some website?"

Even Fletch has the decency to give her a *WTF?* look.

Will's arm snakes around my waist again. Fletch notices, one eyebrow arching as he looks at Will for a message. My date gives no quarter. His hand on my hip silently communicates what Will is saying.

Loud and clear.

I'm waiting for him to defend me. To say something to neutralize the sting of Alisha's words. I didn't earlier, when she was a gadfly, buzzing her nastiness with me, but now there's an audience. My "date" is here, listening to her pettiness, her need to shame someone she hasn't seen in ten years.

This cannot go unchallenged.

That's how this works, right? The nasty insult has to be countered. If one of us doesn't shut her down, she wins. Verbal judo works this way. The hierarchy of high school social groups relies on the mortar of put-downs, squeezed in between the bricks that make up the wall that keeps some people out.

And the select few in.

Without saying another word, Will uses his fingers and arm to turn me away, leaving Alisha's chubby comment hanging there, uncontested. Tears threaten the back of my throat, stupid and childish.

Will leans in and says, "She can't help herself, can she?

Some people haven't changed a bit since high school. She's not worth another second of attention."

"Hmmm?" Worlds are ending inside my throat and heart and behind my wet eyes.

"Attention. That's what she's seeking. That's what that ludicrous put-down was about. The second she gets attention, she's being fed. Good, bad—doesn't matter. Her goal is to make us look at and focus on her. Not going to do it. Not when I have better objects of my attention."

I glance at her, face tipped up, eyebrows knitted as it dawns on her Will is giving me his full attention in every way, shape and form. Publicly.

He squeezes my hip, but—that's not quite my hip.

Did Will just cop a feel?

And did I just move... closer to him?

How can my body seek his touch at the same time my psyche thinks he's rejecting me somehow by not following the rules of the game at which he was a master?

I let out a small laugh through my nose. It hits me.

Because my body is twenty-eight, but my mind is still a teenager.

None of those rules is real. Will just said as much. Alisha is stuck in a reality from a decade ago.

I don't want to be in that club anymore.

"Hey," he says, interrupting my thoughts. I welcome the intrusion. "What's wrong?"

"Nothing."

"Did her comment bother you?" He moves back a foot and looks at me appreciatively. "Because it shouldn't."

"I—"

"It really, *really* shouldn't." Warm eyes meet mine as I look up, caught in his gaze, too many discordant thoughts trying to occupy the same space as the whirling dervish of emotion inside me.

"WILL!" a man's baritone calls out from behind us. Will groans.

"It's going to be like this all night, isn't it?" I whisper as I lean in, the scent of his aftershave and soap filling me, the press of his cotton shirt on my bare palm a kind of foreplay that gets me wet so fast, I blush.

He pauses. Blood pounds through me, my cheeks aflame as each breath closes the distance between high school and now, the way his fingertips brush the soft skin of my wrist an invitation that extends far beyond being his platonic date for a high school reunion.

"It doesn't have to be, Mallory. We can decide how tonight goes. Just us," he murmurs, hot breath tickling the outer shell of my ear, the fine fibers of his shirt turning my skin to a tingly pleasureland as I run my hand up his arm.

Only to be brutally shoved out of the way as a meat wall grabs Will and hugs him.

"LOWMAN!" Michael Osgood screams, looking as much like a pale version of The Hulk as anyone can. Many of the bulging muscles that made him a great nose tackle seem to have migrated to a spot just above his belt buckle. His hair, thinning already by senior year, is largely gone, shaved close to his scalp. He's wearing a navy polo shirt, khaki dockers, and brown leather shoes.

"Ozzy," Will chokes out, giving me a look that either says *Hey, my friends love me* or *Call an ambulance because he just squeezed my spleen until it burst.*

I seriously can't tell which.

Ozzy sets Will down and turns his back to me, Will stretching his neck to peer around the mountain of a man in order to re-establish eye contact with me. Normally, I'd leave, but I'm standing my ground, instantly furious.

Because Michael Osgood is the one who threatened me.

Over *homework*.

Back at the office, when Will asked for the name, I don't know why I clammed up and didn't give it. Now that we're here, and Osgood is just, you know, a *guy* and not a threat, I feel silly. Laughter bubbles up inside me as I stare at his back, thick shoulders moving as he gestures animatedly at Will.

"I run the insurance agency with Dad now, but you wouldn't know that, would you, Lowman? You split the second we graduated." Two towns over, the Osgoods run a well-known insurance office, a franchise of a national company. Osgood knew from day one that's who he would be and where he would work. He doesn't live in Anderhill, or I'd run into him more often.

Thank God he doesn't live in town.

"Well, I'm back now," Will says, giving me looks that say, *Come over here.* His head tilts, a nudge to join them.

"Heard you're managing your parents' property company. Good for you. How's your coverage?"

"Coverage?"

"Business liability. Renter's insurance. Who do you send tenants to?"

Will makes a scoffing sound. Our eyes meet. He smiles at me, the grin fading fast as he turns back and says, "Ozzy, you're not seriously pumping me for business at our high school reunion, are you?"

"No better time, man. We're salespeople. We're always on. Every person in this room is just a dollar sign to me."

"Not me, man. Not me. That's not how I run my business."

"Then good luck ever being successful. We have to be sharks."

"You think that's true, Mallory?" Will asks me as I step closer.

Ozzy happens to move, blocking me from Will. It's clearly unintentional, but it makes me freeze.

I'm a wall, a curtain, a piece of furniture. I'm nothing to Osgood as he talks to Will, the disregard for my existence so evident that I shoot past anger to astonishment.

"Who?" he asks, face blank.

"Mallory Monahan. You remember," Will says, turning politely to me.

"No."

"Valedictorian? In our American Government class senior year?"

Head shake. "Nope." One eyebrow goes up. "Why are you here with *her*?" he asks in an undertone, barely turning away to cover his words. It's clear he feels entitled to say them in front of me. "Look at Alisha. She's hot as hell, and I know she's interested in you, Lowman, because she–"

I walk away.

One step at a time, I just do. Years ago, when Osgood threatened me, I was a trapped rabbit, hunkered down in my warren, waiting for the threat to pass. Like Alisha, Osgood thinks he can say whatever he wants about me because I am unimportant. He has a mental structure that lays out the order of the universe for him, and in that strictly layered planogram, I am nowhere near the top.

He only acknowledges the people at the top.

His top.

"Mallory!" Will calls out as I pick up my pace, feeling the wind outside coming in from an open door. Blood pounds in my ears, the breeze pushing my carefully coiffed hair off my brow. The high heels suddenly feel sturdy, authoritative, the stretch of my stride giving me more boldness than I would have thought possible. I am walking away from high school, from a past riddled with the misconception that I have to let people treat me like Osgood, Alisha, Ramini.

Like Will.

"WIIILLLLL!" squeals a gaggle of women I've just passed, their glittering sequined dresses bouncing light off the dance floor disco balls, my skin cooling as I work my way out from the heat of social clustering.

I'm free.

"MALLORY!" he shouts once more, and then I cut to the left, running on the balls of my feet, my stride boosted by the one force I didn't think could propel me forward, but one with more kinetic energy than I ever imagined.

A broken heart.

Chapter Sixteen

Where are you? Fiona texts me as I sit on the toilet in the women's room at the country club.

In the bathroom, I text back.

Did I hear Will shouting for you? she asks.

I guess. Pretty sure he was eaten by a sharknado of cheerleaders, I reply.

Meow, she texts. *Mallory's getting catty.*

No, I think to myself as I sniffle. *I'm just tired of hoping to be treated differently.*

And then I hear a man's voice call out: "Mallory?" in the hallway.

The *clack clack clack* of jogging footsteps halts, followed by a pause, then the door opens. Heavy breathing echoes in the tiled room, the bathroom nothing more than a temporary sanctuary, stall after stall in a row, the doors too short to provide a real hiding place.

And no way will I lower my dignity further by standing on a toilet seat to hide my location. Who *does* that?

"Mal?"

I hold my breath.

"I can see your shoes. I know you're in there." Through the wide space between the door and the frame I see Will lean his hip against the line of sinks, the counter a gorgeous piece of granite with a faux-broken edge, designed to look raw and natural.

"Do you always lurk in women's bathrooms and stare under the doors?"

"Only when my date's been chased off by an ogre and I should have stepped in sooner to tell him to go fuck himself."

"Did you?"

"Did I what?"

"Tell him that?"

"Yes."

I sniffle again.

"Oh," he says, voice low with meaning. "Are you crying? Damn it."

"Yes, I'm crying. I ate a piece of shrimp and I'm allergic to shellfish, so I came in here to stick an EpiPen in my thigh before anaphylaxis sets in and now I'm crying as I recover."

"I've watched you eat shrimp in your lunch at work, Mal. Bad pretend excuse."

"Well, it matches my bad pretend date."

"Pretend?"

I stand, unlock the stall door, and march out, finger in his face. "We are not having this conversation. You don't get to play Mr. Nice Guy in private and treat me like a cardboard cutout of a human being in public."

"What?"

"You heard me, Will. I'm not a teenager anymore." Pivoting on the slippery piece of new shoe leather under my toes, I spin around to get the hell away from him.

But I can't.

Because he grabs me. Not hard enough to hurt. Using just

enough pressure to keep me in the bathroom, he stares at me with an intensity that shuts me up. Reflected over and over again in opposite mirrors that make us infinite, I can see our misplaced couplehood in stark relief, my face red from crying and anger, his burning with an emotion I must be misreading.

"No, Mal. You're not a teenager. Neither am I. Nothing about asking you to this reunion was pretend."

"Why did you really ask me? Wait." I shake my head hard, just as a group of women burst into the room, one of them shrieking at the sight of a man in the bathroom.

Not just any man.

"WILL!" Alisha gasps. Her eyes don't even bother to cut over to me to take in my existence. "What are you doing in the women's room?" Whipping around, she screams to someone behind her, "OMIGOD, Gemma, I found Will!"

Gemma. Will's girlfriend for part of senior year.

Wrenching my wrist out of his hand, I walk away, head held high, leaving Will Lotham to deal with all the questions from his groupies as they descend on him like fish in a tank as the flakes are being sprinkled for meal time.

Blurred vision from crying makes it really hard to see where I'm going. This country club isn't familiar to me. I need to find the exit, get to my car, drive home, and sit in stunned, ringing silence for a few eternities, right now.

That's the closest I can come to equanimity.

I make a right turn at the end of the hall, the tiled floor changing to carpet. Blaring music and blinking lights make it clear I'm facing the event space, so I turn around.

"Mallory?"

A soft, inquiring voice, feminine and light, stops me dead in my tracks. I'm looking into kind brown eyes, framed by stylish, oversized black eyeglass frames. Long brown hair with curls at the ends, a soft grey dress cut in a tight, flattering peplum style.

"I'm sorry," I say genuinely, smiling with an awkwardness driven both from what's just happened with Will and from having no idea who she is. "Have we met?"

"It's me. Raye."

"Raye?" My eyebrows try to meet as I squint at her, then I do a double take. "Raye? Rayelyn Boyle?"

The eyes widen as she grins. "You do remember!"

"Of course I remember, but *wow*–you look nothing like you did in high school!"

"Is that good or bad?" Her grin is infectious, but her eyes are wary.

"Good! All good! Look at you!" My need to reassure her is total projection. I know this as the words come out. I'm a mess, straddling the past and the present like I'm working on an Olympic-level split for the balance beam, and for a moment, I realize some part of me assumed everyone else is living my reality, too.

Rayelyn–*Raye*–gives me a self-assured look that says she's way more comfortable in her skin than I am in mine.

A woman in golden silk pants, loose at the hips and knees but tight at the ankles, joins us, her flowing white silk shirt embroidered around the neckline with small crystals. Raye's arm goes around her waist in a loving manner, the woman's thick, dark hair in a heavy braid behind her back, long eyelashes fringing minky eyes.

"Mallory, this is Sanni, my wife. Sanni, this is Mallory, my friend from the newspaper in high school. Remember?"

Sanni extends her hand to me, the fingers covered in silver jewelry. Polite smiles are exchanged and they look at me, waiting. There is no pretense. No judgment. No one upmanship.

Just the social nicety of being reacquainted in that slightly awkward way that is normal.

Normal.

"I'm sorry I keep staring, Rayelyn–*Raye*–it's just that you've changed so much. Where do you live now? What do you do for a living?" I'm babbling nervously, authentically happy to run into her. Of all the friends I had in high school, she's the one I've lost touch with but always wondered about.

The kind of person I imagine when I envision reunions.

"We live in the Bay Area. I'm the communications director for an online genetic-testing company, and Sanni is product line manager for a tech company that helps NGOs with refrigeration for public health initiatives."

"Wow." It occurs to me, as the seconds roll by, that they're going to ask me what I do for a living. I knew that would happen, coming to a high school reunion, but so far, this will be a first. I've run into Alisha, Ramini, Osgood, Fletch, and been looked over by a few in Alisha's crowd, and yet–this will be the first time anyone's–

"What about you, Mallory? What do you do for a living? Raye's talked about you ever since the reunion invitation came," Sanni says warmly.

"I remember you chose Brown over Harvard and that was so inspiring," Raye adds with a touch of awe.

–asked about me.

Me.

We come to these celebrations of anniversaries–and yes, a high school graduation certainly falls under that umbrella–not simply to mark the passage of time. *Look at me*, we say when we attend. *Acknowledge me*, we demand when we accept the invitation.

Validate me, our presence insists.

For some people, that need to be seen is physical. External.

For them, it's the crowd who looks, acknowledges, and validates.

For others, it's their own inner teenager who peers with wide, naïve, idealistic eyes, rough edges and bleeding heart frozen in time, needing to see the change in the adult self so she can catch up.

So far, every person I've seen tonight has fixated on Will, other than Fiona and Perky, and they don't count because having them pay attention to me is like asking your mother if you look pretty when you're thirteen. They're constitutionally required to.

Rayelyn is the first person tonight to acknowledge me as important.

"I–I'm in design, actually. Spaces. Homes and occasionally offices. I work for Will Lotham's company now."

Rayelyn's expression is extraordinary. "*The* Will Lotham?" The past comes roaring back into her face, my famous crush indelible in her memories of who I am.

I can't help but laugh. "Yes." Then I sniffle.

Immediate concern radiates from her. "Is something wrong?" Sanni mirrors the compassion, which only makes controlling my emotions that much harder. Rayelyn was my ever-constant friend in all extracurriculars. We were the academic geeks who really enjoyed running a newspaper, sacrificing Saturdays for speech and debate tournaments, writing essays and studying content questions for Academic Challenge. We advocated for pep rallies to acknowledge academic competitions, and aside from Fiona and Perky, I spent more time with Rayelyn than anyone else in high school.

So why is it that until now, I hadn't really thought of her?

A twisting inside me, my skin and blood catching on pieces of memory, makes my nerves jangle, a preternatural knowing pouring into me. As Raye and Sanni watch me expectantly, I blurt out, "Why didn't we stay in touch, Rayelyn? I mean, Raye."

She fights emotion on a face that is clearly not accustomed to doing so. I'm asking a question that pulls her back ten, fourteen years and it's obvious that the Raye—not Rayelyn—before me is all adult when she's not here in her hometown, being yanked back into a time when she couldn't be who she is.

"I don't know. I wondered, too, Mal. You left for Brown and I went to Marlboro and then UC Berkeley. I met Sanni there at the first graduate student union meeting." She squeezes her wife's shoulder. "When I heard about this reunion, I didn't want to come."

"Same here," I tell her, meaning every word. "But I'm local."

Sanni laughs. "We're about as non-local as you can get and still be in the same country."

"My sister lives in the Bay Area. She works for a financial start-up."

"Hasty?" Rayelyn asks, her voice dropping. Years of hearing me complain about my older, domineering sister haven't faded, I see.

Another shaky laugh comes out of me, gaining strength as the conversation continues. "Yes, that Hasty."

"You have a sister named Hasty?" Sanni asks, curious.

"Short for Hastings."

"Ah."

"Do you ever come out to see her?" Rayelyn asks. "If you do, please reach out. I'd love to reconnect. In fact, we're here for a few extra days." She looks around, head turning toward the booming music in the event space. "This is fine, but a quiet coffee shop with good pastries would be even better."

Warmth floods me. "In jeans and t-shirts."

Rayelyn looks down at our high heels. "Yes! And flip-flops!" Reaching into her purse, she says, "Let's exchange numbers right here. I'll call your phone. What's your number?"

I recite it, she taps. My phone rings. I ignore it. The modern version of exchanging business cards.

Then she reaches out for a hug, laughing. Her embrace feels like the past coming into my present and hugging me. "This reunion is pushing all my insecurity buttons," she confesses.

"Everyone told me I had to come," I murmur in her ear.

"Everyone?"

"Persephone, Fiona, and Will."

Astonishment floods her face. "They're all local?"

"Will just moved back."

"Are you two together?" A restrained glee infuses her words, as if she wants to be happy for me if the answer is yes, but isn't sure if asking the question at all is acceptable.

"No," I answer truthfully just as a deep, slightly out-of-breath male voice says from behind me:

"Yes."

One corner of Sanni's mouth goes up in an intrigued smile while Raye blushes hard, looking over my shoulder as I turn to find–surprise!–Will standing there, eyes soulful, hands on his hips, the *yes* hanging in the air like a golden snitch I just have to reach up and pluck.

"Hi, Rayelyn," he says to her.

"Will," she smiles, not correcting him with her preferred name, eyes bouncing from me to him over and over as if she's decoding a secret message that has an answer she thinks she knows.

I, on the other hand, have no idea what is going on.

"Sorry to interrupt, but Mallory and I have some very important unfinished business," he says to Raye and Sanni, pulling me away with gentle firmness that is as impossible to resist as it is paradoxical.

"May I have this dance?" He starts to lead us toward the dance floor.

"What? But I want to talk to Raye and–"

"Dance. Dance with me, Mallory."

"Why would I dance with you?"

"Because you're my date and because I took dance lessons for my sister's wedding and don't want them to go to waste."

"So now I'm a pity dance?"

"You're not a pity *anything*." Carrying beyond the two of us, his voice has an insistent finality to it. As if he knows exactly what's happening and is trying to help, the DJ is playing Ed Sheeran's "Perfect." Will's right hand goes to the small of my back and his left hand takes my right one in his, our bodies making the awkward transition from two people with differing agendas to one couple moving in concert.

Except I'm not melting into him the way a true dance partner would.

"I'm so sorry," he murmurs as we turn in a circle, the DJ's lights blurring and forming a strangely distant rainbow between patches of darkness.

"What? No. I'm fine."

"What Osgood said is *not* fine. What Alisha said is *not* fine. Nothing about this night is *fine*." The words skim over my heart, the touch light and protective.

"No. It's not. But *I* am fine."

His hold on me tightens. That hand flat against my lower back is awfully possessive as he pulls me closer. The thin fabric of my skirt is loose against my thighs, and boy, can I feel the coiled power in his legs.

I'm feeling something else between us, too, and it's turning me on.

I can't. *I can't*. Will was sweet to invite me to this reunion, but what just happened is proof that nothing really changes. I mean, *I've* changed. I've grown. I've analyzed and reflected, but while I'm an adult now, I'm really not all that different than I was ten years ago.

If anything has changed, it's my attitude.

I don't care.

Clarity has a funny way of showing up when you need it most.

Seeing Rayelyn didn't cause a sudden, life-altering realization, but it confirmed what I already know: *I* get to decide who I am. Not this crowd. Not my parents. Not Will Lotham or Perky or Fiona. Me.

I always have.

I just let a lot of psychological clutter get in the way.

Time to clean house.

The music winds down, the slow melody turning into the opening chords of Nine Inch Nails' "Closer."

Ah, irony.

I start to pull away, realizing it's true.

I don't care.

I don't care that Will's wolf pack group of friends from high school is stuck on standards that never mattered in the first place. I don't care that half the people in here have graduate degrees and spouses and kids and houses and I don't. I don't care that my life's trajectory has taken me *way* out of the arc of expectation. I'm not a machine. I'm not an object. The surface of any given scene isn't all that matters.

I am deep ripples in a glacier-carved lake. Most of these people only care about what that lake's shining surface mirrors back to them.

Pulling away slightly, I make sure I can see Will's face. His eyes are unfocused, and he's watching me with the most bewildered look. As we lock on each other, his attention, well...

Deepens.

And then he goes out of focus as he moves in.

Is he doing what I think he's doing?

The brush of light stubble on my jawline makes me start and pull back, nerves like skittish horses in a thunderstorm. I'm so alive in his arms, but stuck in the past on the inside, my heart marshaling my internal troops for a long, steady march into the present.

I'm so many different people, all living memories in disparate times.

"Mallory," he says, pulling me closer until I can't see him, my glasses making him blur. His scent is so delicious, soap and light cologne, his ever-present scent of lime and mint. The low, anguished tone doesn't really match the music, and now our feet are barely moving in spite of the insistent beat. I swallow, hard, as all the people inside me suddenly join together as one, fully present, here and watching.

This is it.

This is real life.

And you know what?

I really don't care.

"I really don't care," he says, like he read my mind. His lips are against the soft skin below my earlobe. I shiver.

"Don't care about—" I hold my breath until I can't take it anymore. "—me?"

"Don't care about Osgood. Or Fletch. Or Ramini. They're all assholes." His nose rubs against my hair and he inhales slowly, a savoring kind of torture that turns every inch of my skin into fire.

"This isn't some teen movie, Will. Kissing me in public isn't going to save the day."

"No, it won't. But it will definitely feel good. I'm about to kiss you because I want to feel good with you. I want to make you feel good. And I'm pretty sure that when we kiss, we'll feel even better." My hands belie my words as he speaks, the folds of his shirt between my fingers, the tight stretch of the fabric drawing him to me.

"Is that how kisses work? They're exponential?" I ask, my voice shaking but full of jokes I don't mean.

"I imagine they are, with you. Now shut up and let's find out."

The space between us folds and he's kissing me, his mouth so perfect, the connection natural and good and how did I ever live without being in his arms? Twenty-eight years without this magic is twenty-eight years of being flat in a world that turns out to be four-dimensional. I didn't know.

I thought I knew.

But I really didn't know.

If people notice, I'm not aware of it, spinning and spinning inside. All the parts of me that have wanted this man for so long cling to him. Fingertips dig into his shoulders, brushing against the ends of his dark hair at the edges where they touch his neck. My breasts flatten against his chest as his mouth moves against mine, arms caging me in like this is his one and only chance to kiss me across all the random chances and infinite combinations of our souls being in the same place at the same time under the perfect circumstances.

And instead of waiting, he's just invented one. Taking the kiss means breaking a spell we didn't know had been cast against us.

Our magic is stronger.

Chapter Seventeen

A rush of whispers fills my ears, like millions of feathers being dropped onto a field of daisies, the brush of one distinct surface against another so different, making a friction that is like a seventh sense. His lips are on mine, then his tongue makes a gentle entrance, a quiet, heartfelt move that crosses the gap from *Let's explore* to *Let's get real*.

His taste is on the tip of my tongue, which is moving against his, my hand that was on his shoulder sliding up his neck, the powerful warmth of his skin heating my blood. Music swirls around us, the DJ's light show the closest we can come to the stars in the sky, my entire world collapsing into all the places where Will touches me.

The music goes quiet but Will doesn't stop. Our kiss deepens, bodies swaying. As time passes I become acutely aware of people in small clusters, some ignoring us, some whispering.

"I don't know how *that* happened," Gemma says to my left, her voice distinct. It always had a Valley Girl aspect to it, anachronistic and nasal. When I met women who'd actually been raised in that part of California, I found myself wondering how Gemma and her sisters had such a stereotypical voice from another place, but at this moment, as Will's pulling back from the kiss and I'm dazed, it's the last thing on my mind.

My eyes shift toward her, anyhow. She's standing with Alisha and a woman who is likely Erin, another cheerleader from back in the day. Erin is hugely pregnant and looks miserable.

"Some people trade down, I guess," Alisha says, giving Gemma a sympathetic pat on the wrist.

Then they both look straight at me.

Raye and Sanni happen to be at the bar, right next to them. Raye overhears everything, face flushing like she always did in high school, emotions all over her face, eyes wide and narrow at the same time.

Will stiffens, fingertips digging into my back with possession. As his heat fades from me, body turning toward his past, a low sigh filled with determination coming out of him, I pivot and leave.

This time, for good.

Rushing out of the room, I practically trip over Perky, who is sitting on the floor, ass against the wall, high heels strewn about her bare feet like adoring fans around a guru. Manoosh Baer, an exchange student from eleventh grade, is next to her, their heads huddled as they scroll through a series of pictures on her phone.

"Eep!" I let out, barely avoiding falling on her.

"Maaal!" she calls out, her voice making it clear she's really availed herself of the cash bar. "Where ya goin'?"

"I'm done, Perk."

Instant sobriety makes her abandon poor Manoosh, who looks crestfallen. Running toward me as I fling open the double doors to the parking lot, Perky shouts, "WHAT DID WILL DO TO YOU?"

"HE KISSED ME!" I scream back.

All the outrage she's mustered on my behalf hovers over her head like a demon who suddenly has no mission. "What? He *what*?"

"HE KISSED ME! ON THE DANCE FLOOR! IN FRONT OF PEOPLE!"

"And you're... mad at him?"

"YES! No! I don't—it's everyone else, Perky! It's the assholes! ALISHA IS AN ASSHOLE!" I scream.

"Well, duh." Manoosh has joined us, standing next to Perky in his suit, tie askew, hair a mussed series of gorgeous waves, big brown eyes aware and curious.

For some reason, his response cuts through everything. I start laughing so hard that my belly cramps, one ankle turning in as my legs can't support so much emotion. Someone's red Corvette provides me with instant stability as I lean against it, giggling my way to tears.

I should never have come to this stupid reunion.

"See? Even Manoosh knows the truth!" Perky screams, hysterical with that effect alcohol has on someone who rarely drinks. Then she adds more quietly, "He was only here for a year and he saw through them. The ones who changed are fine. The ones who stayed exactly the same are so brittle, Mal. They throw stones and hammers because they're terrified you might have the tools and use them first. They have to crack you to feel relevant."

"Will kissed me on the dance floor, Perk. And I heard Alisha tell Gemma he traded down."

Blink.

Blink.

Blink.

Even Manoosh takes a step away from Perky, whose sudden calm is like the eye of a tornado.

213

"I hope she enjoyed those four-hundred-dollar extensions, because they're about to be ripped out at the roots and turned into a merkin I'll apply to her Brazilian-waxed pissflaps with Krazy Glue," Perky declares, turning toward the building and sprinting so fast.

Manoosh gapes.

"Someone needs to stop her," I tell him. "You or me?"

"Damn it," he mutters, taking off, grabbing her by the waist just before she reaches the main doors.

It's kind of a relief to have someone else managing my best friend, the fireball.

But it also feels really good to know her outrage is on my behalf.

Every step toward my car—*uh oh*.

Damn it.

There is no "my car." I came here with Will. In *his* car.

I crack. Right there on the asphalt, barely finding my way to a small island covered with fresh mulch and flowering hostas. My ass finds the cement parking berm and I collapse, knees open, spiky high heels wobbling on the uneven pavement until they settle where they belong, angling my legs into the position that causes the least pain, leads to the least tension.

Leaning back, I let the mulch touch my shoulder blades, dig into the back of my hair, the grounding with the earth affirming and gritty. My tongue presses against the roof of my mouth, fitting into the curves of my teeth. As I move it, I realize how hard I'm pushing. Unconscious pressure inside my body, applied by another part of my body, causes me physical pain.

Why do I do this to myself?

The same can be said for what my teenage self does to my adult self. Insidious and silent, she just acts, forging behavior paths that seem adult on the surface but are driven by a child underneath.

I'm not just done with this reunion.

I am done letting the past dictate my present.

Each breath makes my body feel more real, like those moments when Will touched me. Behind closed eyes, I connect with all the parts of me. Fingertips, toes, lips, ears, belly button–they're all me, and they're all done, too.

Being done means closing a door. And when you close a door, you move into a new space, one you get to assess and experience on your own terms.

"Mallory!" Will's urgent, worried voice startles me, making my muscles constrict, the edges of the mulch chips digging in, scratching me. My thighs rest against the cold concrete edge, eyes opening to find him standing over me, blocking out the stars.

"Did you fall? Are you hurt?" A gentle hand goes to my cheek as he crouches, the faint scent of his cologne, of sweet beer, and a thumping beat between us that has its own olfactory trigger, all coming together.

I should sit up. I should react. I should say something.

Instead, I just look up and stare at him, a bleak hollowness reassuring in its truth.

Anticipation is a two-sided coin that feels like it's all heads or all tails, depending on the situation. What I'm experiencing right this moment, as Will moves his hand from my face and sits next to me, bending back, imitating my child's position on the landscaped space, is the absence of anticipation.

It's so freeing.

"You know," he says with a soft chuckle, "for someone who never left town, you sure do run away a lot."

I don't laugh. I don't say anything. His words don't hurt, but he has a point.

"You're not hurt," he finally says.

"Not my body," I reply with brutal honesty.

"Good. I'm sorry about your feelings."

"Are you?"

"I just told Gemma and Alisha off. Or, well," he chuckles lightly, the sound incongruent, "I came in second."

"What does that mean?"

"Rayelyn Boyle beat me to it."

"Rayelyn?"

"She ripped Alisha and Gemma a few new holes. Didn't make a difference, of course. Nothing you say to soulless Barbies ever does."

"You mean nothing Rayelyn said made a difference."

"No. I mean nothing *anyone* says makes a difference. But you have to say something, don't you? Otherwise, they think it's acceptable to treat people like shit. I thought I was doing the right thing by depriving them of attention. I was wrong."

"They've always been like this."

"I can't believe I didn't see it ten years ago."

I snort. I can.

"Mallory," he says, his fingers scraping along the dirt to find mine. I don't pull away. Twining our fingers, his palm flattens against mine, the connection warming me. "I told Alisha and Gemma they were petty bitches who were embarrassing themselves with their childish putdowns."

"You did?"

"Ask Fiona. She was there."

"I don't need corroborating witnesses, Will. I trust you. If you say you did it, I believe you."

"Why?"

"Why what?"

"Why do you trust me?"

"Because–why wouldn't I? You've never given me a reason to think you're not trustworthy."

"That's your default? Assume trust until someone breaks it?"

"Yes. I suppose so."

"And you make life choices based on what feels right? Inside yourself, intrinsically?"

"We talked about this already," I say with a long sigh. "I know, I know. I turned down Harvard."

He squeezes my hand. "No. That's not what I mean."

"Then what?" Turning toward him, I open my eyes. In shadow, his profile is a work of art, throat moving as he swallows. Greys and browns, black and the flash of light as doors to the building open and close, cars coming into and out of the parking lot, all mingle to make him look like an Escher etching, a Picasso, but 3D and with movement.

"You seem like the kind of woman who likes to take it slow. I've known for a while now that I wanted this," he says, sitting up, hand still holding mine, waving at the ever-shrinking space between us, "and I knew you wanted it, too."

"Then why not say that?" I sit up, too, unable to stop myself.

"I tried. Repeatedly," he says pointedly. "You need a soft sell, though. Pinning you against the wall and kissing you madly next to the coffee machine didn't seem like your style."

"Is it yours?"

"With a woman I want? Who wants me, too? Sure."

My entire body ignites.

"But not with... me," I say slowly, emphasizing the word *me*, setting it apart from the others the way he's setting me apart from his... others.

"You're a smoldering fire, Mallory. Not a sudden blast. You're deep. Shallow bounces right off you. I don't want to skim the surface. I want to explore the uncharted waters with you."

"I don't need this," I explain to him. Beseeching him, really. Almost begging him to understand.

How can he? He's not me. Wasn't me. Never had my role back in high school.

"Need what?"

"For you to make some grand, empty gesture that doesn't mean anything. It's sweet, Will. Really. But I don't need it."

"Did you ever consider the fact that maybe *I* do? Not the empty part. No part of how I feel about you is empty. It's full. Overflowing. So intense that I need help breathing sometimes."

His words are a firehose to the face, a siren to the ear, a million ping pong balls flooding a dorm room through the cracked door. Will is a tsunami of hope carrying me off with the tide, pushing me so far inland I smack against the side of a mountain, unable to climb it to safety.

"To those people–your high school crowd–I'll never be anything more than Mallory Monahan, the high school nerd. The chubby chick who blended into the lockers. I might as well have painted myself blue and turned my belly button into a combination dial," I hiss in his ear, knowing his words are fueled by hyper-emotion. By nostalgia. By the fact that Will is a decent guy who's swept up in the moment and trying to do the right thing.

"You really think that?"

"Your friends just proved it. To them, I'll never be anyone but who I was in high school."

"Seems like it works both ways."

"What do you mean?"

"Sounds like I'll never be the man I *am* to you. That you'll always see me as the teenager in high school. Maybe my friends aren't the only ones stuck in the past, Mal. You're back there, too."

I stiffen.

"Here's the question, Ms. Monahan: where do you want to live? In 2009 or 2019?"

I want to be with you.

I've always wanted to be with you.

The words are stuck, caught at a gate held shut by an enormous deadbolt that my raw, prying hands can't move. No matter how hard I push and shove, heave-ho and grunt, I can't do it.

I can't.

Or perhaps it's more than that: I can't do it *alone.*

"Do you have any idea how I felt about you? In high school? You were my biggest crush." The words whoosh out of me like a hot air balloon descending too fast, rushing toward the ground, out of control. "*Crush.* What a word. It's perfect, really, because the emotions all crush you from the inside out. They crowd out who you really are and put these hollow, carved-out warehouses of hope inside. Impossible hope. I imagined you out of thin air. Created entire worlds— no." I laugh, the sound old and new at the same time. "I created parallel universes where we were together, because it would take quantum physics for that to have happened."

One eyebrow goes up, the cocky look on his face making me mad with desire and equally mad with rage, both feelings true and co-existing inside the very same Mallory here before him, confessing everything, shaking in her heels and all too certain this is the right thing to do.

Feeling the fear, doing it anyway, and knowing she'll pay for it.

"You have no idea. *No idea* how hard it was to say yes when you asked me to be your date to this reunion, Will, because I knew I wouldn't just have to pick a dress and do my hair and makeup. I'd need a U-Haul for all the ghosts and baggage I'd bring here tonight. And it turns out I was right. Ramini and Fletch and Osgood and *you* confirmed it."

"Me? What did *I* do? Or... *not* do?" His eyes search my face for an answer.

"Let me ask you the same question you just asked me, Mr. Lotham. Where do *you* want to live? Past or present?"

"Anywhere you are, Mallory. We're in a parking lot again. This time, you don't get to run away. I shouldn't have let you ten years ago, and I'm sure as hell not going to let you now."

He breathes into me, and I take him in with deep, delicious inhales that slowly surrender. The bolt that has held the gate closed for so long slides open, foot by rusty foot, until one final, coordinated effort removes the barrier and our parallel selves finally meet.

And touch.

With our lips.

No audience this time. No dance floor, no public display. This is about us and us alone. If Will's trying to make a statement to the crowd, he's found an awfully private place to do it. As he kisses me, our breath mingling, words earnest and real, it hits me, full throated and revelatory, the heady feeling of being in Will's arms righting the world.

Because he's showing me our truth.

I *am* the crowd.

Chapter Eighteen

Three weeks later

You ready? Perky texts me as I chop the last red pepper to put in the stir fry. Onions are caramelizing on the stove already, the house filled with the scent.

Will's coming over for dinner. He's ten minutes late and while I'm not worried about being stood up, I have to keep myself busy in order not to spontaneously combust. Chopping vegetables seems like a good outlet for my nervousness.

As long as I don't cut off a fingertip.

The text stands out on the glass screen of my phone, more metaphysical than Perky could ever imagine.

Am I ready?

Am I?

Wiping my right hand on a kitchen towel that hangs on the oven handle, I text back, *Ready for what?*

Sex, she replies instantly. *Third date. It's a requirement. What?*

You really don't know a person until you're naked and in bed with them, she replies. *Third date's a sure thing.*

Is not! I reply.

Is so. You know he expects it, she answers, adding a donut and an eggplant emoji.

Great. Now I'm imagining Will's penis as a big purple nightshade. She's not helpful.

You need to quit reading those erotic sci-fi romance novels where the aliens are blue and purple and have three tongues on their penises, I answer.

Quit deflecting. You have protection? she replies.

From you? I have a sage stick and decaf coffee, I type back.

I get a meme about condoms in return.

You want memes? I threaten. *Because I'm pretty sure you don't want to go there.*

You said you deleted all memes you have about me! You swore! she replies.

Damn. Caught.

I hope he's good in bed, she says. *Did you WD-40 your labia so they don't creak when they open?*

My phone starts to slip and I grab at it desperately, fumbling in my panic to prevent it from cracking on the floor. It falls anyhow.

And... whew. No spider screen.

I resume our texting with, *My cooch is just fine and freshly detailed and I'm sure Will has a huge eggplant cock and knows how to use it!*

I hit Send.

And realize the text window is open to... my mother's phone number.

Three dots appear.

Oh.

My.

God.

Was something wrong with your gynecological parts, Mallory? Mom asks.

No, but there sure is now.

That text was meant for someone else, Mom. Sorry! I reply.

What is an eggplant... you know? Mom asks. *Does Will have some sort of disease that made you sick?*

MOM STOP, I reply, hating Perky, whose texts keep coming through, ever more insistent and graphic about all the ways I need to make sure I have sex tonight.

You initiated the conversation, Mom replies. *You can tell me anything, you know.*

Can I untell you this? I beg.

I'm not sure I understand what THIS is, she answers.

It's hell, Mom. It's hell. We're in hell, this conversation is hell, and my BFF is turning my night into—

Ding dong!

The doorbell.

Will and his purple eggplant cock are here, I text Perky.

Gotta go, I text Mom.

And then I turn off my phone. Power down. Buh-bye.

Will is standing outside my door, head bent as he reads something on *his* phone.

"Hi!" I say, breathless, thrilled to see him as I shove aside the last minute of painful texting.

Gorgeous but very alarmed eyes meet mine. Phone in hand, he turns it around so I can see.

The words *Will and his purple eggplant cock are here* are on the screen.

Oh, no. I texted him by accident.

And, of course, *his* phone is charged to 93 percent. Show off.

"I can explain," I choke out, beyond horrified.

He clears his throat. "Before I come in, I think we need to work on some expectations management for this evening, Mallory."

"It's all Perky's fault."

"Perky thinks I have a purple eggplant in my pants?"

"No!"

"Because we've never dated. I don't think we've even hugged. No way she knows about the purple tuber in my boxer briefs."

"You wear boxer briefs?"

"You'd rather talk about my underwear than my grotesquely huge, extremely thick –"

I kiss him. His arms wrap around me, the crinkle of a paper bag crushed against my back stealing a tiny sliver of my attention away from the taste of Will. My nose picks up the scent of chocolate, his cologne overriding it as my cheek rubs against his.

"If you think kissing me to get me to stop talking about your eggplant fantasies is going to work, you're right." He snuggles in, forehead to forehead.

Inspiration strikes. "Remember that promise you said you'd give me?"

"Promise?"

"Promise we'll never speak of the eggplant again."

He looks down at his package. "I... can't make that promise. It likes to speak its own language."

I swoon a little.

"Well, then, how about we just don't talk about it *now*?"

"Deal." I stand on tiptoes and kiss him lightly. The eggplant stays quiet.

"Now that is a much better way to invite me in," he says, stepping across the threshold into the living room. "I brought dessert."

"You brought brownies?"

He holds up a small white paper bag. "How did you guess?"

"I can smell."

"And a pint of ice cream and some sauces." He also has a plastic grocery bag. Walking into my apartment like he already lives here, he puts the ice cream in the freezer, takes out a small box of baked goods, and folds the bag, setting it next to my coffee maker.

"Why? I–I made dessert already. Pots de crème."

Will comes back to me, reaching for an embrace. "Because," he says, kissing me on the cheek, lips so tempting in my ear, "I want to be clear: I'm a sure thing when it comes to dessert, Mallory. This date doesn't end before that. You told me you never make it to dessert. I'm here to break that streak."

I laugh. "You're not some guy I met online and we're not on a first date. We've had dessert numerous times now."

"No. Third date."

He lets the words hang in the air. I know exactly what he means. Damn that Perky.

"Third date give or take ten to fourteen years," I venture.

His turn to laugh. "Excellent point."

"Good. Because I'm a sure thing, too."

"Then how about we add breakfast to the food lineup?" Self-assurance radiates from him. It's a huge turn-on.

"You want to spend the night?"

"And the morning."

"I'm not sure I have enough coffee to share."

He laughs. I don't. My heart thumps so hard inside my ribs, like a marimba player in a jazz group.

I knew tonight was the night.

I didn't realize tomorrow morning was in the mix, too.

But of course it is. Why wouldn't it be? This isn't just sex.

It never was. Will isn't here for a booty call. We aren't exploring dating.

What we're testing is the long haul.

The long *game*.

"I don't generally let guys stay and use up my coffee."

"Is that a euphemism for some freaky position in bed? 'Use up my coffee'?"

"No."

"Your coffee is *that* good?"

"I guess you'll have to spend the night to find out."

"I don't want a cup of pity coffee, Mallory."

The song changes from an energetic Lindsey Stirling violin ballad to Stephen Swartz's "Hello." The beat takes over, new ukulele sound plucking my past emotions and forming a duet with the very intense present as Will kisses me, slow and deep, our hips meeting in a sway that bends time itself.

Breaking the kiss, he whispers, "Am I coffee-worthy?"

"You're everything-worthy."

"That's my line, Mal. You're stealing all my good lines."

"Then make me stop talking."

"How do I do that?"

"I'm pretty sure you have a few clever ideas. You were salutatorian, after all. Rhodes Scholar. You're kinda smart."

"So I've been told." The smile he gives me—serene, excited, full of promise—intensifies with passion as we hold each other's gaze.

I smell it before I can put words to it. "DINNER IS BURNING!" I scream, fleeing to the stove, where the onions have gone half black and the red pepper strips look like blood on tar.

"It's charbroiled," Will announces, chin on my shoulder as I use the spatula to scrape up what I can and evenly distribute the vegetables.

"You're diplomatic."

"I would never insult another vegetable. They're my people. Purple eggplant, red pepper—we stick together."

An elbow to his gut is my response.

He laughs, moving gracefully across my kitchen to find a bottle of white wine in the fridge. It's already open, stopper in place. Without asking, he looks through my cabinets, finds two wine glasses, and asks, "Wine?"

"Perfect."

Part of the appeal of gas stoves comes in being able to regulate the heat visually, the distribution easier to calibrate when you can see it. Will's body is the same way. Our fingers brush as he hands me the wine, the stir fry saved by my quick movements, the marinated chicken ready to add in a moment.

Steam rises from the rice cooker on the counter behind Will, the aroma of butter and saffron making me smile.

"Smart, sexy, centered, *and* a good cook. I found the whole package." Holding his wine glass aloft in a toast, he waits until I walk to him, the glasses ringing in approval as we cheer each other, sip once, then kiss.

Beep!

The rice cooker is done.

"Can I help?" Will drinks more wine, then sets down the glass, looking at my midsection. "Do you have another apron?"

I point to the row of hooks with five white aprons in a row.

"Wow. You're organized."

"Form and function. I like aprons and I like the look."

Plucking one off a hook, he opens it up and bursts out laughing.

Across the front is a huge Wonder Woman symbol, two giant silkscreened Ws.

Looping the top over his head, he reaches behind himself and ties the strings. "What do you think?"

"You're working it. You could be the next Gal Gadot."

"I'll stick to being Will Lotham. I'm pretty good at that. What should I do?" Unbuttoning his cuffs, he does that slow shirtsleeve roll that looks so sexy on a man who has come over to make love with you after dinner.

Not that I would know.

Because this is the first time I've had a guy overnight. But I'm hoping it's the first of many nights with Will, so I'm going to generalize.

"How about salad, Wonder Will?" I point to the fixings. He gets to work, again not asking, just intuitively knowing what to do in my space.

I like this.

No. Scratch that.

I *love* this.

As I'm browning the chicken in some avocado oil, he asks. "Do these go in the salad?"

I look up. He's staring at a small tray of long, aromatic herbs arranged with other savory bites.

"No. But you can have some now."

"What are they?"

"Basil, mint, coriander, lemongrass."

"Not for the salad? What do you do with them?"

"Eat them. As an appetizer. And we'll have some of the herbs on the chicken." I reach over and choose a sprig of basil, a sliver of ham, and a sesame cracker. "Try it," I offer.

He does. He nods, making sounds of approval.

Is he loud in bed? I wonder as I watch him. Or a dirty talker?

Blood rushes to every pore on my body at the thought, my face feeling like a furnace.

"Mal?" He steps toward me, a predator sensing an opening. "What are you thinking about? You just... changed."

"Changed?" My voice cracks.

He pulls me close. "You look like you just imagined me naked."

"It's the vegetables. Made me think about your eggplant."

A shift in his hips and he presses against me. "You don't need to just *think* about it."

"Aren't you hungry?'

He maintains eye contact as he reaches for his wine, taking a long mouthful. After he swallows, he simply says, "Yes."

"Then let's eat."

"Oh. You meant dinner."

"Is that how this is going to be all night, Will? You'll make sexual innuendos about everything?"

"Yes. Got a problem with that?"

"No. It's just—I think we need to work on some expectations management for this evening, Will."

He bursts out laughing at my use of his own words against him.

I pull back. His grip tightens.

"Where are you going?"

"The chicken needs me more than you do."

"That's debatable." A sweet kiss on my forehead comes before he lets me go, the ukulele music winding down and going quiet.

Five minutes later, we've removed our respective aprons and we're sitting at my four-person table, two seats empty—thank goodness. Tonight is about us and only us, the dinner a perfectly decent performance on my part, Will making appreciative sounds of gustatory happiness.

"The herb tray really adds to this," he says, the compliment hitting home in a way that surprises me.

"Thanks."

"I have to confess, I've never had a date invite me to her apartment and cook me dinner. I wasn't sure how this would go."

"Hold on there, bud. We haven't made it to dessert yet. Don't call this a success before we hit the finish line."

"Dessert isn't the finish line tonight, Mallory."

I fill my mouth with wine and savor it, mulling over his words as my pulse races to settle between my legs.

He stands and holds out his hand, grasping the edge of my empty plate. "Finished?"

I choke a little, a dribble of wine tickling my throat. "Hmmm?"

"Finished? With dinner? You cooked, so I'll clean up." He grabs his Wonder Woman costume—I mean, *apron*—and gets to work.

Openly gawking, I watch as he clears the table, putting dirty dishes in the sink, setting serving dishes on the counter. Opening my lower cabinets, he looks around and says, "Where do you keep containers for leftovers?"

Have I died and gone to heaven?

"You don't have to do that!" I insist, pushing my chair back, abandoning my wine.

"I know I don't have to. I want to." Kitchen skills can't be faked. This is a guy who is comfortable in his own skin, and who knows that pulling your own weight is part of being an adult.

I sit back down.

I sip my wine.

I'm getting even more turned on.

How is that possible? Energy flow is limited by resistors to prevent an overload. Capacitors store energy so it can be released later. I'm ready to explode. I must be short-circuiting.

Maybe that's where tonight's orgasm comes in.

Orgasm*s*.

Please let there be plenty of them.

I finish my wine and move to him, unable to be idle while he does everything. Standing next to each other, we make light work of it, the food put away and the dishwasher humming soon.

Parts of me are humming, too.

Will excuses himself to use the bathroom and I grab the edge of the kitchen counter, reeling, the few moments of alone time crucial for regulating my emotions. My "gynecological parts," as Mom so delicately referred to them, are beyond regulation.

I'm a runaway train of oxytocin and pent-up need.

Nervous, I flit around the room, fluffing my sofa pillows, straightening a stack of books on my side table. I'm good in the grooming department. Condoms and lube in my bedside drawer. Will's comment earlier about staying for breakfast makes his intentions clear.

This is happening.

This is *really* happening.

I need music. My powered-off phone is normally docked into a speaker set, but instead of re-opening a portal into hell with my mother by turning it on, I find my laptop and re-connect to streaming music, picking a soothing jazz-filled station with a little blues, making the air spontaneous and loose. I sit down on my sofa and hold the stemless wine glass at the base, resting lightly in my palm like a man's sac.

It's fragile.

It contains something you swallow.

Squeeze too tight and someone bleeds.

"What are you thinking about?" Will asks me as he walks

in and sits down next to me, body language clear that we're moving on to the sex part of tonight.

Do I tell him the truth?

I blush.

I remove my glasses. He's so close, he's almost crystal clear. If I move three more inches toward him, true clarity will set in.

"Ah," he says softly, looking at me. "You look so much softer. Sweeter."

"Without the glasses?"

"Yes. Younger." He strokes my arm. "Something."

"I can put them back on."

Two fingers touch my face, tracing the cheekbone. "I like you however you are." Before I can react, he looks at the wine in my hand and adds, "Want more?"

I look at his package. I can't help myself. "Yes."

"Now who's making every comment into a sexual innuendo? We're a pair, aren't we?"

Pair. Sac. Testicles.

Oh, no.

How much wine have I had?

He makes his move without any pretense, because seriously–why bother? We both know what comes next.

What comes next is *us*.

A kiss that is a prelude to making love feels so different from any other kiss. Like the first step in a long journey you know will require all the effort, stamina, and fortitude you have, but you also know you'll come out on the other side of it stronger, knowing yourself better, and changed.

From the tips of my toes to the tip of my tongue, this kiss, his breath, the feel of his hands on my body, moving down to my breasts with questions that are too complex to answer with words – it's all about to change me.

For the better.

Smooth and confident, Will takes the wine glass out of my hand, setting it down on the cocktail table in front of us, a mid-century modern piece I picked up at a small second-hand shop in Chelmsford last year. My mind does this—it starts tracking the rooted origin of everything he does. Each physical item in my apartment has a story. Just like me.

Just like Will.

Just like *this*.

The long kidney pillow behind me has a jewel-toned pattern of teardrops, colored in orange, turquoise, amethyst. As it rubs against my lower back, warm from the blanket of his body, our kiss growing more intense, my mind conjures the pattern. Perhaps I'm curating our movements, attaching them to important markers that chronicle what we do.

Or maybe I'm just filled with anxiety because OMG *WILL LOTHAM* IS CUPPING MY BREAST AND WE'RE *MAKING OUT* ON MY SOFA AND WE ARE ABOUT TO BE *NAKED*.

Pretty sure I thought that so loudly Will can hear it from outside my own skull, because he suddenly stops, his hand on my cheek. Looking down at me, eyes filled with an excited, smoky heat, he asks, "You okay?"

"Oh, yes."

"You tensed up."

"I did?"

"We don't need to do anything you don't want to do, Mallory."

"Are you kidding me?" I laugh, brushing the hair off his brow. It's fallen across his eyelashes, the tips moving as he blinks. "Do you have any idea how long I've been waiting for this?"

"Me, too."

"What?" I nearly fall off the couch. "What do you mean, you too?"

"I always wondered what it would be like to kiss you."

"By 'always,' you mean a month, right? Since you saved me from my failed porn career."

He laughs, his warm breath tickling the tip of my nose. "No. Before that."

"Before that, Will, I hadn't seen you since high school."

"That's right."

"You wondered what it would be like to kiss me back in high school?" I squeak out.

"Mmm hmm." He kisses my collarbone. I stare at his thick, brown hair, each strand standing out like a member of a Greek chorus, waiting to chant something incriminating at me.

"Hold up, mister. You can't just drop a fact like that on me without explanation. I confessed my crush on you and you never said a word!"

"Your crush wasn't exactly private," he whispers, the words making every pore on my neck tingle.

"That's not–" I gasp, "–the point." I had no idea a tongue on my neck could do that to me.

"What is the point?" he asks, thumb grazing my nipple until it tightens to an impossibly arousing peak, brushing against my bra with a maddening sensation that makes me want to be naked. Now. With Will between my legs. Now.

Did I mention the *now* part?

"You, um..." Oh, damn. What was I talking about?

"I wondered," he whispers into my ear, mouth on my neck, tongue teasing various soft sections of skin. "I wondered what you were like underneath that shell."

"Shell?"

"You were quiet. Nice. Almost too nice. I didn't think I

knew how to be part of your world." A soulful kiss, then he looks at me, heartfelt and true. "I also didn't have the courage then to break out of my own shell and see what you were really like. And when you rejected Harvard, you set off a cyclone inside me."

"I did? Me?"

"Yes. You. I've thought about you all these years. Not the same way you described your crush on me," he explains, pausing.

Our openness surprises me. *Pleases* me. The sensation is more than intellectual, way more than nostalgic. It's rooted here in the present, the clock ticking and marking this moment, a sentry watching out for me.

Watching out for my heart.

And then Will adds, "More like the feeling that you were the one who got away."

"Really?" This is turning me on more than it should.

No. Scratch that.

This is turning me on *exactly* the way it should.

"I came back to manage the company for Mom and Dad and planned to look you up. I've never been able to get that day in the high school parking lot out of my mind."

"You – what?"

"I almost kissed you then."

My heart stops.

"I wish I had." A quick kiss, a brush of lips against lips, and then he continues, as if his recap of that day during finals week didn't just come careening into the present, wheels peeling on asphalt, racing ten years at lightning speed.

Minus the magenta glitter paint.

"I assumed you'd married long ago. That some lucky guy got you." He pauses to consider. "Or lucky woman." This time, the kiss is long and slow, his hands all over me, moving to the tender, swollen spot between my legs. He stops, stretching over me, our bodies pinned to the sofa, my mind a whirl. "Looks like I'm the one who got lucky."

"You mean finding me on a porn set?" I blink, returning us to banter, because his telling of that moment has all the selves inside me colliding in a mad rush to be fully present, right here, right now.

"That's... not what I was thinking." He laughs. "But I wasn't upset to find you there."

"I'm not sure how to take that statement, Will."

"Then how about I stop talking and show you what I mean."

Closing the space between us, he leads with his mouth, the soft press of his lips against mine extraordinary. This isn't our first kiss and it certainly won't be our last, but it is special. It is special because the gap's been bridged, the question's been answered, the border between my body and his has been crossed. Now it's all about logistics.

And other words that begin with L.

Working the hem of my shirt loose, Will's warm hands are on my belly, moving up to cup my breasts. Once he takes that step, I figure it's my turn.

Oh, my. The bare skin of his back is so hot to the touch, the ridged line of muscles riding up his spine like steel under flesh. Migrating up, I feel his ribs, then shoulder blades, roiling as he moves, my mind transfixed by what my fingers feel. Decoding it as he kisses me puts my body into a state of circuit overload, especially when his fingertips slip under my bra line and I moan.

"The sofa is nice, Mallory," he whispers as we kiss, "but do you have a bed?"

"A bed?"

"You know. A flat, soft surface with sheets and blankets,

where people get naked and do naughty, filthy things to each other."

"Naughty?" And *filthy*? A low, hot clench between my legs is followed by a sudden rush of heat.

"Do you prefer nice?"

"I prefer you."

I stand and stretch out my hand to him and he joins me, leg to leg, hip to hip, belly to belly, then mouths on each other as I walk him backwards to my bedroom. His hips move with fluidity and confidence, a predictor of what's about to happen.

Naked. We're about to be naked, Will's going to be between my legs, and I'm being kissed so hard right now that my hair's on fire. Breasts, too.

And I really need a firehose down below.

Hose. Will. Will's penis.

"What are you thinking?" he asks suddenly.

"Women ask men that question. Not the other way around."

"I'm asking you. You seem distracted. I don't want you distracted during sex. So—"

"I was thinking about your firehose."

"First it's an eggplant, now it's a firehose? Let's get back to expectations management, Mallory. "

I start laughing as he strips out of his shirt like a guy in a naughty soda commercial. It's as if time runs in slow motion and a spritzer machine is on standby in the wings.

Only it's not Will who is wet.

My fingers know what to do, immediately reaching for his bare chest, palms going flat right on his breast bone. His eyes catch mine. I feel him inhale, then slowly let out his breath, the warm air making me lean in.

We have thousands of ways to touch someone. The permutations are endless. For instance, in this moment, Will bends over me, his hands going to my shirt, undoing the buttons one by one as if he's in sync with my heartbeat. Fast, nimble movements leave my skin chilled by the sudden bareness, his chest brushing against mine as he bends down to kiss me while sliding my shirt off my shoulders, down my elbows, my hands forgotten until I remember they exist, his tongue teasing my teeth as I try to remember how to use the rest of my body.

Miraculously, I drop my shirt as my arms band around his waist, head tipped up to take him in.

Reaching the line between your body and someone else's is like crossing an international border, but wordlessly. All the questions and answers are in the form of kisses and caresses, moans and movements.

Will unhooks my lace bra with a quick flick, the cups loosening with a maddening slack that makes my nipples even harder, begging for his warmth, wanting to be cupped by the very same hands that seem to read my mind. Before I can take a breath between kisses, he dips his head down and sucks one nipple into his holy mouth, making me let out a sound I've never made before.

"Will," I gasp, his name so familiar yet so foreign, all four hands between us removing socially required body coverings that serve as nothing more than obstacles between us. Quickly, we're both naked, and Will stops.

He stares.

I stare back.

"You're beautiful," he says, so much emotion in those syllables, earnest and sensual at the same time. His hair is in disarray, dark waves criss-crossing like they've lost direction. Long eyelashes frame intelligent, alert eyes. Appreciative eyes. Eyes that are hot with want to take in every inch of me.

I let him.

I let him look at me.

And I enjoy it.

The first time you sleep with someone new, there aren't just the boundaries between their body and yours. The gaze has boundaries, too. You know exactly what I mean. Stare at someone a little too long–or at the wrong spot on their body– and you quickly learn that invisible lines surround all of us.

Perimeters matter when it comes to defining ourselves in relation to others, even if they appear on no survey map.

"Will," I say again, sitting up to touch him, being the object of his look no longer enough. The whisper of thick hair, spread across his chest with just the right calibration, makes my palm alight with fire. My nipples graze his ribs as he kisses me, a rich, full kiss that really deserves its own word.

Just 'kiss' doesn't begin to describe it.

"Close your eyes," he tells me.

"Why?"

"Trust me."

"That's how all really scary plotlines in movies start, Will."

"I thought trusting people was your default."

"Fine." I close my eyes and smile. "Do we need a safeword?"

Silence. I open my eyes to find Will staring at me with the most complex sensual expression, chest rising and falling with long, deep breaths, setting a rhythm that makes me inhale slowly, with meaning.

I quickly shut my eyes.

And he pulls me up to the top of the bed, my giggles completely unexpected as my bare ass slides against the Egyptian cotton of my comforter.

"Keep your eyes closed," he whispers in my ear, biting my earlobe for emphasis.

I follow his command.

Sound, touch, and scent become my only tools for awareness, each sense heightened by the shutting off of another.
Will's thigh rubs against my hip, the bristly feel of leg hair on
my smooth skin making me shiver. His body crosses over mine
as if he's reaching for something, then I hear a scraping sound,
one I can't identify.

He pulls back slightly, but his body is on mine. A wet,
viscous sound, like gel on flesh. What on Earth is he doing?

A deep huffing sound comes out of him, then a splash of
sensation, like sudden raindrops on my collarbone, my ribs,
my breasts.

I open my eyes to find white goo all over my breasts.

Oh, no.

Poor Will.

It happens to the best of men, right?

"Um, so, it's okay," I start, uncertain how to explain that
while I wasn't expecting a pearl necklace tonight, premature
ejaculation is nothing to be ashamed of, and–

With his fingertip, he scoops up some of the white sticky
stuff and pops it straight into my open mouth.

Perky's advice comes roaring into my mind:

*You really don't know a person until you're naked and in
bed with them.*

God help me, I'm going to have to admit to her that she
was right.

Is this some kind of... fetish?

Taste buds take a little longer to kick in when the brain is
occupied elsewhere, but as seconds pass, I realize the goo is
sweet. Really sweet, like spun sugar.

What does this guy *eat*? I've heard that if men eat a lot of
pineapple, their semen tastes like it. Will must live at the
Necco factory and mainline wafers like a machine if his tastes
like–

"...Fluff."

"Excuse me?"

"Mallory, you're a million miles away. How's the Fluff?"

I look down at my chest. "Oh!" Relief spills through me like adrenaline. "That's *Fluff*?"

"What did you think it was?"

Jaw dropping, eyes going wide, I look away, horrified that I'm in bed with Will, we're both naked, and I have to explain that I thought he popped the stack a little too early. Jumped the gun. Put the cart before the horse. Rode ahead of the hounds.

"Umm..."

Booming laughter fills the room. He's next to me, head propped up on one hand, elbow supporting him. As he laughs, the bed shakes, his abs curling in. My hand is on his chest and I feel his genuine hilarity coming through as he realizes what I assumed.

"Oh, no. No, Mal," he gasps, muscles I didn't know torsos even possessed making their debut before my eyes. "That's not–I didn't already–"

I kiss him.

Hard.

Curling his body over mine, he presses me back against the mattress, belly to belly, lips to lips, tongues moving as we stick together in harmony.

No. Really. We literally *stick together*.

Still laughing, Will peels himself off me, bending down to lick a spot between my breasts. "Mmmmm. We need more."

"You're serious?"

His fingertip grazes my nipple with a decidedly sticky touch. "Of course. I never joke about Fluff. Or sex. Watching you that day you were in my parents' kitchen, licking Fluff off that spoon, made me wonder what you would look like licking it off my cock." His tongue pokes out to swipe a drop from my nipple. "Naked."

I swoon.

"I–" My voice breaks as he sucks the Fluff off my breast, his tongue twirling with a hot, wet warmth that makes me start to shake. "I draw the line at peanut butter."

"Mallory Monahan, the human Fluffernutter."

"Hah! No. Peanut butter is not meant to be combined with marshmallow. It's meant to be combined with chocolate in a Reese's Cup."

"Two great tastes that taste great together," he murmurs as he kisses my belly.

"No peanut butter on my body!"

"Then I guess I have to find another great taste." With that, those masterful quarterback hands part my thighs, and Will uses another body part to display a highly developed skill, his tongue finding me wet, willing, and–*oh*!

Digging my fingernails into his shoulders as he goes down on me is like being allowed to touch a priceless sculpture at the Museum of Fine Arts in Boston. Like I'm alone at an after-hours event for very important guests.

But I'm the only guest.

And the art touches me *back*.

While his tongue paints brushstrokes between my legs, his mastery making me lift my hips for more, his hands roam. Big and strong, smooth and warm, they ride up over my belly, memorizing my ribs, finding my breasts and intuiting what I want–a fluttering stroke, a hard pinch, a smooth, flowing exploration of my ass, my hips and lower back, moving to my forearms and wrists.

When he reaches for my hand and interweaves our fingers, I come.

Hard.

The intensity of my climax catches me unaware, the surprise greater than my own thoughts, pleasure making my body say *Yes*, whisper *It's my turn now*, gasp *Oh, God*, and let this man I've wanted for so long show me how much he wants me, too. Releasing yourself to another person with the fullness of trust makes sex so much better.

And Will's perfect technique doesn't hurt, either.

I'm at that point where wave after wave makes me hypersensitive, my instinct to move away, to stop him, to say *enough* building inside, but then a second burst of pleasure makes me lose myself in his touch, his attention, the way his tongue seems to know exactly what to do to make me want him even more.

Accepting this from Will gives my orgasms an edge that makes me fall in love with him, all the way, without reservation.

Too soon, my mind hisses.

Finally, my heart beams.

He's kissing me, fast and wet, and my hands find his ass, his chest, his jaw, his hair, my mouth smashed against his, the taste of me lingering on him as he whispers my name, "Mallory," interrupting the glow of my skin, the beautiful swell of my heart, the chiseled gorgeousness of his naked body, and the very real moment when I roll a condom over his glorious shaft and invite him in, my legs wide, my heart wider.

And instead of rushing in, he pauses.

The sweetest kiss ever accompanies the slow, steady, sultry feel as Will Lotham makes love to me, all the way.

All the way.

Dropping his chin, he skims it across my nipples, replacing the sandpapery feel with his mouth, the juxtaposition of disparate sensations making me shiver. Heavy above me, but held by strong muscle, his skin is intoxicating. I breathe him in and clench around him as steady strokes build an urgency inside me.

"Will," I gasp, palms loving the feel of his shoulders working as his athletic body moves against mine, the two of us using motion to make something greater.

He stops. "Mal? You want me to–" Gentlemanly and inquiring, he's checking in to make sure I'm pleased.

Widening my hips, I take him in deeper, heels pressed against ass muscles that don't budge. "I want you. This. More of this. I'm so close, Will."

"Again?" Pride makes him grin.

"Again. You seem to know exactly what to do to me to make me feel everything I've ever wanted to feel with you," I confess.

Our gaze fixes for a long time, the deep sense of blending with him, body, heart, and mind making me disappear into him, more real than ever, less distinct, too. We're combining, his mouth on mine for a long, savoring kiss, and then he says,

"Remember what you wrote in my yearbook?" A hot current flows between us, his pause making me feel even closer to him at the same time my body is so, so ready. On edge and half out of my mind, I take in his words and nearly answer with "I love you."

"Yes?" I say instead. It's safer.

"You wrote, *To Will, who always knows where he's going.* When I'm with you, Mallory, that's so true. I feel like I know myself and my path better than ever. But only with you."

I kiss him fiercely, my own words coming from his mouth a connection that closes a circuit, that completes a loop.

Slowly, with a piercing sense of being known to my core, my body joins my mind and heart with a deep presence that touches some equally tender piece of Will, because as our climaxes build, he stares into my eyes. There's more emotion in those beautiful blue-green eyes than I've seen in a lifetime of faces. Soon he's kissing my neck, his low groan meeting my soft cries as we come together.

I didn't know I could feel so integrated. So hot. So turned on.

So *known*.

Peaceful silence fills the air as we breathe our way back to earth.

"That was... wow."

"Yes."

Lifting up, he kisses the tip of my nose, eyes on mine as I stroke his back. He's in me still, hard and touching a spot that makes me shudder.

He laughs. "More?"

Reaching up, I kiss him in answer, then say, "Later."

I expect him to pull out and move. He doesn't, instead brushing my hair around my ear, eyes taking in all the secrets of my face.

Which aren't many when I'm post-sex, in Will Lotham's arms. Sex with Will is a truth serum. I can't keep anything from him.

"I am so stupid," he says, the last words I expect to hear.

"That was anything but stupid!"

Throaty, rumbling laughter answers me, his eyes still on mine. "Not talking about the sex."

"Then what?"

"You."

I squeeze my thighs. "Pretty sure I *am* the sex."

"You're the whole package."

My mouth spreads with a grin. "Thank you. You have a few nice attributes, too." I squeeze one of them until he grins back.

With great care, Will pulls out, takes care of the condom,

and gives me a fabulous view of the same ass my heels couldn't budge moments ago. Electricity finds new conduction paths along my skin as I pull the sheets and coverlet back up, burrowing under.

His eyes light up as he turns back to me, then he joins me under the covers, curling me against his chest. Some of his hair curls in irregular patterns. My nipple sticks to his rib.

Ah, Fluff.

A wave of exhaustion hits me. His breath, too, steadies as we float off. So many firsts tonight. First home-cooked meal. First lovemaking. First overnight.

Please let them all be firsts. Not lasts. I need so much more.

"Mmmmm," he says, the sound fading with a comfort that gives my body another reason to relax. You don't breathe like that with someone you don't trust. He's here. He's falling asleep.

With *me*.

Will Lotham and I just made love.

And my fourteen-year-old self doesn't geek out for a single second of it.

Chapter Nineteen

Until three hours later, when Will is crashed out on my shoulder, his hand near my neck, smelling of, well–*me*.

The ceiling stares back at me, as if I've made it upset by looking at it for so long.

Did that really just happen? Did Will Lotham have sex with me?

More importantly: Did I have sex with him?

And is he really staying the night?

This is too easy.

Way too easy.

The spot above my heart, where ribs and cartilage form a protective cage over the strongest and most vulnerable muscle in the body, feels like someone is trapped in there, banging on the bars of a prison. Will's body spreads over me, possessive, vulnerable, his sleep so natural.

His presence so abnormal.

People have a strong need for the familiar when they're put in unknown territory. We assimilate quickly–those of us who adapt are the ones who pass on our DNA, evolutionarily. I can adapt.

I can definitely adapt to making love with Will.

Just did.

But what takes time is the mental shift. The slow comprehension that this isn't an anomaly. The new normal for me will be unfettered access to Will's naked body.

And inviting him into my own.

What *is* familiar, then? I'm in my own home, sure. But I need more comfort.

I need chocolate.

Now.

Peeking under the covers, I take in the sight of my naked thigh covered by Will's naked thigh. I blink. I blink again, imagining my eyes are a camera, memorializing this image. Yes, it's silly. Yes, it makes me smile.

And yes, it's perfect.

He's spending the night. Expecting breakfast. Maybe some morning nookie.

Scratch that.

Look at that body again. Did someone carve him out of ivory, soapstone, a big old chunk of solid testosterone?

Definitely some morning nookie.

The rasp of my own breath in the back of my throat is all I hear as I move my hip just so, trying not to wake him.

Midnight expeditions for chocolate when you are alone are easy. Cravings hit. Emotions overwhelm. We aim for the fix that makes the storm of impossible feelings calm down from a whirling tornado to a wind gust.

But turning to a theobromine therapist when you're stuck to your lover–the residue of Fluff mixed with other, lovelier fluids–is layered with obstacles.

Getting my hands on those brownies in my kitchen is a journey akin to traveling through Jötunheim in *God of War* to reach the highest peak.

Will lets out a long sigh at the exact moment I manage to get the sole of my left foot on the ground, his hand migrating to my breast. I'm on my back, his thumb sliding across my nipple like he's ready for round... for round...

Oh, man.

I lost count.

Will's breathing settles back into the cadence of deep sleep, his hand moving enough to make me suppress a moan, stomach gurgling. I burned two brownies' worth of calories from all that sex, right?

Maybe three?

He withdraws his arm and I take my chance, my ass hitting cold air as it slides off the bed, my glutes engaged in ways that make them scream as I work to wiggle out, then stand.

Whew.

I look down.

I'm naked. And is that a hickey on my boob?

The thought of Will's lips on my skin makes me start to want him again.

Brownies.

Will.

Brownies.

Will.

Brownies–

Damn.

My refrigerator draws me like a moth to a flame. I'm just being considerate, right? It would be rude to wake him up to ask for another ride on the Willmobile.

Oh. My. God.

My inner voice has turned into Perky's.

I made the right choice.

Brownies it is.

The light from my fridge as I open the door shows my

creamy thighs, the tops a little red. A smattering of love bites cover my breasts. Or maybe that's just my splotchy skin. I shiver, then pull out the white baker's box and a bottle of milk.

My carefully constructed pots de crème are sitting patiently, waiting their turn.

"I see you," I whisper. "Don't worry. You're next."

One minute later, I have a full glass of cow juice, an open box of brownies, and my inner voice has been silenced with the classic witch's brew of sugar, chocolate, and disbelief.

There's a soft aqua throw on the end of my sofa, slumped and disheveled from our earlier make-out session. How quaint. Hours ago, being touched and kissed so deeply by Will was extraordinary.

What just happened in my bedroom?

It was even better than any fantasy I've ever had.

Grabbing the throw, I drape it around my shoulders, the fringe tickling the tops of my thighs. Digging in the box for brownie number two, I take a bite and sigh, letting my shoulders drop, my butt bones melting into the chair, guard down for just a moment as the throw slips to the floor in a puddle, gone as I descend into a sweet haze.

Until I realize I'm not alone.

"What are you doing awake?" he asks, rubbing his eyes. A completely naked Will stands before me as I eat brownies directly from the box, caught red-handed and chocolate-mouthed. I don't even have a robe on. No draped sheet around me. Mallory Monahan is one hundred percent unclothed, bent over a white pastry box, smelling like sex and gorging on brownies while her hot high school crush is standing in her kitchen with questions.

Naked.

And... *hard.*

"Uhhhh." I can't say anything else because my tongue is currently occupied by cacao-inspired bliss and crushing embarrassment at being found shoveling sugar into my face like a desperate addict fighting withdrawal symptoms.

His eyes dart to the box. "Ooh. Great idea. I'm starving." Palm flat on his belly, he moves it, a gesture of hunger.

It makes his erection a focal point. Evolutionarily speaking, we're drawn to look at movement, right? Survival instincts are hardwired. The memory of staring at him for years in high school is a deep groove in my brain matter.

So it's not *my* fault that I stare.

My amygdala is my favorite scapegoat.

"Like the view?" Will says as he bends over my shoulder, breaks a brownie in half, and lifts it to his mouth. His chest brushes against my shoulder before he pulls back, but then he purposely leans against me, heat pouring off him.

"Hmmm?" I ask, playing dumb. A big glass of milk in front of me becomes my haven. I drink until my mouth is clear.

Will saunters over to the fridge, opens it, and the refrigerator light should also play the "Hallelujah Chorus," because my God, what an ass he has. It's the kind of muscle structure that deserves gallery showings.

Though I would prefer to be a private collector.

With the glass bottle of milk from Hesserman's Dairy in one hand, he moves over to my cabinets, opening one. I lick my upper lip, finding a rich crumb of brownie on it. A tingling sensation starts in my inner thighs and travels up the midline of my body, spreading out as our nakedness begins to seem normal. Will emerges from the shadow of the cabinet door with a tall glass, setting it on the counter and pouring.

He gestures to mine. "Want a refill?"

"Seconds are always good," I murmur.

"Oh? You want seconds of everything? That can be arranged." To my surprise, he's not being porny.

He's in the fridge again, beautiful backside on display, grabbing the plate of herbs and a small wheel of ripe Brie.

Agog, I stare for too long, until he gives me major side eye, one eyebrow shooting up, eyes clear and amused. "What?"

"You took a pass on my perfectly good pass?"

"We can have sex any time. Fresh herbs, though... they wither." Plucking a stem of basil from the plate, he combines it with a torn-off piece of brie. "Mmmmm."

I look at his midsection. No withering going on there.

"You're choosing cheese over *this*?" I gesture to my body, licking the corner of my mouth to catch another taste of chocolate.

"I'm choosing cheese *and* you. It's not a competition," he says, though his words are muffled. "Mmmm, though. This is delicious."

Befuddled, I mirror him, trying mint and cheese.

It's *good*. The chocolate lingers on my tongue, the cheese rich and creamy. Mint gives it a burst of energy.

He comes up behind me, hands on my shoulders, and twists to kiss me.

"You taste like basil."

"You taste like mint."

"The combo is really interesting."

"We need to test this more."

"But no peanut butter, Will."

His laugh is potent. Strong. Like the flavors in my mouth, it combines disparate elements and turns them into an alloy that is better than the individual parts. Sexy and real, Will is in my kitchen, hip against the island, noshing on leftovers after we took our bodies to an ultimate level of intimacy, higher than skin and bones alone can achieve.

And this is the *next* level.

Milk tastes pure when it washes down chocolate. Everyone knows that, the cool baptism of the liquid passing over my teeth, down my tongue, swallowed into the belly. Will finishes his glass and leans forward, palms flat on the counter, chest rising and falling as he watches me with an intensity that belies the hour. People shouldn't be so awake after giving each other so much of their biology.

He had my blood, my bones, my tendons and arteries, my nerve clusters and nipples, my tongue–my whole being entwined in his. He played me to pleasure until every cell sang, a rhythm and frequency Will invented on the spot, sexual improv at its finest.

We should be loose and sleepy in bed, breathing into the new space we made.

Our eyes lock, and before shyness can stop me, I say, "This is so much better than any of the thousands of daydreams I had about you."

His shoulders drop. "Whew." Hand pressed against his heart, he licks his lips. "I wouldn't want the real Will to disappoint after so many years of being Fantasy Will." One fingertip draws a line from my collarbone down to my shoulder. "What did you imagine?"

"Everything."

"Everything? You daydreamed about having sex with me?"

"When I was younger, I thought of it as making love. Not sex."

Mischievous delight fills his eyes. "When I was eighteen, there was no distinction."

"What about now? What was that?" I nod toward the bedroom, heart booming in my chest.

A long, slow breath, brought in and out by emotion, threads its way through time. "That was making love. The first time, at least. Sex the second. The third time, it was – " He squints one eye, as if deliberating.

Playfully, I smack him. He grabs my wrist with a light, happy touch.

"How about you tell me every dream you ever had, and I make them all come true right now?" he whispers in my ear.

"Now?"

"And tomorrow. And the day after that."

"Every dream?"

"Yes." His eyebrows go up. "You have a specific one you're thinking about?"

"Yes."

"Go ahead."

I stand on tiptoe, my lower lip brushing against his earlobe, the scruff of his chin scratching my neck as I say the words, "I love you, Will."

Instead of tensing, instead of pulling away, instead of making all of the heartbreaking choices he could possibly enact, Will moves slowly, tenderly, until our eyes meet.

Fingers settle under my chin, his eyes studying me. The words are out there now. Too early?

Or too late?

"It's crazy, Mallory, but I feel it, too. I love you. It seems like I've loved you forever and am only now discovering it. But I do. My heart fell for you long before my stupid mind caught up."

I love you. The three simplest words.

The three hardest words, too.

As he gathers me in his arms, the press of his erection against my hip a startlingly fine sensation, his lips more intense as they kiss me, I realize that the space we make together will work like this every single time.

We invent it anew.

Again.

And again.

And oh, yes–*again*.

Chapter Twenty

One year later

It's the Dance and Dairy festival, the one I missed last year for the high school reunion. And the best part of this annual ritual, something I adore and will exploit for every single one of the eight concerts on the town common, involves deep-fried-Twinkie-and-pickle sundaes.

That's right.

No, I'm not pregnant. I just love the cart that comes to the common and parks next to the seasonal stage for bands and sells fried-Twinkie-and-pickle sundaes.

I served my two-hour shift at the Habitat for Humanity table, recruiting two new volunteers for a house being built in Stoneleigh. Duty done, it's now time for pigging out.

"Mallory! Will!" Philippe is on the stage between dance performances, waving madly at us. Dressed in his master of ceremonies outfit, he looks oddly elegant for the setting, complete with a top hat and red cummerbund.

I wave.

Will cuts him a look I don't understand.

I take another delightful spoonful, making sure it has a little hot fudge, a little vanilla bean olive oil ice cream, plenty of Twinkie cake, and just enough pickle to complete the mouthfeel of perfection.

"Mmmmm."

Will looks a little green.

And *then*.

And then he begins cracking his knuckles. He pops the index finger and starts on his middle one but stops himself, furiously stuffing his hands in his front pockets.

I pause.

"Wa sum?" I ask through my currently occupied mouth, spooning up the perfect ratio and holding it out to him.

He winces, then laughs. "Uh, no, thank you. I'll be gallant and let you enjoy it."

Perky appears to the left, holding an enormous fried thing, about a foot long and the diameter of a soda can, on a giant marshmallow stick like you use for roasting over a campfire.

"Preparing for pregnancy?" she says to me, making a sour face at the pickles. "No. You're just being Mallory. You've eaten that crap every year since fifth grade."

"No," I correct her. "I missed last year." I study the thing on a stick she's holding. "Either that is the biggest fried Twinkie ever, or you've cut the head, tail, and legs off a dachshund and deep fried it."

"It's my new dildo," she informs me with an outrageous sniff.

Will doesn't laugh.

Peering at Will suspiciously, I can't help but wonder what's up. The weirdness he's displaying is *so* out of character.

"Mallory! You and Will need to come up here!" Philippe shouts. For fun, Will and I have been taking tango lessons at

Bailargo. Philippe uses the story of how we "met" at his studio in online advertising.

Bonus: it's quickly edging out the porno-set shot of me with Will and Beastman as the number one online photo of me. Between Fiona's brother and his reputation-management work and Bailargo's ads, Mallory the Porn Queen is finally on page three of search results for my full name.

Which means it's in the internet Doldrums.

Will takes my hand, his palm slick. I don't mean to, but I flinch and pull back.

"C'mon!" he says with a smile that makes me even more wary.

Will Lotham never has sweaty hands. *Ever*. If his palms are wet, it's because he's showering, we're in the middle of sex (TMI, but whatever), or he's helping to shove a beached baby whale back into the ocean on Cape Cod.

I'm not making that last one up. He's *that* perfect.

So why is he so nervous?

"May I have your attention, please!" Philippe says, his expression like an impish nine-year-old with a few shots of coffee in him, at a big chocolate-egg hunt on Easter. "We have a special tango demonstration for you!"

I look at the people assembled on stage.

Not one is under seventy.

"Gladys and Lou are doing tango now?" I ask Will, knowing they're in the contra-dancing group, puzzled by the sudden change.

"Not them," he says, gently taking my hand, his skin dry and smooth now. "Us."

The first few notes of "Por una Cabeza" float into the air, making me smile reflexively.

Philippe catches my eye and winks.

Will takes my hand and pulls me close, belly to belly, his

belt scratching my navel, his hand on my back tight. Firm. Unyielding.

Claiming.

As he spins me, thighs crashing into each other then holding steady, I look for the other dancers. This is the point in the song where everyone joins in, the empty dance floor filling, like ants to a pinch of sugar.

But no one does.

It's just me and Will.

Have you ever had a man who knows how to dance carry you across a dance floor on your own feet? I don't mean lift you up–I mean make you *glide*. His hands are in synchrony with the music, with his feet, with mine. The miracle of a choreographed dance is that you are taking two bodies and creating art with them in one motion.

It's like sex.

Only more complicated, and with an audience.

He dips me, the crowd cheering, my eyes catching my mom and dad near the stage, holding hands. Half the town is here–maybe even most of it. Even Will's parents, Helen and Larry, stand over by the garden club tent, watching us. They're in town for a week, visiting Will and some old friends. Larry is behind her, the same strange smile on his dad's mouth that Will just had.

Perky is ignoring her fried dildo, staring up at us with a silly grin. I've spent the afternoon running into everyone I know.

And loving it.

When Will pulls me back up, I giggle, his laughter infectious, the heat of his body against mine reigniting me. Every time his shoulder bumps mine, it becomes more real. Each time his foot nudges mine with a strong beat in the score, it echoes in my bones. We become the music, and it becomes us, until–oh, *until*.

Until he lets my hand go as I whirl, coming to a standstill, the dance routine ruined.

Questions pour out of me like fireworks, but I don't say a word, because he drops.

He *drops*.

I know what it takes to be so graceful, his thigh muscles in perfect alignment, the strong knee bending with calibrated perfection that makes proposing look like a part of the dance. The music rolls on, sustaining the show while we break choreography. Light shines off the waves of his hair just so, as if Mother Nature decided to be a costume designer for this moment.

This unbelievable magic.

Our eyes meet.

He's nervous.

Why is he nervous? Does he seriously think I would ever say *no*?

"Mallory Monahan," he says, strong and loud, dark hair blown to the side of his cheek by a sudden wind.

People start to turn toward us, eyes narrowing, ears sharp. A few women have expressions like their hearts are melting.

Me, too, sisters. Me, too.

Sighs accrue, growing as they ripple through the townspeople at the craft tables. Vendors start to stand, looking at the dance floor we're on.

"Mallory Monahan," he repeats, so loud that it's like a bullhorn, a public address system, a roar of joy. "Fifteen years ago we met for the first time in the hallway of Harmony Hills High. You had the locker next to mine. Eleven years ago we graduated and I left. One year ago I ran into you again – "

Half the crowd snickers. Clearly, the half on social media who saw the infamous Beastman picture.

"And I reversed my stupidity."

Snickers turn to laughs.

"You are a delightful, brilliant, extraordinary force, Mallory. You know who you are and what you like and you use that as a divining rod through life. Every part of you is so true, so real. I want to be real with you, and true to you."

Now sighs and sniffles fill the air. Including mine. His eyes are worlds, spinning and spinning, eternity inviting me to come in, find a comfy chair, have a cup of hot chai and stay a while.

In his arms.

"Will you do me the honor of becoming my wife? Mallory, will you marry me?" The jeweler's box appears as if conjured, the glint of sunlight on the diamond so blinding. All I see is Will and the bright light.

Our bright future.

"Oh!" A woman's gasp of joy makes me look to the right.

It's Mom.

My parents are standing there, Mom's hands over her mouth, Dad's eyes shining.

Oh, my God.

This is *real*. Will Lotham is proposing to me at the Dance and Dairy festival on our town common.

In front of the whole community. My town.

Our town.

Love pours out of those handsome eyes, so pure, so true. He's looking up at me, on one knee like a gentleman, a champion, a knight kneeling before his queen. For the last year, I've lived a fairy tale, but one rooted firmly in reality. He's become my new best friend, my hot lover, my smart business colleague, and now–

–my *husband*?

The word *yes* sticks in my mouth, like honey, like too much taffy, a jar of Fluff, like all the peanut butter in the world and none of the water. *Yes*, I want to say, elongating the word until it stretches back fifteen years to the first day of ninth grade, when I met Will Lotham in homeroom and realized my life would never be the same.

And I was *right*.

It wouldn't. It would never, ever be the same.

It would be so, so much better.

Green and blue speckled eyes meet mine, staring up at me with sweet love that glistens, Will's chest rising and falling as if the very air he breathes is produced by my answer. As if I alone make his reality.

Never in my life have I actually held fate in my hands. My mind reaches out to the speech center of my brain for an offering, waits for my mouth to take those signals and form a response.

Wind blows as the music, intense and dramatic now, punctuates my state.

"Yes," I whisper, bending down to accept the ring, Will standing up to take my face in his hands and kiss me until he breathes in my air, as if the answer can only be truly understood by infusion.

"Yes." The ring is cold as he slips it on my finger, its heaviness contrasting with the helium that fills my heart, his arms around me, his boisterous laugh bordering on incredulous.

"MALLORY!" Mom screams, jumping up and down, Dad's hands on her shoulders, his expression pure joy. Helen and Larry are hugging, her face buried in her husband's chest, Larry giving us a thumb's up.

The audience bursts into spontaneous applause as Will kisses me blind, the sound deafening, pushing out every other noise in the world, until all I hear is his heartbeat, all I feel are Will's hands and mouth.

"You said yes," he murmurs, throat clicking as he swallows, my eyes closed. I just want to breathe once more, twice–no, three times, with my eyes closed, sensing who Will is in the space I create.

"Of course I did. You're making all my dreams come true, Will."

"Same here, Mal."

"You didn't have a crush on me for four years."

Will kisses me. The crowd goes nuts.

He ignores them and whispers,

"No. But I will for the next sixty or so."

Chapter Twenty-One

Epilogue.
Or stinger.
You decide.

THREE MONTHS LATER

We're holding a pre-rehearsal dinner for all of the groomsmen and bridesmaids. No parents. No flower girl or ring bearer. The wedding is supposed to be fun, but Will and I know that the actual day won't be fun for *us*.

That's where the honeymoon comes in.

But the big day should be a party, right? And nothing makes a party like knowing who you're having fun with. The better the groomsmen and bridesmaids all know each other, the more extraordinary our special day will be.

Plus, it's an excuse to have a grown-up event with our friends.

Anyhow—we're at a small farm-to-table restaurant that opened six months ago in a renovated barn on a local nonprofit community-supported farm, waiting for all ten invitees to show up, the small banquet room perfect for privacy... when Parker Campbell walks in.

I nearly drop my artisanal blood orange martini on the floor.

"Skip! Great you could make it!" Will says, giving him a genuine hug that goes beyond polite back smacking.

Skip. This is *Skip*? I rub my eyes, careful not to smear the five layers of mascara Perky applied to my eyes half an hour ago. Nope. It's definitely Parker Campbell.

The guy who ruined Perky's life five years ago.

Our eyes meet. His smile has layers, going from polite to apologetic to nostalgic, settling finally on uncertain charm.

"Mallory," he says simply, dimples on display, looking every inch the young lawyer who was an assistant to the right congressman and filled his seat in a special election after an untimely tragedy.

"Let me introduce you," Will says. "Mallory, this is—"

Not baring my teeth is really, really hard.

"Will you excuse us?" I say to Parker, grabbing Will's arm and giving no one a choice in the matter. Will's a strong, tall guy but right now, I've got Hulk-level rage running through my veins as I pull him into a hallway near a stack of high chairs.

Where we run straight into Perky.

"What the hell is *he* doing here?" Her eyes are laser beams focused across the room.

Parker should be a smoldering piece of carbon right now.

"He's in the wedding party," Will says, bewildered. "One of my groomsmen."

"How do you know Parker?" Perky asks Will like she's asking him why he's holding a bloody murder weapon.

"We met in grad school. We worked on a project together in a supply-chain management workshop. How do *you* know him?"

Perky is agog. I can see her back molars from three feet away. She closes her mouth.

Around a beer bottle. Her throat is a metronome of perfect tempo as she swallows all of the contents, then sets down the bottle.

Did Will's shoulders drop in relief?

"You never mentioned Parker was coming!" Perky gasps, then belches, polite enough to keep it contained, which is really unusual given her propensity for burping contests no one else ever participates in. "You didn't say anyone named Parker. You told me I was paired with some guy named Skip," she whisper-yells at Will.

"Skip is his nickname. Short for Skipper. We went sailing on a long weekend vacation and when we came about, he didn't duck. Threw him off the boat. Skipper stuck. We shortened it to Skip."

"That is such a stupid nickname," I inform him. "Why does everyone have to have a nickname? Can't we trust our parents' judgment and just go with what they gave us?"

"And Perky is so much better?"

Did Will just go there?

Yep. He did.

"Are you—are you making fun of my friend? The one *your* friend nearly destroyed with revenge porn?"

Will and I have never had a fight before. I feel one brewing.

"Revenge *what*?" Will's eyes pop out and his voice drops. "What are you saying about Skip?"

"You really don't know?"

"I know that Skip is a member of the U.S. House of

Representatives for a district in Texas. Is there something else I'm supposed to know about him?"

"Oh, my God," Perky groans. "Damned if we tell him, damned if we don't."

Fiona chooses that exact moment to rush over to us and hiss, "What the hell is *Parker* doing here?"

Will gives me a *help me out, honey* look. "Mal, I don't understand what you guys don't like about Skip."

Perky answers for me. "He's a dirty, filthy, disgustingly immoral sonofabitch who is also–"

"So happy to see you." Parker's words cut Perky off and suddenly, he's kissing her.

And from the looks of it, she's kissing him right back.

Which is fine.

Until she hauls off and punches him.

:)

Curious about Perky? Watch for her eponymously titled standalone novel wherever you read books:

AN ALL-NEW STANDALONE FROM NEW YORK TIMES BESTSELLING AUTHOR JULIA KENT

One hundred years ago when I was young and impulsive (okay, it was five, alright? *Five* years ago...) I let my boyfriend take, let's just say...compromising pictures of me.

(Shut up. It made sense at the time).

Surprise! The sleazy back-stabbing jerk posted them on a website and, well, you can guess what happened. That's right.

I'm a meme. A really gross one.

You're seen the pictures. And if you haven't – don't ask. And don't look!

As face recognition software online improves, I get tagged on social media whenever anyone shares my pictures. You try getting a thousand notifications a day, all of them pictures of your tatas.

So. I'm done.

It's time for revenge. Let him see how it feels! But how do you get embarrassingly intimate pictures of your jerkface ex who double-crossed you five years ago?

Especially when he's a member of the U.S.House of Representatives now?

Getting sweet between the sheets with a congressman is pretty much every political roadie's dream, right? I'm one in a crowd.

Except to this day, he swears he didn't do it. Pursued me for months after I dumped him five years ago. Begged me to take him back.

And I almost did it. *Almost*. I was weak and stupid and in love a hundred years ago.

Okay. Fine. *Five*.

But I still have the upper hand. Second chance romance has all the emotional feels, doesn't it?

I can't wait to punch him in the feels.

All I need to do is sleep with him once, take some hot-and-sweaty pics of him in... *delicate* positions, and bring him down. That's it. Nothing more.

Pictures first. Revenge after. And then I win.

At least, that's how it was supposed to happen. But then I did something worse than sexting.

I fell in love with him. *Again*.

Find Perky now !

Audiobook narrated by Erin Mallon!

Other Books by Julia Kent

SUGGESTED READING ORDER

Shopping for a Billionaire Boxed Set (Books 1-5) (a New York Times Bestseller!)

Shopping for a Billionaire's Fiancee

Shopping for a CEO (A USA Today bestseller)

Shopping for a Billionaire's Wife (A USA Today bestseller)

Shopping for a CEO's Fiancee (A USA Today bestseller)

Shopping for an Heir (A USA Today bestseller)

Shopping for a Billionaire's Honeymoon

Shopping for a CEO's Wife (A USA Today bestseller)

Shopping for a Billionaire's Baby (A USA Today bestseller)

Shopping for a CEO's Honeymoon

Shopping for a Baby's First Christmas

Shopping for a CEO's Baby

Shopping for a Yankee Swap

Shopping for a Turkey

Shopping for a Highlander

Love You Wrong

Love You Right

Love You Again

Love You More

Love You Now

Little Miss Perfect

Fluffy (A USA Today bestseller)

Perky (A USA Today bestseller)

Feisty

Hasty

Our Options Have Changed (with Elisa Reed) (A USA Today bestseller)

Thank You For Holding (with Elisa Reed)

In Your Dreams

Her Billionaires: Boxed Set (A New York Times Bestseller!)

It's Complicated

Completely Complicated

It's Always Complicated

Eternally Complicated

Random Acts of Crazy (A New York Times Bestseller)

Random Acts of Trust

Random Acts of Fantasy

Random Acts of Hope

Randomly Acts of Yes

Random Acts of Love

Random Acts of LA

Random Acts of Christmas

Random Acts of Vegas

Random Acts of New Year

Random Acts of Baby

About the Author

New York Times and USA Today bestselling author Julia Kent writes romantic comedy with an edge. Since 2013, she has sold more than 2 million books, with 4 New York Times bestsellers and more than 21 appearances on the USA Today bestseller list. Her books have been translated into French and German, with more titles releasing in the future.

From billionaires to BBWs to new adult rock stars, Julia finds a sensual, goofy joy in every contemporary romance she writes. Unlike Shannon from *Shopping for a Billionaire*, she did not meet her husband after dropping her phone in a men's room toilet (and he isn't a billionaire in a rom com).

She lives in New England with her husband and children in a household where everyone but Julia lacks the gene to change empty toilet paper rolls.

Join her newsletter at http://www.jkentauthor.com

9 781638 801320